THE SHADOW OF A SMILE

THE SHADOW
OF A SMILE

KACHI A. OZUMBA

ALMA BOOKS

ALMA BOOKS LTD
London House
243–253 Lower Mortlake Road
Richmond
Surrey TW9 2LL
United Kingdom
www.almabooks.com

First published in UK by Alma Books Limited in 2009
Copyright © Kachi A. Ozumba, 2009

Cover design: Øivind Ovland
Author picture: Chiemeka Ozumba

Kachi A. Ozumba asserts his moral right to be identified as the author of this work in accordance with the Copyright, Designs and Patents Act 1988

This is a work of fiction. Names, characters, places and incidents either are the product of the author's imagination or are used fictitiously, and any resemblance to actual persons, living or dead, business establishments, events or locales is entirely coincidental.

Printed in Great Britain by TJ International, Padstow, Cornwall

ISBN: 978-1-84688-089-6 (trade paperback)
ISBN: 978-1-84688-097-1 (mass-market paperback)

THE SHADOW OF A SMILE

Beside me, in the queue, there was a woman with blue lips. She had, of course, never heard of me; but she suddenly came out of that trance so common to us all and whispered in my ear (everybody spoke in whispers there): "Can you describe this?" And I said: "Yes, I can." And then something like the shadow of a smile crossed what had once been her face.

Anna Akhmatova, *Requiem*

The Middle World

New Man

The policeman motioned with the rifle hanging from his shoulder. "This way mister man."

Zuba stepped into the dim corridor. His steps echoed on the pockmarked concrete floor strewn with pieces of broomstick. The yellow walls had a thousand blotches like the albino skin of the policeman. A smoky amalgam of stale sweat, urine, fermenting faeces and desolation hung over the passage.

"You think rich man son no go cell?" the policeman called after him.

The words did not sting this time. Zuba had been lashed with dozens of them during the interrogation and had got used to them. He walked down the corridor, staring blankly. Ike followed behind him, his face tight with rage. The imprint of the interrogator's palm was still visible on his cheek.

The smell intensified as they passed the rust-and-dirt-coloured bars of a cell door. Bare-chested men squatted on the floor in the dimness beyond. The words "New man" floated out – whispered, repeated, passed from mouth to mouth. Bodies began to stir within the cell.

"Idem, they say you suppose get space for your cell for this two," said the albino when they got to the office at the end of the corridor. He placed a white sheet on the counter before a chubby-faced man in police uniform. Then he studied an almanac on the wall with its photos of gaily dressed women: NIGERIAN POLICE WIVES

ASSOCIATION 2000. The nose-crinkling scent of mosquito coil struggled against the odour oozing from the corridor.

Idem looked down at the sheet. "Hmmmnh, threatening violence and stealing." He looked up and glanced at Ike's glowering eyes. Then his gaze settled on the softness of Zuba's face, at the eyes that seemed to stare back at him from a dizzying distance, and down at the gold cufflink that winked at him from the manicured hand Zuba had placed on the counter. "Undress, undress!" he barked. "Or you want enter cell with your fine-fine dress? Bring your money and valuables too."

His words must have carried down the corridor. Shouts erupted from the cell:

"If you people dare to come in here without your *cell-sho* we'll pummel you till you forget your mothers' names."

"Make sure you bring your *cell-sho* or we'll dip your head into our shit bucket."

"We'll kill you here today…"

Zuba and Ike exchanged glances. The dread they had nursed beneath their calmness, hidden like some venereal disease, broke out in a rash of symptoms. They forgot to feel embarrassed as they stared at each other with gaping eyes and palpitating hearts.

"D-Do you understand what th-they're saying, Zuba?" Ike's usually robust voice was whispery.

Zuba smelt the fear in Ike's breath. He did not trust his own voice. He shook his head. His rigid fingers unbuttoned the striped white shirt he had on over black trousers. None of the detention stories he had read, none of the tales he had heard, had ever spoken of "*cell-sho*". He leant towards Idem. "Please, what… what are they saying? What is '*cell-sho*'?"

"Cell-show. You'll find out soon enough what it is," Idem replied in perfect English.

"Please, have you any advice for us? We've never been in this kind of a situation before."

Idem's lips stretched in a sad smile. He shook his head slightly, to himself. "What's your name?" he asked.

"Zuba."

"OK, Zuba, give me one thousand naira from there to give them," he motioned with his chin at the wad of money lying on the counter. "That should help take care of things."

Zuba counted out twenty fifty-naira notes from the wad. The money quivered as he handed it to Idem.

Idem collected the money. "You no remove your trouser?"

Zuba shook his head. "I'm OK." He ran his hand over his white vest and black trousers. Beside him, Ike had stripped to the black shorts underneath his trousers.

"OK, remove your belt. Belt is not allowed in cell. Someone fit use it hang himself."

Zuba unbuckled his belt and pulled it free. He unstrapped his watch; the automatic Seiko stainless-steel watch his father had given him four years ago, a month after his eighteenth birthday.

"You people sure you bring all your money?" Idem asked. "They go take everything from you once you enter cell o."

Ike nodded. Zuba nodded too. He exchanged a glance with Ike as he felt the warmth of the money spread out evenly in the two back pockets of the denim shorts under his trousers. He rubbed the keloid on his face. A spindly wasp hummed before its mud nest behind Idem, at the point where the yellowing ceiling met the yellow walls, the sound amplified in the confined space.

9

KACHI A. OZUMBA

The shouts coming down the corridor had petered out to intermittent calls.

"Zuba, please allow me to manage the situation when we get in there," Ike said.

"No, Ike. No. Don't worry. I can manage the situation."

"I understand this people better than you do. Let me. Trust me." There was a stubborn streak in Ike's eye which Zuba knew too well. This was survival, not some official matter.

"OK," he said.

They signed beneath the list of their belongings, then followed Idem as he led the way to the corridor. The jangle of keys, the squeal of rusty hinges, the clang of metal against metal as the iron door swung shut. Zuba and Ike were in the dark stench of the cell. Five men stared at them. Three of them were seated, their bare backs resting against the wall. The fourth man was stretched out on the concrete floor. His six-foot body bisected the cell, with his head propped up against one wall and his toes brushing the one opposite. While the fifth man, who had risen from his post before the doorway to allow them to enter, was standing by the door. He was burly and light-skinned, and had jutting cheekbones, bushy hair and beard.

Zuba felt for the secure coolness of the cell wall behind him. His gaze roved from one face to the other. Beside him, Ike stood ramrod-still.

The burly light-skinned man took his place again before the entrance, resting his left elbow on the bars of the door.

"You, take—" Idem handed some money to him through the bars. "Make you treat them well."

Idem walked off.

10

"What's this? Two hundred naira?" the prefect barked, after the echo of Idem's boots had died out in the corridor. He waved the money disdainfully at Zuba and Ike.

Zuba's heart thumped in his chest as he stared back at the prefect with a blank face.

Ike stepped away from the security of the wall. He stood in the centre of the cell, between the outstretched legs of the other inmates, and looked around like an architect on his building site.

Zuba could hear Ike's brain cranking behind a fake smile. *Say something quick*, he commanded Ike in his mind.

"I said, what is this?" the prefect repeated, his voice rising. "Mike," he called.

The man beside him got up. He was tall and dark, and the contours of his large bones showed clearly through flesh that was stretched too tightly over them. His only clothing was trousers, worn inside out and folded at the hip to keep them from sliding down. The cream pouches of the pockets looked comical against the black fabric. "You see this?" Mike said, pointing at an inscription in chalk on the wall. "CELL-SHOW = N500," he read out.

"Oh. So this thing is still here," Ike said. The smile on his face grew wider. "I wrote it."

Zuba's heart skipped. The buzzing of flies became the only sound in the cell. Ike remained where he was, rocking on his feet while returning the stares of the other inmates. One of them laughed – Zuba was not sure who. He had just begun to relax, hoping Ike had called the bluff of the inmates, when Mike's hand rose in a swing while the inmate lying on the floor lunged for Ike's crotch.

"Ike!" Zuba screamed, and began bawling: "Police! Police! Idem!"

11

Ike leapt. Mike's punch missed his face and landed on his shoulder. The hand from below grabbed at his crotch and yanked, transforming his shorts into a skirt.

"What's happening there?" Idem called as his steps thudded down the corridor. "I say, what's happening? Where you? Zuba?" He stood before the iron bars.

Ike's assailants had sat back down on the floor, staring straight ahead. Ike returned to the security of the wall beside Zuba, panting.

"Em... It's OK now," Zuba said. He poked his head before the bars to reassure Idem.

"I say I no want any trouble in there. I no want hear any noise again. Otherwise I go throw tear gas in there." Idem turned and left. His footsteps had barely faded when Mike and his co-assailant came at them again.

Zuba held out his left hand. "OK, OK." He slid his other hand under his trousers and retrieved the wad in one of the back pockets of his shorts.

Mike snapped the money out of Zuba's hand and counted it. "Thank your Creator," he said, and wagged a finger at Ike's face. He took the money to the prefect. "One thousand one hundred naira."

The prefect collected the money and recounted it. He nodded.

"Won't you find me something?" a female voice called from outside the cell.

The prefect crumpled a note and flung it towards the cell opposite. A young lady seated behind the bars reached out and picked it. "Bless you," her voice rang out again.

The prefect turned back to Mike. "Give them seat," he said.

Mike went over to the old man seated last in the row. "Shift, shift, Papa," he barked at the man, kicking him twice. "You will still be the last. And if by the end of the week you're still here without completing your *cell-sho* we'll give you only standing space." He beckoned at Zuba and Ike. He placed Zuba fifth on the line, and Ike after him. Then he returned and took his place between his co-assailant and the prefect.

Zuba lowered himself to the ground. He could feel the warmth of the man who had just vacated the position. He stretched out his legs before him.

"This people wanted to turn me into a eunuch," Ike muttered beside Zuba, holding together the torn crotch of his shorts. "Thank Heavens I'm wearing a pant underneath. What would I have told my wife?"

Zuba forced a soft chuckle through his lips, thinking it would help Ike feel better. But the expression on Ike's face was still that of shock. It was not an attempt at humour, Ike was just mumbling to himself.

"New man, you in white vest, come here," the prefect said.

"Get up! Get up!" Mike waved at Zuba. "Obasanjo is calling you."

Zuba scrambled to his feet. He had heard that cell prefects were called presidents. But he never thought they actually took a sitting president's name. He stood straight before the prefect. "Mr President sir!"

A smile softened the prefect's features. "What's your name?"

"Zuba."

"What kind of a name is that? Is it Igbo?"

"Yes. Short for Chikezuba."

"What does it mean?"

"The Lord created enough wealth."

"Did He?"

13

Zuba rubbed his keloid.

"What kind of a lump is that on your forehead? Or is it a scar?"

Zuba snatched his hand off his face. He shook his head and said nothing.

"What happened to your forehead?" the prefect persisted.

"It's from an accident, when I was a child."

"What brought you people here?"

Zuba hesitated. Wasn't it the case that people were sometimes beaten up if they claimed innocence? "A case of stealing."

"What did you steal?"

"They said we stole money, and personal goods, from a family."

"Did you?"

Zuba hesitated again. He shook his head.

The prefect stared long and hard at him. "Well, it happens," he said. "Do your people know you're here?"

"No. But I'm sure they'll find us soon."

"What do you do for a living?"

"I just finished from school, still studying."

"So you're one of those who never get tired of school, eh?"

"Why not wear your trouser inside out to save it from dirt, so it will still look clean when you leave?" Mike said.

"It's OK," Zuba answered. "I don't mind looking dirty when leaving." He paused, then made an attempt at a joke: "Even Obasanjo himself was once in cell."

The prefect smiled. The inmate beside Mike smiled too, looking so unlike the person that had made for the balls of his fellow man minutes earlier.

14

The prefect threw his head back and yawned. "You can return to your place," he said.

Zuba sat back in his position. The floor felt grainy against his palm. He looked around the cell, beginning from the extreme right corner of the opposite wall, which he had avoided focusing on since they came in. A filthy metal bucket stood where the two walls met, spewing its foulness into the air like a noxious fountain. The square piece of plank that served as its lid failed to sit well on its bent rim. Flies buzzed around it and in it. The outstretched legs of the elderly man last in the line were just inches from touching it.

The walls were dank and dotted with dried blood. Chalk and charcoal graffiti stood out in white and black on their dull dirty yellowness: BADBOY BAHODA LIVED HERE. DERICO NWAMAMA WUZ HERE, and the like. They reminded Zuba of his last days in secondary school, when some of the students had gone round scribbling such graffiti on walls. The students were mainly the dull ones. He could still recall one of them murmuring to himself as he scratched his name on the hostel wall: "The principal said I cannot leave an impression on the school, so I will leave one on its walls."

The graffiti that held prime place on the cell wall was a life-size charcoal portrait of a man's head and shoulders. The face was angular, with jutting cheekbones and chin. The width of the nose nearly matched the width of the frowning but grinning lips; the squinting eyes gave a thoughtful expression. BUGA IN CELL, said the words beside the drawing. THE GODIAN PROPHET FROM THE HOLYLAND. NO PLACE LIKE HOME.

Zuba rested his chin on his knees. He wondered if his sister, Nonye, and the handyman who sometimes doubled as driver for Ike, were close to locating him. A policeman had waved a gun at them, warned them against following, as he and Ike were being driven away. "Inform Barrister Chigbo," he had managed to call out to her.

Footsteps thudding down the corridor. Idem appeared at the door and slid three metal plates under the bars. The plates grated against the concrete floor, jarring on Zuba's nerves.

The prefect picked up a sachet of water from one of the plates and bit it open at one end. His Adam's apple bobbed up and down as he drank. Mike picked up another one and drank too. The other inmates watched. When the prefect removed the sachet from his lips, only half of the contents remained. He squeezed some water onto his right hand and washed it into the plate, then turned towards the two inmates between Mike and Zuba.

"Okpu-uzu, Chemist, now we have money. I'm sure you people will prefer to wait for Madam Food," he said.

"Sure," the ball-grabber answered.

Okpu-uzu... Zuba and Ike exchanged glances. So the ball-grabber was a blacksmith, with hands hardened by handling iron.

The prefect pushed the plates towards Zuba. "Pass them on to that papa. You people will get something better to eat when Madam Food comes."

Zuba stared into the plates. One was filled with *garri*. The *garri* had not been stirred as was customary: it stood hard and flat in the bowl. There had been an attempt to eke out the okra soup in the second plate. A clear layer of water lay over it. Two half sachets of water lay on the last plate. Zuba passed the plates on.

The papa took the plates. He was a short, slight man with a sprinkle of grey in his hair. His arms and legs were stocky, and seemed to belong to another body; his movement was lethargic, and the sadness didn't leave his face even as he swallowed outsized dollops of the *garri* in noisy gulps.

Idem's voice drifted down the corridor: "Madam, wetin you cook today?"

"Na *ogbono* soup o."

"Oya, put for me, with two extra meat."

When footsteps headed down the corridor, people began to stir.

"Madam Food, you have come," the prefect greeted.

A middle-aged woman stood outside the bars. Her face shone with the warmth of hearths and kitchens. The smell of firewood smoke and condiments trickled into the cell from the wrapper around her waist. The cloth was so faded that the jumping horses on the fabric looked spectral. A heavily laden metal tray with a broad turned-up rim rested on her head like a sombrero.

"Yes o. How are you? How are you all? Are you buying any food today?" She lifted the tray off her head and lowered it to the ground. Smoke-blackened pots, plastic plates, cutlery, a tiny blue bucket and a jerrycan filled its circumference.

"Nwamaka, I hope all is well. You're quiet today," she said, casting a glance into the opposite cell.

"I told you I won't talk to you again." The clear soprano of the speaker came as a mumble.

Nwamaka. A child is good. The stresses in the name could be placed differently to make it mean: "This child is so beautiful". Zuba bent forwards to get a better look at her. She was young; her skin glowed. The floral dress that hugged her, outlining her ample bust, was faded but clean. She looked like she was new. But Zuba knew she wouldn't be occupying the prime position in her cell if that was the case. Only the cornrows on her head were unkempt. He estimated she was between eighteen and twenty-two. But the way she stared up at Madam Food with Betty Boop eyes, while holding her lips together in a sulk, made her seem no more than twelve.

Madam Food laughed. "Nwamaka my child, please forgive me. I came with something special for you today. Let me quickly serve Peter and his mates, then I'll take my time to serve you specially."

The pout on Nwamaka's lips dissolved into a smile. Three older-looking women seated after her leant forwards to stare at Madam Food.

"What's in your soup today?" the prefect asked.

"It's dried fish and pork meat. Very sweet."

"Give us" – he looked back into the cell – "six plates of food."

"I don't—" began Ike.

Zuba nudged him. "My partner and I had lunch a short while ago, we can share a plate." He was surprised that the prefect included them on his feeding list and did not want to rebuff the gesture. He and Ike had prepared to go without food for the rest of the day. They had taken Coca-Cola and bread, bought from a shop in the police station, after their interrogation, and then swallowed tetracycline capsules obtained from the same shop, to seal off bowel movement – something that had always worked for Zuba whenever he had a runny tummy.

"OK. Bring five plates," the prefect said.

Madam Food slid the plates of food under the bar along with a bowl of water for washing hands.

"It will be nice if you can come earlier tomorrow," the prefect said while handing her some money. "I've added some extra. And Mother Food, please give your boy tissue paper, candle and matches to bring for us when he comes to collect the plates."

"I have heard," the woman said. She squeezed the notes into a ball and tucked it into her bra.

Slurps and lip-smacking arose around Zuba and Ike. Zuba swallowed the saliva that the stench in the cell had caused to pool in his mouth, and examined the food: a steaming mound of yellow *garri* and a gelatinous soup with two Maggi-cube-sized pieces of meat. He wanted to ask the woman for a fork. But after a glance around, he thought it unwise. He set to work. "Ike don't leave it all for me o," he said.

They ate slowly, blowing at hot, soup-moistened balls of *garri*. Mama-puts, as food hawkers such as Madam Food were called, were reputed to possess certain native skills lost to chefs of expensive restaurants, and the food would have tasted good under different circumstances. But Zuba was discovering the dynamic of taste and cell-smell. With the food's aroma smothered by the general stench, the *garri* tasted revolting and the soup's gooey texture reminded him of mucus.

Mike pushed his clean-licked plates towards the door. His body was covered with sweat. He licked his fingers and rested against the wall.

The other inmates followed suit. Zuba and Ike gulped down what was left of their food. "Thank you," they said to the prefect. Mike took their plate and slid it under the door.

Zuba's buttocks throbbed against the hard floor. He shifted and tried to adjust his legs. A hand clamped down on his thigh.

"Careful! Watch my foot. Don't upset my wound," Chemist said.

Zuba stared down at the foot. Chemist's ankle was twice its normal size. A wound, the size of a fifty-kobo coin, festered upon it. Black and glassy-yellow scabs of dried blood and serum were crusted around the opening.

Zuba's face convulsed. "What happened?"

"They shot me. During interrogation. And said I was trying to run away. The bullet is still in there. They had arrested me from my chemist shop saying I had been treating armed robbers. I know it is the work of my enemies. They have been envious that my shop was making great progress just two years after I completed my apprenticeship."

Zuba examined the swollen ankle. There was no exit wound. If Chemist had been shot during interrogation, then he was probably shot at close range – so wouldn't there be an exit wound? Or did it depend on the kind of gun used?

The boy came to collect the used plates, bringing the matches, candle and tissue paper. The prefect tore off a long sheet of tissue and began to twist it with his fingers. When the tissue became a long white cord, he put it aside, tore off another long sheet and began twisting again. He hummed under his breath, and worked with a deliberate slowness, as if he wanted the task to last for ever.

Zuba and the other inmates watched each twist of the prefect's fingers.

The prefect pushed himself to his feet. Seven cords of tissue, as well as matches and a candle, were clutched in his hands. He took a step forwards and placed the objects at the foot of the opposite wall. He lit the candle, waited for some wax to gather at the base of the flame, then poured the melted wax onto one end of a tissue cord and stuck the cord to the wall. He repeated the process until the seven cords were trailing, bright-white, against the dull yellow of the wall. They made the Buga graffiti, inches above, look like a totem in a shrine. "It's for the smells. Wait till the morning and you'll see," Chemist muttered when he saw the question in Zuba's eyes. The prefect returned to his post. He sat down and gazed at his handiwork. He gave voice to the song he had been humming, singing in a low husky tone:

Jesus, my rock of ages
The pillar of my life
I run to thee, I shelter in thee
There's nothing the world can do…

The sound of a car halting outside floated into the cell. Doors slammed shut. Zuba sat up. Muffled voices. He strained his ears. Footsteps in the front office.

"Good evening, Sergeant. I'm Barrister Chigbo…"

Zuba exhaled. Warmth spread through his chest.

"…I'm here to see my clients. Two men: Zuba Maduekwe and Ike Okoye, just taken into your custody."

"Your people have come," the prefect said, turning to Zuba and Ike.

Zuba nodded. He held his lips between his teeth. Beside him, Ike stared towards the door, a new light in his eyes.

"Only their IPO can allow you to see them," Idem said.

"Good. They're here then. We'll go and get their Investigating Police Officer's consent."

"Can you please pass this food on to them?"

Zuba closed his eyes – Nonye!

"No. I have told you, nothing-nothing without their IPO."

"We'll be back," the barrister said.

"It's almost closing time at the office. You may not get him today."

"We'll still try."

The footsteps started receding.

Zuba jumped to his feet. "Barrister!"

"Zuba, are you OK?"

"Zuba!" Nonye's voice rang out, thick, sagging under the weight of her anguish.

"Nonye—" Zuba began.

"One more word and I'll throw tear gas into that cell," Idem shouted.

Zuba's lips found each other again.

"Just hold on, Zuba. We'll get you people out soon. We'll be back," Barrister Chigbo shouted.

Car doors slammed shut and the engine coughed to life. The car drove off.

Zuba clung to the sound of the receding car, following it far into the distance until not even the faintest hum could be heard. He sat down, pulled his knees to his chest and wrapped his arms around them. He stared at the wall in front of him. The Buga graffiti stared back, thoughtful, wondering with him when his people would be back. Zuba rubbed his keloid. He looked up at the darkening patch of sky visible through the tiny window.

"They'll be back tomorrow morning." Ike said.

"I guess so." Zuba bowed his head till it rested on his knees. He rubbed his keloid against the callused skin. When he lifted his head a few minutes later, Buga had faded into the darkness.

The sixty-watt bulb hanging from the ceiling came on, casting an oily light.

Mike yawned. He stood up and headed for the slop bucket. His pee hummed against the metal. He returned to his position and stretched out on the floor. Other inmates followed. Chemist pushed himself up with difficulty and hopped to the bucket. He stood on one leg as he peed. Zuba was the last to head for the bucket after Ike. He expected to be hit by a pungent stench, but the smell that rose to his nostrils was weak. Was there a relationship between light and smell? Do smells go to sleep at night?

He returned to his position and lay on his back. He had never been able to sleep on his back. As kids, he and his brother, Chuu, had tried sleeping on their backs with their legs together and their arms by their sides, after they had seen Yul Brynner lying that way in *The King and I*. They had called it the Royal Sleeping Posture. They had not succeeded, but now he had to succeed. He wouldn't rest his belly, his cheek on the dirty floor.

The bulb went off. In the blackness, Zuba realized that a radio had been blaring at the front office. And there were voices. He heard a man curse at the radio's poor reception. A beam of a flashlight cleaved the darkness. Then the crackle of a match being struck. The voices at the office resumed their conversation. From the tiny window up on the cell wall, a cool, rain-washed breeze drifted in bearing the sounds of rustling leaves, shrilling crickets and the piercing squeaks of bats.

Zuba shut his eyes. He wondered how Nonye was faring. She would be too scared to sleep in the house all by herself, and the housemaid had travelled home for a sister's marriage ceremony. He should not have done this to her. He should have listened to her.

Tears stung his eyes as he thought of their father on his hospital bed. How much different, how much better their lives would have been had his father's big ego not driven him to quit his university job and start a secondary school. He felt the hot rush of bile at the thought of the school principal, Mrs Egbetuyi, and her husband sleeping comfortably on some downy bed somewhere. Perhaps he should have followed his police friend's advice, and gone along with the "selling marijuana to the students" scheme, since he could not stomach the "poisoning of students' food" scheme. Then Mr and Mrs Egbetuyi would have been the ones lying on a cold concrete floor.

Zuba rubbed his keloid. To his left, two of the inmates snored a duet. To his right, Ike kept twisting and turning. He wondered what Ike was thinking about. The Egbetuyis? Or his pregnant wife and child?

Mosquitoes swarmed upon the cell like the fourth biblical plague. Huge mosquitoes with needles for proboscides, and sirens for whines. Their buzz was infuriating. Why couldn't they go straight to business without announcing themselves?

"When they cry in your ears, they are asking: "Are you *asleeeeeeeeeeep* yet?" his mother used to say. "So if you don't swat and let them know you're awake they'll get to biting you."

"But Mummy, all I hear is a long whine, I can't make out any words," he had said.

"That's because they speak *mosquitolese*, not Igbo or English. So swat and keep swatting at them to make them know you are awake. Otherwise they will give you malaria and I will give you injections with big needles."

In the cell, Zuba kept swatting and swatting.

"These things won't allow somebody to rest," Ike muttered as he slapped at the mosquitoes.

Zuba's right arm started aching, and he switched to swatting and slapping with his left. Hours later, however, he and Ike became still like the other inmates of the cell, too tired to react to the needles drilling and re-drilling into their bodies in search of succulent veins.

The Outside World

Keloid

An oil tanker hurtled towards them. Zuba was just able to glimpse the NIGERIA GO SURVIVE splashed on its bumper before the impact.

The acrid fumes of petrol mixed with the smell of mangled metal, stinging the insides of his nostrils as he whimpered, dazed, in the back seat with Nonye. A stranger was trying to force the door open. They had barely been pulled from the wreckage when it burst into flames. The air filled with the scent of burning flesh.

"My mummy and brother are in there!" he cried. He struggled to return to the flames, clawing and biting at the hands that held him until the blood trickling down his head blinded him.

He was pulled away to a car. Nonye was already there, trembling in the arms of a large woman. A crowd of onlookers curtained off the accident site, but not the dark smoke billowing into the sky. His mother's scream before the impact continued to play in his head.

"*Gini?*" their mother had yelled at the tanker. It was what she always said when startled. *Gini?* What? Presenting a fearless front. Querying the unknown that suddenly confronted her. "Don't you know that it pays to present a bold front even when one is all jelly inside?" she had once said to Zuba. "It can stave off dangers." But there was no staving off that hurtling tanker, and the last syllable of her exclamation, the *gini*, had gone shrill and off-key. Unlike his kid brother Chuu's elemental

29

"*Mummee!*", beseeching Mummy's magical ability to protect.

The wound which Zuba sustained when his forehead rammed into the car door window refused to heal for a long long time. It was stitched up, cut open and stitched up again. When it finally healed, the scar, rather than fade into the skin, grew bigger and bigger, into an itchy mound that looked like a leech fastened to his head.

"Keloid," the doctor said. "Such scars are called *kee loids*," he repeated, staring at Zuba and his dad as if they were interns. "They're notoriously difficult to heal. Even when they are surgically removed, oftentimes they grow back. He just has to learn to live with it."

Zuba got home from the hospital and withdrew to the darkest corner of his room. He yanked off his shirt and slumped on the floor, resting his back against the blue wall, where a dark smudge, the size and shape of his bare back, was visible.

When Nonye came into the room and saw her brother's glistening face, she joined him on the floor. He threw his arm around the padded hardness of the cervical collar on her neck, and they cried.

It was not the attention-seeking crying of children. It was silent like the bleeding of wounds.

When their housemaid came into the room and saw them, she gathered them into her arms and carried them to her bed. She sang them to sleep with ancient lullabies, her sweet voice keeping out the mutterings and curses that wafted down the corridor as their father began his nightly pacing of the house.

* * *

One day in the month of March, just before the rains, when the heat and dryness were at their peak, and the grass on the lawns and bushes had become brown and brittle, Zuba and Nonye returned from school. Zuba sat on the floor of his mother's study and selected one of the medical textbooks scattered before him. He opened the book at a folded page and leafed through the colourful pictures, mouthing certain words. After a few minutes, he reached for a hand-mirror on the floor and held it to his face while he fingered the growth on his forehead.

"I am now ugly," he cried as the housemaid entered the study. "And the doctor said that it cannot be cured. But there has to be a cure. There has to be."

"Don't mind the doctor." She planted a kiss on his head and removed the mirror from his hand. "If we keep rubbing and massaging it like this," she used her forefinger to rub the keloid in a circular motion, "it will eventually go down."

Zuba purred while her finger worked on his face. His eyelids became heavy, and he rested his head against her breasts.

"Now, come and have your lunch," she said finally.

"I am not hungry."

"Come and try, my dear. You have not been eating well. I promised to tell Nonye a folktale if she eats. You have to join her if you want to listen."

Zuba shook his head.

"OK. Come and eat only the chicken and leave the rice."

Zuba lifted his head from her bosom.

At school the next morning, during break, Zuba withdrew to the shade of a mango tree. He sat on one of its gnarled roots, away from the tailor ants commuting on the fat furrowed stem. The thick leaves of the lower hanging branches reached down around him, shielding him from the bustle of his mates playing in the distance. He retrieved a mirror from his pocket and held it before his face. Had the time he spent rubbing his keloid the previous night yielded any result?

"Hey, look who's here. It is Scarface." A stocky boy waddled towards Zuba, swinging arms that seemed to reach down to his knees.

Zuba looked up at him, at the thick drooping lower lip that made it look as if he was sneering at everything, and at the two boys grinning behind him in their grubby blue-and-white uniforms. He slid the mirror back into his pocket.

"So, you love your scar so much that you sneak off to a cosy place and admire it, eh?"

"It is not a scar. It's a *kee loid*."

"It's a scar!"

"A scar, a scar, a scar. You're Scarface, Scarface, Scarsface," they chanted.

Zuba ran towards his classroom, trying not to cry. He sat brooding in class for the rest of the day, watching a lizard that had crawled up the wall to shelter from the blazing heat outside. When his teacher used the word "oftentimes" he sat up and rifled through his memories.

"Yes, oftentimes," he whispered to himself. "The doctor said: oftentimes they grow back."

He dreaded raising his hand; everyone would stare at him. He scribbled his question on a sheet and passed it to his neighbour.

His neighbour's hand went up.

"Yes?" the teacher said.

"Aunty, what is the meaning of oftentimes?"

* * *

Zuba went home and paced about, waiting for his father to return from work. But when he saw his father stepping out of the car, his tongue failed him. He decided to wait for another day. Three days later, his father returned with a less forbidding expression on his face. Zuba followed him around the house.

"You have something to say?" his father asked.

"Yes, Daddy. I want this *kee loid* removed. It has made me ugly."

He was startled by the roar of his father's laughter.

"You mean you've started thinking about girls? At this age? What are you, ten or eleven?" He laughed some more. "Zuba, just study hard, work hard and become successful, then you will be a handsome man to any girl you meet. A man's beauty lies in his pockets, not in his face."

"But I still want it removed. They call me..." his voice fell to an inaudible whimper.

"Have you forgotten that the doctor said it will grow back if removed?"

"The doctor said 'oftentimes', which means" – he paused to remember the definition he had memorized – "many times, again and again – but not every time."

"You're not a girl. You're a man, and men don't do plastic surgery. So, my son, just study hard and become successful."

The result of the entrance exams came out and Zuba passed. He nodded to himself. Secondary school would be a new beginning.

"It will do you much good, Zuba," his father said of his decision to send him to a boarding school for boys.

"You need the fresh air of a new environment, to meet new people and make new friends, to become a man."

Zuba rubbed his hands together as he surveyed his new shoes, crisp uniforms, and cartons of goodies: cornflakes, milk, chocolates, biscuits and fruit juices. His eyes glowed as he felt the weight of his new leather wallet and filled his nostrils with the fresh mint of his pocket money. The thought of leaving home to become his own master, master over his money and goodies, got him cackling with excitement. Nonye's sulking about being stuck all alone with the housemaid at home, with her goodies rationed, increased his excitement.

"Grow up quickly then. But, wow! You still have four years, four whole years before you get to my position," he said.

Zuba arrived at the Immaculate Conception College, Enugu, in the south-east of Nigeria, on a day when the sun seemed at its most radiant. He felt his keloid itch as he was introduced to his house prefect. But he held his hands together. This was supposed to be a new beginning; he was not going to draw attention to it.

Yet the first question the prefect asked after introductions was:

"What kind of a scar is that on your face?"

"It's not a scar, it's a *kee loid*."

The prefect looked at him strangely. "Well, whatever. This is your bed and that is your locker." He tapped on the top of a double bunk, the last in a row of five, and pointed at a white wooden locker that stood out against the green walls. Then he left the cubicle.

He reappeared seconds later. "Hey… you… you… what's-your-name-again… Scarface!"

The students in the cubicle squealed with laughter. Zuba knew from experience that such laughter would confer longevity on the name. He looked at the prefect waving at him from the door.

"Don't forget to see me in the morning for your exeat card," the prefect said.

Zuba nodded.

"Let me take my arrival refreshment," he said. The giggles ended and his neighbours sat up on the beds beside him. He reached for his beverages, his biscuits and pastries, and gave himself and his neighbours an extravagant treat. He was later to recount to his sister, Nonye, that the beverage he took that night was so thick with powdered milk and cocoa that he had to drink it with a spoon, like custard.

Afterwards he changed into his pyjamas. He stared at his fat wallet for a minute or two, stroking it, noting the tiny lines that criss-crossed the shiny black leather. He put it away and climbed up to his bed to lie down, heavy and happy like a python that had swallowed a calf. He waited for sleep to overtake him, staring at the fluorescent tube at the centre of the ceiling, and at the brown moth that danced around it oblivious of the gecko inching closer.

The wind howled outside, heralding a September rainstorm. The glass louvres chattered; the air became chilly. Zuba reached under his pillow and retrieved a wrapper. It was one of his mother's old *ogodo*: the long, ankle-length cloth wound around the waist beneath a matching blouse. He threw the cloth over his body, and her scent wafted into his nostrils. An emotion he had never experienced before rose from the pit of his stomach with the speed of vomit. He pressed his head into his pillow.

"Home. Home. I want to go home. Daddy, Nonye..." Minutes later, the emotion was joined by a more familiar grief, and he began to mouth into his tear-soaked pillow: "Mummy, oh Mummy."

When he woke in the morning, the fresh smell of the newly washed air and wet earth rushed into his nostrils. But he did not feel refreshed by it, then or on other days. He took to shuffling to the shower, and on to breakfast and classes, like an apparition in the middle of a bustling market. Week after week, month after month, his sandals scraped along on the dusty school grounds.

"Look, if you're homesick, it is normal," his older neighbour advised him one morning while they made their beds. "But try and get over it. You don't have to carry your grief on your face all the time."

Zuba thanked him for his advice. He picked up his mirror and studied his face. His eyes were puffy and his keloid had increased in size. It now looked like a leech that had gorged itself to bursting point. He lifted his eyelids a bit, showing more of his sunken eyeballs. Then he parted his lips slightly, enough for the whiteness of his teeth to show through and brighten his face. He nodded and put the mirror away, squared his shoulders and strode out of the room, his new look plastered on his face. But his stride kept relapsing into a shuffle, and his shoulders into a droop, even after his pillow had forgotten the salty taste of his tears.

One afternoon during his second year, his house prefect came into his cubicle.

"Scarface! Get up." He kicked the stand-alone bed on which Zuba was stretched out. "Scarface!"

Zuba squinted at the prefect with drowsy eyes. "My... My name is Zuba."

"OK. Zuba or Zoo-bat or whatever you say your name is, I need your bed. You have to move to the lower bed of a double bunk."

Zuba recoiled at the thought. He had woken up one morning in the previous term to find himself drenched with urine from the bed above. No doubt the prefect wanted to give the bed to his second-year student pet. He looked around the cubicle at the other second-year students sprawled out on their stand-alone beds observing their siesta. There would be fiery protests if they were to find themselves in his shoes. He took a deep breath and tried to kindle such a fire in himself. Instead, his hand flew up to rub his keloid as he said, "Senior, I'm sorry. I can no longer sleep on lower bunks. I have lung convulsion."

"What about short convulsion?" the prefect sneered.

"I mean lung, l-u-n-g not l-o-n-g, convulsion. If I sleep on the lower bed of a double bunk and breathe in the dust from the mattress above, my lungs will start convulsing."

The prefect stared at Zuba for a while. He scratched his head and walked away.

A long-forgotten feeling of triumph awakened in Zuba. The feeling grew with each successful encounter with the school prefects, building in him the confidence of Houdini. But the senior prefect's knots were usually harder to slip out of.

"Oh, sorry, where do you have the abscess?" the senior prefect had asked in a sympathetic tone during one of their encounters, when Zuba claimed to have an abscess in order to avoid being flogged on the buttocks.

"Here," Zuba had answered, placing his hand gently over a spot on his right buttock.

"Don't worry then, I'll flog you only on your left buttock." He squatted before Zuba's buttocks and dealt him the strokes, holding the cane vertically. "Steady now," he had said, like a nurse administering an injection.

* * *

37

One evening during housework the house prefect was bent over a large map of the school farm, calling out the students one by one and allocating them plots of land to cultivate. The junior students stood in a mass, holding grass-cutting knives bent at the tips like scorpions' tails, and chattering with fresh tales from their midterm break. The senior students strutted around with canes, which they wielded with the excitement of four-year-olds holding new water pistols.

"Scarface, this is your plot," the prefect said, chuckling while he mapped out a large trapezium on the farm.

Zuba felt his keloid itch. His plot was the only part of the farm overgrown with wire grass.

"Why are you still standing there? Get to work!" he barked.

Zuba rubbed his keloid. "Senior, you have forgotten my boil." A large boil had grown on his right arm, close to his elbow, before the midterm break.

"What boil?" The prefect walked up to him. He grabbed Zuba's arm and twisted it to get a better look.

"Ouch," Zuba said.

"What is ouch? The boil is no longer there. It has healed."

"Yes." Zuba touched his elbow gingerly. "But the doctor said the root of the boil went so-ooo deep that it weakened my elbow joint. He said I should do nothing strenuous with the arm."

"What is wrong with this boy?" the prefect screamed, turning to the crowd of students. "He's always dodging from everything, takes part in nothing. Always at the fringe of every activity. He has asthma and cannot sweep dusty floors. He has an abscess when all others are being flogged on their buttocks. And now he has a weak elbow and cannot cut grass." He turned back to face Zuba. "You know what you are? You're a fringe-man!"

The students doubled up with laughter. "Fringe-man," they repeated, pointing at Zuba with one hand and holding their bellies with the other.

In his final year, when his mates' shoulders began broadening, when their voices deepened and their heights increased and their chins sprouted hair, Zuba realized that the name, Fringe-man, was loaded. It not only referred to his disposition to keep to the fringe of events but to his size as well. He was passing out of the school and entering university, but he was just five-feet-four-inches tall. And, unlike other short people who made up in girth what they lacked in height, he was fish-bone thin.

Yet any name was better than one that referred to his keloid.

What the Doctor Ordered

A high fence enclosed the eight-hectare estate. Coral vines, nourished by the abundance of the rainy season, ran wildly, intertwined along the fence. Fat carpenter bees buzzed and perched on the vine's flowers, their black and yellow contrasting with the lush pink blossoms.

Zuba's father, Professor Chukwueloka Maduekwe, strutted around the fifteen buildings that comprised his own school – offices, classrooms, dormitories and staff quarters. He no longer regretted giving up his academic career at the University. He kept grinning and rubbing his palms together. In a few years, no doubt, he would repay the loan that had enabled him to renovate and expand his late senator father's estate. He stopped at the centre of the compound and inhaled deeply. The air was heavy with the sharp scent of paint and with the fumes heated up from the fresh tar on the roads. It gave the compound the smell of a newly unwrapped gift pack. He nodded. An orange-headed lizard nodded back at him from its perch on the office wall.

The Professor resumed his walk, occasionally patting the trunks of the neem trees that framed the driveway. He stopped again when he got to the gleaming black front gate. A wide signboard, spilling over with the smiling, happy faces of well-fed children, proclaimed in bold blue letters: COROLLA SECONDARY SCHOOL FOR BOYS AND GIRLS: *where your child wants to be!*

When Zuba came home from university he saw from the bounce in his father's step that the school had taken off well. It was similar to the way his father used to walk beside their mum during family outings, especially when other men were looking.

Nonye teased their father about his new gait. "*Daddy, I buzikwa bobo*," she said, calling him a cool dude.

Their father threw back his head and laughed so hard that Zuba saw his tonsils, the way he used to laugh when their mother was around. It made Zuba recall what his kid brother Chuu had told him about being woken up in the night by Daddy's laughter and going to his room to find Daddy wrestling with Mummy under the bed sheets.

"Mummy is stronger than Daddy," Chuu had concluded. "She was winning, she was on top."

Zuba too had a lightness in his walk. He had had an essay published in his university's biochemistry journal – a rare feat for an undergraduate – and his Head of Department was encouraging him to take up a career in science, and offering his services as mentor. Zuba had spent a great deal of the last semester with the man he had come to call his school father. He showed his father the journal during a rare father-son outing to a pub.

"Hmmm. 'Exploring the Biochemistry of Keloid and Scar Formation'. Excellent!" The Professor closed the journal and placed it beside his glass of beer. He extended his hand for a presidential handshake. "Congratulations. Making good in your course, are you?"

"Yes, Dad. But it's more than just a course to me. It's what I want to do with my life."

"Writing scientific essays?"

"Researching and writing. I want to be a researcher."

Professor Maduekwe laughed. "So you will like to spend the rest of your life as a lab rat, locked away from people, with microscopes, test tubes, slides and pipettes for company?"

"No, Dad. I will not only research. I will lecture too, like... like..." He rubbed his keloid. "I'll lecture too," he said, stopping himself from mentioning the name of his school father. His father might put the man down as "a colourless fellow" – a tag the Professor used for many of his ex-colleagues, some of whom now laughed at him behind his back. (News had got to the Professor that his former rival for the Vice-Chancellorship of the University of Nigeria, Professor Umeadi, had said, "The last Dean of Education wanted to become Vice Chancellor so badly that when he lost to me, he left to become Vice Chancellor of a secondary school").

"Lecture? Well, that's good. But you'll be frustrated. Like I was. Universities are no longer what they used to be in the good old days. The President hit the nail on the head when he said lecturers today do nothing but sell handouts, drink beer in the staff club, harass female students and go on strike. And the lecturers proved him right by going on strike to protest his utterance."

A man in a green apron glided past the tables and placed two wooden bowls before them.

The meaty aroma got Zuba's stomach yearning. He washed his hands and started on the dish.

The Professor watched with a smile as his son chewed on a succulent piece of tongue. He picked up the tongue in his own bowl and moved it, dripping with spicy emulsified palm oil gravy, into Zuba's bowl, soiling the white plastic table top in the process.

Zuba avoided his father's stare. A young couple was seated at the other end of the pub, beneath a banner that said: CENTRAL INN, OJOTO, ANAMBRA STATE. BEST IN TOWN FOR GOATHEAD PEPPER SOUP. They were singing along and giggling over some memory called up by the highlife music playing in the background. He focused on them.

"How old are you now, son?" the Professor began again.

Zuba stiffened. His father used the expression "son" the way a farmer uses water on sun-baked soil: to soften it before tilling and sowing. "Twenty-one," he said, still averting his gaze.

"And you'll be graduating later this year?"

Zuba nodded.

"You know, son, I was thinking the other day how nice it would be if you got more involved in the school now. I will make a call to my old friend at the National Service Directorate and have you posted to our school here for your Service. What do you say to that, son?"

Zuba rubbed his keloid. He had been dreaming of his National Service, and could still hear his school father talking about his own Service: "It was a once-in-a-lifetime experience, Zuba, living unfettered for a year as an unknown in an unknown place." He nodded and said, "Yes, Dad, let me work and help out now during my holidays. But when I'm due for National Service, I'd like to be my age and take a break for a little adventure, to go to whatever nice new place I'll be posted."

Professor Maduekwe's lips stretched in a slanted smile. He lowered his voice as he said: "I know, son. You want a little wild time of your own, away from the reach of Daddy's prying eyes. I understand." But something in Zuba's expression made him ask, "Or did I get it wrong, son?"

"Dad, it will just be a little break to help me refocus."

The smile faded from the Professor's face. He would have gladly let his son go elsewhere for National Service if, at last, Zuba wanted to do what other young men did: play and sow their wild oats before settling down. All he knew about his son's sex life came from Nonye teasing Zuba with imitations of the housemaid: "Zuba, I have an itch in a place my hand can't reach, come now and help me scratch it?"'

The Professor studied his son's face while sipping his beer.

"And after Service? You have any plans?"

Zuba wanted to travel far from home, to see more of life, to spread his wings without fearing they would get in his father's way. "Like I said earlier, Dad, I will want to research and lecture in a university."

"That's good. Your interest is in education, like mine. But you know, son, the school I've started is just the lowest rung in a ladder. Once it takes off fully and stabilizes, we could move another rung up, into higher education. And then, you can lecture in your own school. In your own university. How about that?" Professor Maduekwe's eyes were now aglow. He gesticulated wildly, inflicting chops on the air as he spoke. "Welcome on board the ship, son."

On the day that Zuba came home after graduation, his father did not seem himself. Professor Maduekwe was shuffling about, seething and mumbling to himself. Anything in his path received the caustic blast of his bitterness. Zuba, Nonye and the housemaid moved about the house on tiptoes. Even their clothes seemed to match the colour of the walls, as if they were trying to blend in and vanish once they heard his footsteps. Unfortunately, it was at this time that a classmate of Nonye's came to visit.

"So you did not see her enough while in school, eh?" Professor Maduekwe barked at the boy. "You have to chase her all the way to my house. You don't want her to study in peace for her matriculation exams." The Professor looked Nonye's friend over again, from his glistening jheri curls to his shiny patent-leather shoes. "Yes, I know your kind. You're looking for a girl you will send to an early maternity. Well, not my daughter." He stormed forwards, mistaking the boy's dumbstruck stare for defiance.

"Daddy, no!" Nonye screamed.

The boy started and ran off.

The Professor chased him out of the compound, then walked back to the house. "Yes, I knew it, I knew it," he muttered. "That's the problem with mixed schools. I should have sent her to a girls' school. She would then not have boys sniffing after her like he-goats, following her scent to this house." He stepped into the parlour.

Nonye was on the sofa holding her head while her body shook with her quiet weeping. Zuba's arm was around her shoulders. He was wiping the tears off her face and murmuring consolations.

Professor Maduekwe shifted on his feet. He fought off the urge to rush over and wrap his arms around them. Such displays of softness were unmanly. He swallowed saliva to dissolve the lump forming in his throat. But when Nonye raised her teary face and stared into his eyes, he rushed over anyway and swept them up in his arms. "It's for your own good. Believe me, all I do is for your own good," he moaned into their hair.

Professor Maduekwe rested his head against his children. His breathing was laboured. The sixteen-hour days, the problem at the school, the skipped meals and the mislaid blood-pressure tablets... the whole burden of his rage descended upon him in a splitting migraine.

"Zuba... please... the car keys," he whispered. "Let's go to the hospital."

Zuba hesitated. There was something strange in the wording of the request. His father had not said please since their mother died.

They spent the night in the hospital, the Professor on a drip in the hospital bed while Zuba and Nonye slept in fits, huddled on a couch. By morning, the Professor had bounced back and insisted on being discharged.

He took the car keys for the drive back to the house, avoiding Zuba's eye. He stared ahead as he drove and said nothing. Zuba glanced at him. Was he embarrassed by that intimate hug with his children, as if it was a one-night stand?

After a hurried breakfast at home he rushed off to his office, summoning some of his staff along the way for a brainstorming of the current problem facing the school, even though it was a Sunday morning. For the school had been brought to its knees by the antics of its first principal, Mr Iweobi.

He had come highly recommended from the State Ministry of Education. At the age of fifty-six, he had over twenty-five years' experience in the education sector, twelve of them as principal at various schools.

After working with him for two terms, a disappointed Professor Maduekwe had called him to his face "a dyed-in-the-wool *state*-school principal with a lazy public-service mentality that does not fit in with the challenge and dynamism of the private sector". The Professor had decided to lay him off by the end of the session. Mr Iweobi – then barely on speaking terms with his employer – had left quietly.

The next term only twenty-six of the fifty-six pioneer students returned. The former principal had fed their parents lies about the school, advising them to transfer their children to other schools. It was this news that had driven the Professor into his latest rage.

Now alone in his office after a protracted meeting with his staff, the Professor felt the beginnings of a headache. He retrieved a blood-pressure cuff from his desk drawer. The school nurse was away so he fiddled with the contraption himself. His wife had always checked his blood pressure for him and, many years after her death, he was yet to master the contraption. He used to enjoy the way she would insist on his cooperation, even when he was dog-tired. Sometimes, he would put up a show of resistance just to get her going. Then she would pout her lips and use every arm-twisting technique in a woman's book to get him to budge. He would budge with a frown on his face and a smile in his heart, and occasionally on one unreasonable condition: that she dressed in some of the lingerie he had bought her, or in nothing at all. He would admire her curves and contours as she wrapped the bandage around his arm.

The Professor wiped tears from his eyes. He focused on a photo on the wall. It showed a younger-looking him in a Savile Row suit, being sworn in as Commissioner for Education before the Executive Governor of the state. His life had been one long tale of joys nipped in the bud. But he would not allow his joy to be extinguished so soon this time around.

With a few trusted staff, he set about contacting the affected parents to enlighten them as to the true state of affairs in the school. Eleven of the withdrawn students returned.

"The next principal should be a woman," the Professor mumbled to himself after the episode. "Yes, a woman. They're more honest, straightforward, and less likely to cause problems. Easier to handle, too."

He got home one evening, weeks later, and in a joyous mood announced to Zuba that he had interviewed a new principal for the school.

"In fact, I believe she is, like they say, what the doctor ordered for the school."

The new principal, Mrs Egbetuyi, came on a visit to the Professor's house with her husband.

"Good evening. You must be Zuba," she said, looking Zuba straight in the eye and smiling as he let her into the house. "Your father has told me much about you."

"I hope he didn't tell you the bad things," he said, returning her smile and the firm grip of her soft hand.

"Oh yes, he did. That was the part I enjoyed most."

Her husband followed her. He walked with his hands intertwined before him like a child that has promised to be on his best behaviour. He was just a bit taller than Zuba's father, but some kind of medical condition – acromegaly? – had enlarged all his extremities and made him look like a hulk. He squeezed Zuba's hand. His palm was callused and Zuba almost winced. The man grinned.

They sat on a sofa beside the bubbling aquarium, smiling as they took in the angelfishes that swam backwards, and the guppies with red, blue and orange markings and spade-shaped mouths.

They seemed an incongruous pair. The principal, short and slim, radiated an air of intelligence. She paid little attention to her appearance; with a little care, she could have looked pretty. Her hair was bobbed and combed forwards. Perched on her nose was a pair of thick-lensed glasses whose arms strained towards her ears at an obtuse angle.

Her husband sought his wife's gaze every now and then, and a small smile would move his lips each time. His left hand rested on her knee. He looked fortyish. His hair was smoothed backwards above a granite face with its king-size nose.

"I just left the army last year, Professor, after sixteen years of the most exciting service," he said, and went on to regale them with tales of his travels on hazardous peacekeeping missions. His wife kept nodding beside him, her eyes shining with pride.

Zuba shifted in his seat; there was a flicker of bitterness in his father's eyes. It was obvious that Mr Egbetuyi reminded his father of that terrible time years ago, soon after he was sworn in as Commissioner, when the military, having sacked the government, had clamped him in jail along with other corrupt politicians.

"Your daddy has gone abroad," Zuba's mother had explained, but later Zuba heard his dad's name on the network news.

"Mr Egbetuyi," Professor Maduekwe said, "you're still young, how come you left the military then?"

"It's a long story, Professor. It was in Liberia." He grimaced. "During Operation Thunderbolt. I was asked to waste a woman caught spying for the rebels. Yeah, she was a prostitute. But her country was a war zone, and it was through such liaisons that she managed to feed and preserve her children and husband. I kept thinking: this is somebody's wife, just like my wife. Heaven knows I cannot bear the thought of anyone hurting my wife in any way, how then could I harm another man's wife? I refused, Professor. And, in the end, I suffered dearly for it. Became jobless."

Mrs Egbetuyi laid a hand on her husband's knee. Her husband's hand was still on her knee, so her arm crossed his, forming an X. Zuba had heard that lovers who took a blood oath of loyalty would hold their arms in that manner, their blood mingling at the point of intersection from earlier incisions.

As always happened when confronted with such displays of emotion, Professor Maduekwe felt uneasy. He exchanged a glance with Zuba – didn't it all sound too Hollywood to be true?

"Well, Mr Egbetuyi, I have some contacts and will let you know of job opportunities that might interest you and... Aha! I wanted to ask about your children."

Mrs Egbetuyi stiffened. Her husband began to rub her knee. "Children? We'll have children when we're ready for them, Professor," he said in Igbo.

The Professor's eyes widened. So did Zuba's.

"You speak Igbo?" the Professor asked.

"Yes, Professor. And Hausa too. I picked them up in the course of my military postings."

After some more chit-chat, Mr Egbetuyi declared, "Permission to fall out, Professor." And they took their leave.

A few weeks after their visit, Zuba understood a little more about their curious reaction to the question of children.

Anxious for his National Service call-up letter, Zuba collected the keys to the school's post-office box one evening and drove to the post office. He found his call-up letter in the box and restrained himself from tearing it open. He had promised Nonye that they would open it together. He collected two other letters for Mrs Egbetuyi, and headed back to the school.

The principal's lodging was a concrete version of the traditional Igbo hut. Its roof, made of asbestos, was peaked at the top, and stretched down and wide around the house. It kept the rays of the sun off the walls of the building, ensuring coolness even in the hottest weather.

As Zuba approached the steps leading up to the veranda, he heard a woman's voice raised in argument:

"...we are no longer asking you to end your marriage to her. All we are saying is that you agree to our marrying another wife for you in the village. She will live with me and bear your children. You must not shirk your duties..."

"Mama, I can't take any more of this. You'll have to leave tomorrow morning. I did not invite you down to our new base to start talking to me about this again. Well, soon, my wife and I shall be out of your reach, and you'll never see us again."

"Son, if your father had not got me to give birth to you, you wouldn't be here today. You too have to—"

Zuba rapped on the door.

Mr Egbetuyi yanked it open. He regarded Zuba with bloodshot eyes.

"Sorry to disturb you. But these letters are for your wife." Zuba held out the letters.

The man took the letters and turned back inside.

Zuba left the veranda and hurried home.

"Nonye! Nonye!" he screamed.

Nonye ran out from her room. "What is it?"

"My call-up, my call-up."

They sat together on the sofa, and Zuba tore open the letter.

He had been posted to serve as a teacher in Lokomo, a village in the south-west of the country. The village had been in the news a few months back when the inhabitants demonstrated over their lack of amenities. It had no electricity or pipe-borne water. It was flanked by a river that served for drinking water, laundry, bath and latrine. The people still lived in mud huts.

Professor Maduekwe celebrated when he learnt of his son's terrible posting. He waited silently, expecting his son to come whining to him; then he would call his friend at the National Service directorate to effect a change in the posting and have Zuba sent to his school. But Zuba did not whine. He started packing his bag, and the look in his eyes awakened a sense of déjà vu in the Professor, who had seen that look before, in a shaving-mirror, the morning he had decided to quit his job at the University after losing his bid to be Vice Chancellor.

Presidential Slaps

The school's back entrance looked different from how Zuba remembered it. Clumps of elephant grass that had once lived up to their name, towering proud, lush and green on both sides of the culvert, were stooped and broken in spirit, fried brown by the dry-season heat. Further down the right side of the culvert, heaps of oily red earth lay beside an extensive excavation.

Zuba rapped on the gate. The echoing boom reminded him of a metal gong. He heaved his bulging bag off his shoulder and dropped it on the ground. A cloud of dust swirled around his boots. He undid two buttons on the faded khaki top of his National Service uniform, revealing a white vest that was soaked with sweat. He rapped again on the gate.

"Who be that?"

"It's me, Zuba."

A face appeared in the chink where the two gates met.

"Heeeey! Oga! Na you. Welcome sah." The gate squealed open. The gateman reached for Zuba's bag.

"No, don't worry. Thank you." Zuba lifted the bag into the compound.

He met only the housemaid in the house.

"Daddy collapsed this morning and was rushed to the hospital," she said. "Nonye and the driver are still there with him."

After a bath and a light meal, Zuba picked up the keys to one of the cars. What could have caused the breakdown this time? He drove slowly through the school compound, heading towards the front gate. He waved at the principal. Her hair had grown longer. She was on a cane chair on the veranda of her apartment, reading from a book on her lap, while her husband was seated on the bare floor at her feet, staring ahead into the compound.

The compound was bright and noisy with students in their blue-and-white games wear. A jubilant scream came from the volleyball court as one of the teams scored. The players danced and hugged each other before returning to their positions for another round. Further ahead, the games master coached a group of students in football. They bantered and laughed as they passed the ball among themselves. Their vests were dull with sweat, and their faces shone with such joy that Zuba could not help feeling pride for his father's work. The school was doing well. What then could have caused the breakdown?

He arrived at the hospital as Nonye and Ike were about to leave. Stella, the school bursar, was with them.

"You've become thinner than a fish bone," Nonye exclaimed, running up to embrace him. "Were they starving you in that your exotic village? And what's with the new glow? Have you won a lottery?"

Zuba grinned. "Let's save the story for later, fat girl," he said, and pinched her upper arm.

"Ouch! Your fingers pinch like pliers."

She went back into the hospital with him, Zuba wrinkling his nose at its antiseptic smell.

His father was on a bed in the private ward. A drip fed into his arm. His face looked handsome and serene as he slept. Zuba smiled. How nice it would have been if this were his father's usual expression. He laid a hand on his father's arm. It had been long since he last saw him.

He felt happy, and looked forward to telling him about his latest article on keloids, 'Biochemistry and Keloid Formation: A Freshman's Perspective', published in *The International Journal of Biochemistry* just four months into his service year, and the UK university scholarship he had secured in its wake. He could imagine receiving a presidential handshake.

The doctor came into the room. "Your father may be needing a longer rest this time," he said, after the preliminary greetings. "You're now a graduate, Zuba? And... how old are you?"

"I'll be twenty-three in October."

"Good. I'm sure you can keep an eye on your father's work in the meantime. You're now a man."

You're now a man. Zuba liked the sound of the words. "Of course, doctor," he said. "I definitely will."

Zuba walked out with Nonye to meet Ike and Stella, the bursar, still waiting. "What caused it this time?" he asked.

"What else? It's the school," Nonye said. "The new principal, this time around. Let Stella tell you what happened."

"It's Mrs Egbetuyi o," Stella said, and shook her head. Her Bob Marley weave-on braids dangled over her cheeks. "She was running a secret racket, collecting 'Special Lesson Fees' from parents. I discovered this three days ago while she was away for the All Principals' Conference. A parent had asked if he could pay to me since she was not around. Rumour has it that she and her husband are trying to raise money for their migration to Canada."

The Professor had seethed and raved for two whole days while awaiting her return from the conference. He collapsed on the third day as she reappeared. Mrs Egbetuyi had just been in time to see her boss being carried away, unconscious, from his office.

Nonye joined Zuba in his car. He drove behind Ike and Stella, chatting with her as they tried to catch up on each other's lives.

"Wow! So you'll be travelling again. Overseas, this time."

"Yes. By September. Can't wait."

"Congrats! But I'll stow away in your luggage. I don't want to be all alone again."

"Don't worry." He patted her on the knee. "I'll keep in touch better than I did during National Service. The nearest post office was an hour and two hundred naira away."

Nonye stared up at the evening sky. "I smell rain. We may have the first rain tonight."

The next morning, Zuba arrived at his father's office and found, lying on the mahogany desk, a file with the fresh-looking inscription: Board of Governors. His father must have initiated moves to constitute a board for the school, something he had deferred until the school had really taken off. Beside the file was another with the inscription: Egbetuyi, Adebisi Omolola (Mrs). Steering clear of his father's swivel chair, he reached for the file. The intercom crackled and the secretary announced the presence of the school contractor.

The contractor handled most of the school's minor construction works. After preliminary greetings, he informed Zuba that he needed more bags of cement for the storm drains he was building outside the school fence, along the erosion-ravaged road that led down to the local stream. The drain was necessary to protect the fence from caving in under the pressure of rain flood. Zuba assured him of the supply of cement, and accompanied him to the site at his request.

They were inspecting the site when the secretary rushed out through the back gate.

"Zuba, Zuba, please, you have to come, hurry. There's trouble in the office."

"Don't tell me that's where all that noise is coming from," Zuba said, starting to run. He had been hearing the occasional cry, screams and shouts, but had thought that the villagers were at it again. Perhaps another land feud or a robber being dealt instant justice.

Approaching the staffroom, he glimpsed desks and chairs lying on their sides, books and papers strewn all over the ground. Part of the brown carpet had been torn up, exposing the bare grey floor and the wires that criss-crossed it. The curtains lay in a grumpy heap beneath the windows.

The principal stormed past Zuba as he stepped inside. Her husband followed.

"Mrs Egbetuyi, Mrs Egbetuyi," Zuba called after the principal. "What happened?"

She turned and regarded Zuba with rage-red eyes. "Please excuse me," she said, and sped after her husband.

There were four people in the staffroom: Nwandu, the vice principal, Effiong, the clerk, Mrs Iwenofu, the maths teacher, and Stella, the bursar.

Nwandu and Effiong straightened up from their squatting positions, shock and outrage on their faces. Neither of them said anything – not even Effiong, who was noted for his loquacity. Stella's weeping competed with the drone of the refrigerator.

Zuba knelt before Stella. Her cheeks were red. Her head, which only yesterday had borne glorious Bob Marley braids, now displayed the receding hairline of a granny. Scattered on the ground before her were some of the black weave-on braids. She held up her torn blouse to shield her bra.

Zuba placed a hand on her shoulder. "What happened?"

"The principal and her husband beat me up," she said through sobs. "I... I didn't do anything to them. Ask them." She motioned towards Mrs Iwenofu and the other members of staff in the room.

"What happened?" Zuba asked again, straightening up and facing Mrs Iwenofu. Mrs Iwenofu took a deep breath.

"Stella had come to see me in the staffroom and we were seated, talking, when the principal came in and made straight for her. 'What right have you to interrogate my visitor, eh?' she was saying. 'Don't you have any respect for me as your boss? What right have you to insult me and call me a troublemaker before my visitor?' You see, a visitor had come in earlier to the staffroom asking for the principal. Stella had asked the visitor if her business was private or official. When the lady said private, Stella didn't take her to the principal's house, saying she wanted no trouble – you know they're not on speaking terms because of the 'Special Lesson Fees' issue.

"Well, the principal slapped Stella when she denied the accusation. 'Liar! Liar!' she shouted. 'Come on, apologize, I'm your boss.' Stella got up from her seat and went to another. The principal followed her. Slap! again. 'Open your mouth and say you're sorry.'

"Then Stella gave her a shove. The woman crashed into a desk, screaming and falling over with it, pulling down the curtain with her. Stella ran out of the room. Haaaaa! But you know, no one knew the woman had come with her husband, and that he was waiting quietly outside, peeping from the window. Stella ran straight into him and he dragged her back to the staffroom by the hair. Hmmmnh! The man was livid. 'You dared to touch my wife,' he shouted. 'You dared to assault my wife?' You won't believe the slaps he gave Stella. Stella ran around, screaming and trying to get out of the staffroom. But the man blocked her path to the door.

"It was not until Effiong came in and, together with Nwandu, was ready to take the man on in a fight that he let Stella go."

"Did any of the students witness this?" Zuba asked, his head swimming.

"I don't think so, they were all in their classrooms. They must have heard the screaming though."

Zuba shook his head. No, this could not be. There had to be some other explanation. He consoled Stella and helped her to a chair, then he left the staffroom.

The school compound seemed strangely deserted. Zuba's steps echoed on the tarred road leading to the senior-staff quarters. Why weren't there any birds chirping on the neem trees? Even the squirrels that scampered from branch to branch were nowhere to be seen, and there were no skinks and lizards sunbathing on the road. Had all the screaming shocked them out of the compound?

He knocked on the door of the principal's apartment.

A peep through the window preceded the opening of the door.

"Good day, madam," Zuba said. "I'd like to have a word with you."

Mrs Egbetuyi led him to the living room and sat down beside her grim-looking husband.

Mr Egbetuyi was sitting complacently on the settee. Too complacently for a man who had ceded his position as breadwinner to his wife. Yesterday Nonye had explained how the man had rebuffed their father's attempts to get him a job – he had described such attempts as "an interference in the logistics of my family life" and "an attempt to mess with the territorial integrity of my family". His right arm, thrown carelessly over the headrest of the settee and resting on the shoulder of his uptight wife, together with the jaunty cock of his head, seemed to proclaim: "Yeah, I'm in charge".

Sizzling sounds – the sound of a pot boiling over – and the pungent smell of sweet basil came from the kitchen. The principal excused herself.

Zuba looked around the room. The only addition to the basic school furniture was an old radio set. It sat on a shelf beside a framed picture of a younger-looking Mrs Egbetuyi and her husband on their wedding day. On the side stool beside his chair, a news magazine was open on the classifieds page. One of the adverts caught Zuba's attention:

YOU CALL YOURSELF A MAN?

Before you can answer yes to this question, naturally it is when you can win your partner in four or five rounds of sex. But many kinds of staphylococcus in the body make this impossible by causing difficulty in going more than one round with sex partner, premature ejaculation, weak erection, watery sperm, etc. Visit Alhaji Dr Fasuba, Indian-trained homeopathic doctor, for a permanent solution! Home service also available nationwide. A trial will convince you...

A pot cover clanged down and the principal walked back into the room. Though she now walked with a slight limp, there was still a self-assurance in the way she carried herself, which melted away as she sat beside her husband.

"Em..." Zuba began. "Madam, what happened in the staffroom? What was the cause of the commotion?"

"Are you querying her? What's your position in the chain of command in the school? Or are you asking as an ally?" Mr Egbetuyi said.

The lips of his wife, which had parted to give a reply, came together again.

"You should allow her to answer. This is an official school matter and she understands better how things stand," Zuba replied, ignoring the challenge in the man's voice.

"But you can't question her over school matters. She doesn't report to you. She reports only to your father, not to you."

"I don't think she shares your viewpoint. She knows that under certain circumstances I can act for my father..." Zuba stopped. He chose another approach to avoid a deadlock. "Anyway, I'm only asking to know what happened, as many others will ask."

"Can you imagine that diabolic old prostitute they call Stella interrogating my sister and insulting me before her?" the principal began. "This is neither the first, second nor third time that she will be looking for my trouble. The other day I heard she said I was a witch. And even when I try to keep out of her way she keeps interfering in my work."

"But don't you think that resorting to violence was taking it too far? You could have reported her, and disciplinary action would have been taken against her after due investigation."

"I had reported her several times to your father to no avail. I was so angry this time that I slapped her. That was all I did. Whereas she pushed me down, and I'm still limping from my sprained hip."

"Look Zuba, It is quite usual for a boss to slap his subaltern," Mr Egbetuyi began again. "I even heard that your father has slapped his staff before. And it was in the papers the other day that the president slapped his ADC. Believe me, the slap was long overdue. Stella will be tame and respectful to my wife as her boss henceforth."

Zuba opened his mouth but no sound came out.

"She really got us angry. We're only human, you know," the principal added.

The "Special Lesson Fees" case – which, no doubt, her idle husband drove her to – was yet to be resolved, and they were already entangling themselves in another matter. Zuba shook his head; his father would destroy them, like a shiny-eyed kid tearing apart a daddy-long-legs.

He rubbed his keloid as he said, "Well, madam, the important thing now is that work in the school should continue peacefully, we must keep the school going until my father returns."

The Egbetuyis exchanged glances. Something like surprise flickered in their eyes.

"Thank you for your understanding," Mrs Egbetuyi said.

As Zuba left the building, the man's voice filtered out through the open windows:

"...If the boy wants, let him not wake up to reality. His father is gone. That was how my father was carried away and he ended up in a mortuary."

62

Zuba smiled. They did not know that such hospital visits were common with his father.

He caught sight of the maths teacher's husband as he made his way back to the office block. Clad in a loincloth, the man was seated on the veranda of their apartment reading the paper. He was a lecturer at the nearby Nnamdi Azikiwe University, and claimed to be giving only three hours of lectures a week. He waved, and Zuba waved back.

No doubt, he would easily secure a lecturing position when he had his UK master's degree. Then he too would enjoy the quiet university lecturer's life that would give him time to pursue his research. Of course, he would remain at the fringe of all administrative responsibilities.

Zuba walked on towards the offices, dreaming about his future three-hours-of-lectures-a-week life: walk into class, give his lectures, walk out again, mark and submit his papers, collect his salary, go on holidays, and also show solidarity by going on the extra strike-holidays with his colleagues. Such strikes were the reason why he had ended up taking almost six years for his four-year BSc programme. His lecturers had been on strike with pay for four months in his first year, seven months in his second year, and five months in his third year.

He got to the staffroom and urged the members of staff to attend to their work as usual. "My father will be back soon to handle the case," he assured them.

"The Disciplinary Committee should look into the matter," Mr Nwandu, the vice principal, suggested. He was also chairman of the Committee.

Zuba searched Nwandu's face. His eyes still burned with indignation over the event. Zuba had reservations about the success of a disciplinary sitting. From the little interaction he had had with the principal and her husband, he doubted they would cooperate. Nevertheless, he gave the go-ahead for the sitting.

"Zuba, welcome," Nonye said as she let him into the house after the close of work.

"Thanks, Nonye. What a day."

He made straight for his room, tugging at his tie. He nodded a greeting at the picture hanging on the eastern wall of his room. The picture showed Gandhi leaning on his cane, and had the caption: Mahatma Gandhi, Father of Non-Violent Change – An Eye For an Eye Will Make the Whole World Blind. Stuck onto the lower left corner of the frame was a Post-it with the handwritten inscription: 5 f 4 in tall.

He pulled off his shoes and clothes and put them in their places. He removed his watch and placed it on top of Coetzee's *Life & Times of Michael K* on his bedside table. He remembered he was close to finishing the book and wondered if he would be lucky again on his next visit to the bookshop: to pick a book, flip it open, and discover a physically flawed character in the first sentence.

Two Left Feet

Zuba was awakened by loud voices coming from the direction of the general-staff quarters. He picked up his watch: 6.27 a.m. He was still dressing, wondering what could be the cause, when a knock sounded at the main door. Thomas, Stella's fiancé, stood outside.

"Zuba, good morning," he said, panting. "Please, you have to come quickly. The Egbetuyis are out to engage us in a fight."

"Are you serious?" Zuba exclaimed. He found a pair of slippers and followed Thomas out, buttoning his shirt as they raced to the staff quarters.

Dressed in a faded blue tracksuit and brown canvas shoes, Mr Egbetuyi paced back and forth before Stella's apartment, banging intermittently at the door.

"Where are you? Don't just hurl a threat and run. Come on out! Let's settle this mano-a-mano, once and for all."

Leaning against the wall, a few paces from him, was the principal. Her gaze was fixed at the door of the apartment, unmoving, like her puckered lips.

Staff and their children stood in front of their apartments, watching with chewing sticks in their mouths and sleep in their eyes. A group of students returning from their morning prep had also stopped to watch.

Mr Egbetuyi caught sight of Thomas. "Coward, coward," he shouted. "Why did you run away? Why did you run away?"

"Mr Egbetuyi, Mrs Egbetuyi, what's the meaning of all this? I thought we had settled this yesterday," Zuba said.

Mrs Egbetuyi fiddled with her fingers. Her husband stopped his pacing and regarded Zuba over flared nostrils.

"Yes," Mrs Egbetuyi began, "but—"

"Come, come and explain to me," Zuba cut in. He led the way to their apartment.

When they reached the veranda, Zuba blurted out, "Mrs Egbetuyi, what happened again? How can you behave like this? You're supposed to be the principal of this school, for goodness sake."

"I'm sorry Zuba. But can you imagine that whore's lizard of a twentieth boyfriend threatening us last night? It was about 7 p.m. and my husband and I were going to shop down the road. As we made to pass the gates, we saw Stella and her boyfriend coming in. Her boyfriend stopped and stared hard at my husband and said, 'You have seven days.' 'Seven days for what?' my husband asked. Thomas said, 'I'll show you that I'm a son-of-the-soil here. And your wife too. I'll teach you what the English people mean when they say you cannot beard a lion in its den.' Then he stormed off with Stella. 'Wait, wait,' my husband called after him. 'Let's talk this over.' But he ignored us."

Mr Egbetuyi, who had been pacing back and forth while his wife talked, stopped and said, "You see, Zuba, I spent sixteen years in the military, and we're trained not to take threats lying low. I tried, really tried to overlook the man's threat. But it haunted me all night. It is one thing for a man to threaten me. I'm a man, and I can wait to see if the man will dare approach me to make true his threat. But for a man to threaten my wife! I've been awake since 5 a.m. this morning.

"Since the man did not want an amicable talking-it-over, well..." the principal added.

Staring at the large frame and granite face of the man, Zuba found it hard to believe that the skinny bespectacled architect, Thomas, would so challenge him. Mr Egbetuyi looked like he would have jumped at such a heaven-sent opportunity to pulverize the fiancé of his wife's enemy.

"Did anybody else witness this?" Zuba asked.

"No," the principal answered. "We were alone by the gate and it was already getting dark."

Zuba pushed down the annoyance building up in him. His father would handle them when he returned. Once more he tried to play things down: "He must have been trying to save face before his fiancée," he said. "Mr Egbetuyi, as a man, surely you can understand that. Anyway, the thing is, the proprietor's absence is not an opportunity for us to do whatever we like. We can't allow this place to descend into anarchy just because he has been taken ill. I will hand over to the police anyone that disturbs the peace of the school again."

Zuba left the Egbetuyis and headed for Stella's apartment.

"I never made such a threat," Thomas insisted. He shook his head so hard that Zuba thought his glasses would fall off. "We passed each other at the gate but we did not exchange a single word. It must be his conscience worrying him. Like our people say, when a fowl farts it is chased by shadows."

"Besides," Stella began, "Zuba, do you really think that if Thomas had made such a threat Mr Egbetuyi would have waited till this morning to react? He would have started a fight immediately."

That made much sense. But Zuba repeated his earlier warning to the Egbetuyis, that he would tolerate no further disturbance in the school.

Fifteen minutes later, Zuba was being driven to the hospital by Ike.

"We have to put fuel in the tank."

Zuba glanced at the fuel gauge. "Oh no. What about the queues?"

There was fuel scarcity in town. Even at the inflated price of thirty-five naira per litre – fifteen naira above the official price – only very few filling stations were selling. Cars, buses and motorbikes queued before the fuel pumps, stretching out into the roads and obstructing the traffic. Drivers assaulted the lines from many points in an attempt to jump the queue, provoking fights, protests, pleas and obscenities. Hawkers moved from car to car, announcing their wares – the filling stations had become open markets.

"Let's head for Nnewi," Zuba said. "If Uzoil is also as crowded as the stations we've seen, then we'll have to settle for black-market fuel."

Ike made a U-turn and sped off. He spat out of the window as he passed a mound of burnt and blackened human body parts, chopped up and arranged at a road junction – trademark of an execution by the dreaded local anti-robbery vigilantes, the Bakassi Boys.

The Uzoil filling station only had five cars jostling to get to the pump. They were healthy-looking cars, unlike the usual second-hand cars, jalopies, and "management cars" – cars that you had to drive while managing one fault or the other: faulty steering, overheating engines, backfiring exhausts, squealing bushings or epileptic carburettors

– that dominated the roads. No commuter bikes, buses or taxis seemed to have discovered this oasis in the fuel drought.

Ike veered into the station and joined the queue behind a glistening grey Honda Accord. Zuba sighed with relief.

"How much is it?" Ike called out to the pump attendant.

"It's fifty naira per litre o," the attendant said.

"Fifty naira!" Zuba exclaimed. "No wonder only bourgeois cars are here. Ike, what do we do?"

"Let's buy it here. It's still cheaper, and certainly more reliable, than any fuel we can get on the black market. Or do you want me to drop you and return to one of those crowded stations with my sleeping mat to take a holiday from work," Ike said, chuckling.

Zuba laughed. "Ike-power, no holiday o."

Ike grinned and rubbed his hand over his face. He was tall, with a slenderness that belied his strength and capacity for wildness, and was always happy to recount how soft and mousy he had been when he first came to the Onitsha-Ojoto area. The road touts, street urchins, fake tax agents and fake parking agents had picked on him until he had learnt to fight back – learnt that bravado, the loudest voice, and the fist, usually carried the day. Zuba's feeling towards him was fraternal, because of Ike's doglike loyalty to his father. Zuba had seen Ike go the extra mile to protect his father's secrets – secrets that his father would never know that Zuba knew – and even sacrifice his own reputation to preserve that of the Professor.

They got to the hospital in good time. Zuba met the doctor on the corridor leading to his father's room.

"How is he, doctor?"

"Zuba," the doctor said. "I'm afraid he has had a stroke."

"Stroke?"

"Yes. He was already hypertensive. He pushed himself too far. I had warned him several times to take things easy and pay more attention to his medicine. But you know your dad. He never listens. At the moment, the right side of his body is paralysed. I'm sorry. We can only hope the damage will not be permanent."

Zuba quickened his pace to his father's room, Ike following behind. The doctor's words were difficult to accept. No, his dad had simply stressed himself out as he usually did, and now needed some rest. He burst into the room and made straight for the bed.

His chest constricted as he stared down at his father. The right half of his face was twisted out of shape and drooped downwards. Spittle dribbled from his lips in a slimy, elastic string. Zuba collected some tissue and wiped the dribble off his father's mouth and chin.

"Dad, good morning," he said.

His father stared at him with the passive eyes of a geriatric. Gone was the restless fire that made his gaze so engaging.

"Daddy... Daddy..." He brought his face closer to his father's. "It's me, Zuba. Daddy..."

It was like a punch in the belly when his father's eyelids came down, shutting him away from his father's new world.

"Doctor, did you see that? He doesn't recognize me. My father no longer recognizes me." He laid a hand on his father's shoulder and shook him lightly. "Daddy, say something. Please, do something. Tell me you know it's me. Show me you recognize me!"

The doctor placed a hand on Zuba's shoulder and led him to a chair.

"Doctor, don't tell me that my father can no longer recognize me. I thought you said he was only paralysed. Did it also affect his mental capacity?" The tears were now trickling down his face.

The doctor ran his hand over what was left of his hair. "I'm sorry, Zuba, but I cannot yet say. More time and tests will be required before we know the nature and extent of the brain damage. And we lack the equipment here to carry out some of the necessary tests. I'll have to refer you to another hospital at Enugu."

Zuba wept silently beside the bed, staring at his father.

"Take heart my child, I believe it shall be well," the doctor said.

Zuba glanced at Ike. Tears had made glistening patterns on Ike's face. He was leaning against a wardrobe in the room, staring down at his boss.

"Take heart, I say, my child," the doctor said. "It may take a while, but he may make a substantial recovery. You should know your father. He has always been a fighter, and will not give up easily. Let's hope he will be back on his feet within a couple of months."

"Months?"

"You have to take care of his work. You know how dear the school has been to him. You have to make sure he has something to return to."

Zuba and Ike drove back to the school in silence.

Nonye wept and wailed like one bereaved. "Daddy, oh Daddy. Lord, how can life be this cruel to us? Oh Daddy…"

"But Nonye, Dad is still alive…"

She broke away from his embrace. "You call that life? Tell me, Zuba, you call that life?" Her eyes were demented.

"What greater punishment could anyone inflict upon him? O Lord, are we to become as orphans? Mummy, oh Mummy, how I wish you were here, how I wish you had not left us." She began to sob again.

Zuba pulled her back into his arms. "Nonye, don't cry so," he said while trying to stem the flow from his own eyes. "Believe me, he'll be OK, he'll be back soon. You know Daddy. He won't give up. He will fight to get up. For us. For the school. Believe me, Nonye, he will. He knows he's all we have left. Let's be strong, Nonye, strong for him while he recovers."

They fell asleep in each other's arms, huddled on the sofa beside the aquarium. By the time they awoke, the evening was half gone. Ike drove Nonye to the hospital, where she spent the night sitting up beside their father's bed.

Zuba stayed back to keep an eye on the school. He went to bed after a walk around the compound. He slept badly, and at four in the morning was staring into the darkness, twisting and turning. He could hear the usual voices and footsteps outside the compound as the villagers walked down to the stream to fetch water. The first rays of light were yet to streak the sky. He sat up on the bed, turned on the reading lamp and began to stroke his keloid.

He had no choice. No, he had no choice. Like his father used to say, he had to dance to the new beats that Fate was drumming for him. Even if he had to do so with two left feet.

Lying on the floor beside his bed was his admission letter, and the UK university brochure, its gloss thumbed off by his fingers. It was April, and he was due to go in September. He reached for the documents and cuddled them in his lap. There was a bold-lettered sentence in his scholarship letter: "Deferral of the award to a later academic session is not permitted". He pulled open the drawer on the table, arranged the documents within it and pushed it shut. They would be safe in the drawer. Along with his dreams. For weeks, a few months, perhaps. But definitely not for more.

He slumped back on the bed.

Runny Tummy

By the time Zuba woke up, his earlier feelings of sorrow and dread had been replaced by an inexplicable elation, an intuition that his troubles were fleeting. He had had a dream. It had been Nonye's matriculation party, and she was dancing with their dad. Their dad's movements had been lopsided – his right hand, stiff. But he was smiling, happy, as was Nonye. Yes, their father would be well and up in no time, their lives would return to normal. Yes! Zuba glanced at his watch. 9.22 a.m. He sprang from his bed and rushed to the bathroom. Then he dressed and stepped out.

The lawns twinkled, emerald-green and shiny, surrounded by the dark-green leaves and screaming-red flowers of the Ixora that hedged them in. Sprinklers hissed and whirled, creating a light mist. Agama lizards hung on the walls where they had woken up, grey and dour, waiting for the lazy rainy-season sun to call them out to the road. Neem trees swayed by the roadsides.

Two students were walking down from the road that led to the hostels. "Good morning, Uncle," they greeted as Zuba approached.

"Good morning," Zuba answered. "Shouldn't you be having a lesson now?"

"Yes, Uncle. I went to get the key to my locker. I forgot it at the hostel," one of them said, and dug out a bunch of keys from the pocket of his trousers.

The other pulled out a calculator from his shirt pocket, "And I forgot my calculator."

Zuba noticed the tiny flakes that surrounded their lips and smelt the chocolate in their breath. He smiled. "OK, hurry to your classes then," he said.

The students sprinted off.

Zuba ascended the steps to the office block. In his hand was a reporter's notebook, open at a page on which he had written in bold black letters: "To Do":

1. *Ensure all is well in the school*
2. *11 a.m. appointment with dad's lawyer: inform him about dad's stroke. See if you can sack principal. VP to act in her place*
3. *1 p.m. appointment with Dr for dad's transfer to a better hospital in Enugu.*

He saw the principal through her office window. She was dressed in a peach skirt suit, and was engrossed in a document. She put the paper aside as Zuba walked in.

"Good morning, madam. How is the school today?"

"Good morning, Zuba. Everything is as it should be."

This was the first time he had seen her office so quiet and empty. It usually bustled with members of staff seeking advice or discussing one issue or the other with her. He nodded to her and moved on to his father's office.

A memo from the chairman of the Staff Disciplinary Committee lay on top of other documents in the in-tray on the desk. He pulled a straight-back chair to the side of the desk, sat down and skimmed through the memo. Stella had accepted the committee's invitation, while the principal had spurned it. "A high priest cannot be tried by his Sanhedrin," she had responded.

75

There was a soft rap on the door. Stella walked in, panting.

"Zuba, a policeman is here to take Thomas to the station," she said.

She had barely finished speaking when Thomas appeared in the doorway. A man in faded jeans trailed behind him.

"Zuba, please can you accompany me to the local police station?" Thomas said. He glanced behind him, through the open office door. The man in jeans had taken a seat in the secretary's office.

Zuba did not want to go with Thomas to the station. But there was an appeal in Thomas's eyes that made it difficult for him to decline his request. Zuba tried to do it in a roundabout way. He walked up to the policeman.

"Good morning, officer. I'm Mr Maduekwe. Zuba Maduekwe, acting director of the school."

The policeman rose from his seat, sizing Zuba up from head to toe, surprised. They shook hands. "I'm Detective Sergeant Akume, sir, from the Ojoto Police Station."

There was tobacco in his breath, and it mingled with the strong incense smell of his perfume.

"Thomas says you have invited him to the station. I hope there's no problem."

"No problem at all, sir." The policeman broke into a smile that was supposed to be disarming. "Someone reported threat-to-life case against him. We just want to ask him some questions. That's all."

Zuba returned to his office. "You see," he said under his breath, "there's nothing to worry about. They just want to ask you some questions."

"Zuba, you can never trust these people. Please accompany me."

"Zuba, please go with him," Stella pleaded.

Zuba glanced at his watch. "All right, let's go," he said. He walked to the principal's office to tell her that he was going out. But her office was locked and she was nowhere in sight. He got into the back seat of Thomas's Passat, behind the detective in the front passenger seat, and they drove off.

The police station was situated off the Nnewi old road; one of the two tarred roads in the town, it led to the bustling industrial town of Nnewi, hometown of Emeka Ojukwu, leader of the Igbos during the Biafran War. Shops, residential buildings and cassava farms flitted by as they drove. Bare-chested men stooped over newly cleared plots with hoes, raising mighty mounds for the yam-planting season.

A sheet-metal signpost, painted in the official colours of blue, yellow and green, proclaimed: The Nigeria Police Ojoto. The station occupied the ground floor of an uncompleted one-storey building. Windows, without glass louvres, stood agape. Cars from accident sites, squashed and mangled in every conceivable way, littered the compound, decaying and sprouting weeds.

Zuba was surprised to find Mr and Mrs Egbetuyi sitting on a bench in the station.

"You left the school without telling anyone," he said.

The principal stared in surprise. "Please bear with me, Zuba. You see, like my husband said, we cannot take a threat to our lives lightly. Our minds have not been at peace since the threat. You know we're strangers in this part of the country. So we have to take every possible precaution."

Mr Egbetuyi's nostrils quivered as he regarded Zuba.

"Don't be worried, Zuba," Mrs Egbetuyi continued. "You needn't have bothered coming with him." She nodded contemptuously towards Thomas. "We just want him cautioned, and the incident documented by the police so that if anything happens to us the police will know where to look."

Thomas sat down behind a brown classroom desk. Above him, a poster proclaimed: BAIL IS FREE. A policeman emerged from an inner room. He placed two sheets of paper on the desk before Thomas. "Read this," he said, thumping one with his forefinger, "and after, write your statement here."

Thomas bent over the paper. Two minutes later, he was scribbling on the blank sheet as they all watched and waited. It was a quarter of an hour before he handed the sheets back to the officer.

The officer took his time to read through the document.

"So you're denying everything, heh?"

Mr Egbetuyi muttered in Yoruba to the policeman. The policeman replied in Yoruba too and looked at Mrs Egbetuyi. She nodded.

Zuba shook his head in frustration. Although he had spent his National Service in the Yoruba-speaking southwest of the country, his grasp of the language was limited to a few basic greetings and many swear words.

"I have already told you, I did not threaten anybody," Thomas said.

"All right. You must wait with us while we investigate."

"Wait?" Lines appeared on Thomas's brow.

"In cell. Till we finish investigation."

"But you know where I live."

"And how do we know that you will not run away?"

"That's preposterous!"

"Look, Mr Whatever-is-your-name, this does not call for big grammar. Don't try to show me how learned you are. I'm following normal procedure."

Zuba walked to the desk.

"Officer, don't take it that way. We are a school and we all live in the school. I am Chikezuba Maduekwe, acting director of the school. Like any other organization, we have our own way of handling matters such as this. So please, this is evidently a minor misunderstanding that can be settled in the school without making a federal case out of it. I assure you that if the school is unable to reconcile the parties we would report the matter to you ourselves."

"Look, Mister, don't tell me how to do my job."

"OK," Zuba said. He walked past the man, went down a corridor, rapped on a door and stepped in.

It was a small cluttered office. The head of the station sat behind a desk strewn with files and papers. He was a wiry man with a spotless, fair complexion – the kind of complexion that many black girls covet. The plaque before him read: A.C. Okonkwo. Zuba smiled and greeted him warmly in Igbo.

"Young man, what can I do for you?"

"Please, I need some assistance with a little matter. A Yoruba employee has reported a minor matter to one of your officers who is also Yoruba. I don't know what they discussed in their language but now the officer wants to detain my Igbo friend instead of granting him bail."

The head of station grunted and summoned the officer, gesturing for Zuba to wait elsewhere. Zuba walked out of the station and sat on the car bonnet. It was half an hour before Thomas hurried out.

"Zuba, please can you lend me two hundred naira? I have only three hundred naira, and the man is asking for five hundred before he can release me on bail after I sign an undertaking of responsibility for whatever harm may befall the Egbetuyis."

Zuba gave him two hundred. Thomas hurried back in with the money just as the Egbetuyis came out.

"Zuba, please understand. Like I said, we're strangers in this part of the country and cannot take any undue risk. With the signing of an undertaking by Thomas we now feel safer," Mrs Egbetuyi said.

"Yeah, such defensive moves are necessary in unfamiliar terrain," Mr Egbetuyi added.

"Your defensive moves had better stop with this," Zuba said.

"You know we're a peace-loving couple, Zuba. There'll be no further problems," Mrs Egbetuyi said.

They walked down the denuded red earth on the side of the road, chatting in vernacular. They stopped outside a convenience store with the bold sign, DAILY BREAD SUPERMARKET, and flagged down two motorbike taxis to take them back to school – the riders of these *okada* would weave through the tightest traffic jams, leaving a train of curses and scratched paintwork behind them if necessary, to make good time. Ike had a horsewhip on the dashboard for warding them off.

One of the riders tilted his bike towards Mrs Egbetuyi while she held onto her husband with one hand and hitched up her skirt with the other, revealing robust thighs with a lighter complexion than her face. Mr Egbetuyi mounted behind his rider with dexterity, and the bikes zoomed off.

Thomas came out of the station. "Thanks so much, Zuba. You've saved me from these people. Thank you." He pumped Zuba's hand.

"Oh, it's nothing," Zuba replied. He glanced at his watch as they headed for the car. A loud banging was coming from the mechanic workshop nearby. A man was

beating out a dent from the panel of a commuter bus
while his apprentice watched. Zuba and Thomas got into
the car and drove off. The pound-pound of the mechanic's
hammer followed them, sounding like the beating of a
heart in mortal fear.

At home, Ike was waiting beside the car. His wife and son
– a full-bodied woman with a crown of plaited hair, and
a toddler of about two years of age – stood close to him.
Oby's stomach was swollen in pregnancy. On sighting
Zuba, she handed a set of keys to Ike and took the little
boy by the hand.

"Let's go," she said.

"No, I want to go with Daddy in the car," the toddler
shouted, and wrapped his chubby arms around Ike's leg.
Ike lifted him into his arms. The boy clung to his father
like a koala.

"Junior, how are you?" Zuba called.

The boy ran to Zuba, drawing his hand back and
slapping it with all his might into Zuba's palm.

"Strong boy," Zuba said, shaking the tiny hand.

"Good morning, sir," the woman said.

"Oby, how are you? Hope all is well?"

"Yes sir, we're fine." She took her son's hand and they
walked away.

Zuba glanced at his watch. "Just in time for the lawyer's
appointment," he said.

"Please wait for me," Nonye called, coming out of the
house and locking the door. Her voice was hoarse and her
eyes had the soreness of insomnia. She hid the key inside a
flowerpot that bore a leafy dieffenbachia plant.

"Don't you need to rest after your night at the hospital?"
Zuba asked.

"I don't want to keep thinking about Dad. That's all I do when I'm alone."

"Nonye, brighten up, be positive. Dad is going to be all right. I've seen it; I felt it in my bones this morning, and still do. Everything will be all right soon."

Chigbo Chambers was tucked away in a sprawling bunga-low in the Government Reserved Area (GRA), an exclusive part of the neighbouring Onitsha. "The only sane part of Onitsha," Zuba could recall his father saying, the last time he had accompanied him to the Chambers before his National Service.

A life-size portrait of Barrister Chigbo hung on the wall of the reception. It showed him in full ceremonial attire clutching a diploma that conferred on him the rank of Senior Advocate of Nigeria. Beside the portrait, carved in shiny black wood, an image of Justitia hung above the words:

> It is for us
> Most auspicious
> That Justitia
> Wears a blindfold
> And can't behold
> The dementia
> And deeds of shame
> Done in her name.

Zuba and Nonye waited on a settee, steering clear of a wet smudge on the wall left by some greasy-haired client. He opened a newspaper on the coffee table and found a handbill tucked between the pages. IGBOS INCH CLOSER TO BREAKING AWAY FROM NIGERIA: Movement for the

Actualization of the Sovereign State of Biafra (MASSOB) Opens Biafran Embassy in Washington. He sneered as he went through it. He dropped it on the table and buried his face in the newspaper. Nonye stared at the opposite wall.

The door leading into the chambers swung open. A tall, dark lady stepped in. As she shut the door, a book slid out of the files she held and landed beside Nonye's feet.

Nonye picked up the book for her. Coetzee's *Disgrace;* Zuba wondered if the book had a physically flawed protagonist like the other Coetzee novel on his bedside table. He gazed at the lady. Her white blouse was crisp and well-ironed over a black linen skirt that reached to her knees. Long dark braids hugged the sides of her lean face. The arm she stretched towards Nonye was slender.

"Thanks," she said. "Clumsy me."

The Niger-Delta lilt of her voice, the strength in the set of her slim lips, and the alluring squint of her eyes – the kind of squint that comes upon the eyes with a smile, though she was not smiling – caused something to stir in the pit of Zuba's stomach.

He stared at the panelling of the door that she went through. The floral scent of her perfume hung in the air. He held the air longer in his lungs each time he breathed in.

"I need to use the toilet," he murmured to Nonye, and made for the door.

The corridor was dim compared to the reception. When he reached the open door of the lady's office, he slowed his pace. She was bent over an open file. The tip of her pen rested on her lip. He walked past quickly as she began to raise her head.

At the toilet, he washed his hands and examined his keloid in the mirror. The skin on the growth shone like patent leather. He wiped his oily face and dabbed a wet piece of tissue on the keloid. He stared into the mirror again. Then he stuffed his hands into his pockets and returned to the corridor. He moved past her office without slowing his pace.

Nonye was leafing through a magazine filled with gossip about the lives of local celebrities. He sat down and picked up his newspaper. After a minute, he realized he had been reading the same sentence over and over.

"Excuse me again,"

"Any problem?" Nonye asked.

"Uhhhh!" He pressed a hand to his stomach. "It seems I have a runny tummy. Good job they have a decent toilet here."

He went into the corridor and made straight for her office. He had barely appeared in the doorway when she said, "Come on in."

He squared his shoulders and walked in. Her smile made the warmth in his stomach spread up to his head. There were three padded chairs before her desk. He went past the one opposite her and sat on the one to her left. The novel that she had dropped in the reception lay on top of a shelf stuffed with fat legal books.

"Hi," he said.

"Hello. Can I help you?"

"Em... Yeah... Em... I saw your... book. *Disgrace*. I am reading a book by the same author."

"You go for literary fiction too?"

"Sure. I can't stand commercial fiction..." He pulled himself back. Why was he lying? He enjoyed most fiction, especially novels with physically flawed characters. *It's not a lie, it's a hyperbole*, another part of him said.

"I just love books. That's probably why I researched into the copyright laws protecting books for my final-year project at school."

"Which school was that?"

"University of Nigeria. At the Enugu Campus."

"Oh. I visited it a few times as a child. I grew up in Enugu."

"Nice and peaceful city."

"Yes."

"Which university did you attend?

"Benin. I read biochemistry. We used to call it buy-your-chemistry."

She chuckled, revealing white shapely teeth. "You know, I don't have a clear idea what biochemistry is? I mean, what do biochemists do?"

Zuba smiled at her directness. "Well, they become lab rats."

He watched her braids jiggle, and soaked up the sound of her laughter. "At least, that's what I want to do with it," he added.

"You mean research?"

"Yes, and lecture."

There was a lull. Zuba racked his brains for something to say. He pushed his hand deeper into his trouser pocket to keep it away from his keloid. She stared calmly at him, a light grin on her lips. Finally he said, "I wonder why I never bumped into you during my previous visits to this office."

"I just started here a few months ago."

"Excuse me," a voice said behind Zuba.

Nonye was standing at the door.

"The receptionist said we can see Barrister Chigbo now," she said.

Zuba turned back to the lady. "My kid sister."

"Hi," she said.

"I've got to go," he said. "It's been really nice talking to you." He didn't move.

"I may not be here by the time you finish with my principal. But I'll look forward to your coming around again." She extended her hand and Zuba took it.

"Tanna," she said.

A quizzical look jumped into Zuba's eyes.

"Short for Lotanna," she added.

"I'm Zuba. Chikezuba." He held her hand a few seconds longer.

"Hurry along then," she said. "My principal doesn't like to be kept waiting."

Zuba stepped out of the office and turned right.

"You like her," Nonye said as they walked down the corridor.

"What?"

"I said you like her."

"Well, yes. I like her. I like many people."

"You know what I mean. You'd like to go out with her."

"I just met her. And have not given it a thought."

"You're lying."

"What do you mean? Standing there and saying I'm lying. Are you in my mind?"

"You're rubbing your keloid."

"And so? It itched me."

"Runny tummy indeed. Just don't try to play big brother with me when I get my own runny tummy."

Barrister Chigbo was bent over the desk in his large office. Shelves of books covered the walls. On the shelf tops, trophies and plaques reflected the light glowing from the ornate holder on the ceiling.

"Good morning, barrister," Zuba said.

"Ahaa." The barrister looked up. "Zuba, how are you? You came with your sister. How are you, my daughter?"

"I'm fine, sir," Nonye answered.

Zuba stared down at the shiny pate in the middle of the barrister's head. The thick black hair surrounding it was like the luxuriant vegetation around a lake. He remembered how the man's full crown of hair had stood out in his father's wedding picture.

"I called at the hospital this morning, on my way to work," the barrister began after Zuba had taken a seat. "I saw your father. He was asleep. The doctor said his vital signs are good. He'll be all right, he'll be all right. It's only a matter of time. The doctor said you will be transferring him to Enugu this afternoon."

"Yes," Zuba said.

"He'll pull through, surely," the barrister continued. "I have seen worse cases. The important thing is that you keep things going in the interim. And, as you know, I'm here to give you all the support you need."

He spoke slowly. His voice was barely louder than the hum of the air conditioner on the wall. But he was renowned for being fiery in court. Did he have a special voice for litigation, which he hung up after court like the black robe on a hook behind him?

"I was sorry to hear about your problem with the principal. I am hopeful that I can resolve it." He rose, walked to a filing cabinet and pulled out one of the drawers, talking all the while: "You're lucky – or rather, your father is lucky. He can trust you. The two of you agree. That is remarkable in today's world. My son doesn't listen to me. He spends all his time playing basketball. Where can basketball take him in life?"

Zuba lowered his gaze to the table.

"Your father's main worry about you," he continued, walking back to his seat with a file, "is, as he put it, that you are 'not wily enough for the world'. But you're still young, and that is sure to change."

He sat down, stretched across the table and placed a sheet before Zuba.

Zuba studied the sheet. It bore the heading: *Power of Attorney.*

Fifth Columnists

Professor Chukwueloka Maduekwe flicked open his eyes. He batted his eyelids several times to clear the drowsiness. The ceiling above him was like a spotless bed sheet. It seemed so far away, like the clouds, undulating before his gaze. The cream-coloured walls stretched down for metres and metres and metres, and rippled gently, like curtains.

Light poured into the room through a window on his right. The louvres glinted with sunlight and cast shiny rectangular patterns on the adjacent walls.

He was on a bed. Yes. Bare-chested. He could see the curly hair on his chest. He was on a bed. A wide bed. With cream railings at its foot. A... tree made of metal. Yes, metal. Stood by his bedside. His eyes passed up the trunk to its solitary branch. It held the strangest-looking fruits. Large, pouchy. One was the colour of water. The other was... brownish. Transparent vines travelled from the fruits, down the stem of the tree and on to him. He shuddered as he realized that one of the vines was attached to his arm.

People. Their voices echoed from a great distance. Garbled. Like words carried on desert winds. They shouted, they whispered. Voices. There they were. The speakers. Wavy like spirits. Ephemeral, like soap bubbles that could burst at any time. There were three of them. A lad, an older man and a woman. A woman wearing a yellow-and-blue patterned *ogodo*. The lad was talking to the older man. The older man was dressed in white and had a metal rope dangling down to his stomach from his neck. His face was the colour of a freshly sawn plank; his eyes were the colour of the sea. His hair was brown like jute, straight, as if it had been stretched with a hot comb. The lad. Something about the lad made him smile. But his lips did not move. The lad's eyes... He knew the lad from somewhere. He loved him. But did not know why. The lad pointed at his open eyes and the people all moved towards his bed. They looked down at him. He was the newborn baby in a cot. Their faces swam and melted before his gaze, merging and separating, like their voices. The man in white lifted the end of the metal rope and pressed it against the wiry hair on his chest. He looked at a band on his wrist, holding the end of the metal rope pressed to his chest.

A smell. Yes, yes. What was that smell? Where was it coming from? There. Another person by his bed. A young girl. A pleasant warmth spread through him. Warmed his heart. His heart. He could feel it beating now. He was alive. But what was happening. Aaah! The smell was stronger. She was leaning over him. He wanted to pull her to his face. Fill his nostrils, his being, with her scent. Unravel her mystery, and the mystery of his condition. Why she smelt like him, and yet not him. He tried to lift his arm. But his body felt as though it had been cast in concrete, as if it was not his. He made another effort to lift his arm. And blacked out.

* * *

The rain came down in heavy drops. It beat upon the earth, rooftops and windowpanes like a thousand drumming hands. The sky was overcast, and the temperature cool.

It was the kind of Sunday morning to be spent lying in in bed, but the Egbetuyis had requested to see him "on a matter of importance".

"You've been scarce these past few days, difficult to get hold of," Mrs Egbetuyi said, raising her voice above the patter of the rainfall.

"Yes, scarcer than an American visa," her husband added. They chuckled and glanced at each other.

Zuba smiled. Mr Egbetuyi looked warm and affable, different from the surly man Zuba had met at the police station two days ago. "Can I offer you anything?" he asked.

"It's still too early, Zuba. Don't bother," Mr Egbetuyi said.

"OK." Zuba reclined into his seat.

"How is your father? By the way, thanks for having our salaries paid so promptly this month," Mrs Egbetuyi continued. "It must be difficult for you, monitoring the school and caring for your sick father at the same time."

"He's making progress, though slowly. We transferred him to a better hospital on Friday and..." A crash of thunder rendered the last part of Zuba's words inaudible. It rattled the French windows that were being whiplashed by the rains.

"Yes, my doctor friend tells me that progress is usually slow for those of his age."

"You know, Zuba," Mr Egbetuyi began, "I lost my father to a stroke. He died after spending four months in a hospital. Indeed, I am car-less today because I had to sell my car to clear his hospital bills. So I can empathize with your situation."

"And your father was such a good boss," Mrs Egbetuyi said. "The best I have ever had in my career. Yes, we had our problems, our misunderstandings and disagreements. But they were usually caused by the lie-peddlers. The envious, scheming, non-progressive elements..."

"Fifth columnists," her husband added.

"But we always overcame such misunderstandings in the end, becoming even closer in the process." She shook her head with sadness.

"Believe me Zuba, my wife was almost in tears last night as we considered your father's condition. And your own plight too: a handsome young man, full of promise, fresh out of school, having the world out there to explore, to catch some fun like other youths of your age."

"And suddenly finding yourself saddled with a burden that would turn your hair grey overnight," Mrs Egbetuyi added.

"Without having really lived," Mr Egbetuyi concluded.

Handsome young man? What, with the leech he carried about on his head? Zuba sat up in his seat. The talk was going contrary to his expectation. He had suspected Mrs Egbetuyi was going to tender her resignation, thereby saving him the trouble of presenting her with the notice of dismissal lying on his desk ready for Monday morning. But now, he was no longer sure. "Thanks for your sentiments and concern," he said.

There was a long silence. The Egbetuyis exchanged glances. Then Mrs Egbetuyi began:

"Zuba... In view of the unfortunate situation regarding your father, I... we are suggesting that I offer myself, my experience and expertise, to serve you in the upgraded position of Director of the school. I can, with support of my husband—"

"And a reorganized platoon of staff," Mr Egbetuyi added.

"—oversee and manage the affairs of the school, giving you periodic reports as required, so that you'll be free to devote yourself to the demanding task of caring for your father, and to do other things you, as a young man, might desire."

"Of course, it is expected that this new commission will go with a higher remuneration, perks and benefits," said Mr Egbetuyi.

"But it may only be temporary," Mrs Egbetuyi continued, "pending your father's recovery, or permanent, as you wish. If you give the go-ahead, we can start right away and reposition the school for greater success."

"What do you say, Zuba?"

Zuba took a deep breath and held it in. Then he rose from his seat. "Excuse me for a minute," he said as he walked towards his room. Another thunderclap rattled the windows and the power went off.

He returned with a white envelope.

"The events of the past few days have been unfortunate—"

"Unfavourable," Mr Egbetuyi said, nodding vigorously.

"—and I'm sorry to say that, in the light of those events, I have had to take some hard decisions." He locked eyes with the principal. "Madam, this letter was to have been handed to you on Monday morning. I regret to let you know that the school will have no further need of your services. You are to receive a month's salary in lieu of notice, and are expected to vacate the staff quarters immediately." The last part of his statement sounded louder than he intended, since the rain subsided suddenly.

Mrs Egbetuyi became a statue, unable to lift her arm to collect the letter. Her husband's gaze fixed on Zuba with a red ferocity.

Zuba dropped the letter on the table. It fell with a thud in the silence.

"Is this some joke?" Mr Egbetuyi asked.

"I'm sorry," Zuba said. "No school can tolerate such serious misconduct from its principal."

"No, no, you can't sack her like this. I thought we had put all that behind us. You can't sack her like this." His voice rose suddenly, startling them all.

"It will be cruel and heartless of you, Zuba. I don't believe you can do this." He stared at the letter on the table. "I wish your father were here. Before I allowed myself and my wife to redeploy six hundred kilometres to this place, I interrogated your father over her job security and prospects, and he assured me that we should have no worries about that. He even paid for our redeployment." Mr Egbetuyi was on the edge of his seat now. "My wife had a great job, with excellent prospects, in Lagos. In Lagos! She left it, sacrificed everything, to come to this forsaken backwater village to work for your dad after he had worked on her with his sweet tongue. And now you want to terminate her commission."

His wife reached for the letter on the table. Mr Egbetuyi smacked her hand away.

"No, Zuba. Take back this letter. Please, please, take back this letter. I thought we were allies. Believe me, you don't want to go there. You don't want to go there. I won't take such an injustice to my wife. I am prepared to place myself in the line of fire for her. Nobody, I repeat, nobody will treat my wife like this. Not while I am alive."

Zuba looked at the picture on the wall: his father, shining eyes and smile, in his Savile Row suit, being sworn in as Commissioner by the Executive Governor of the state.

"Mr Egbetuyi, I thought you were sympathetic to my situation. Don't make this any more difficult for me. Understand. I'm sure you would do same if you were in my shoes. I cannot withdraw the letter."

"Very well," Mr Egbetuyi said. "Go on, open it," he said to his wife. "It is your letter."

Mrs Egbetuyi took the letter from the table and tore it open. She lowered her sad, sorrowful eyes onto the sheet. Seconds later, when she raised her head and stared at Zuba, her eyes were full of hate.

Mr Egbetuyi snatched the letter off her hand. He read it hurriedly, moving his lips like a child learning to read in silence.

"OK. We shall leave," he said. "We shall leave. I see you've made up your mind. Besides, who wants to remain in this backwater village anyway? But you must discharge my wife honourably, pay her her full severance entitlements, not a miserable one month in lieu of notice."

"Your wife knows well enough that based on her conditions of service she is, strictly speaking, not even entitled to the stipulatory one month in lieu of notice, since she is being dismissed due to misconduct—"

"You will either give her six months to put in her resignation, during which time we can make arrangements for our redeployment and for a new commission, or you will give her six months' salary in lieu of notice, and some money to cover our relocation costs. That will be about... two hundred thousand naira in all."

Mrs Egbetuyi nodded.

"You can't be serious. Your demands have no place—"

"I've simply told you what to do if you want us to leave peacefully."

"You'll be hearing from the school lawyers then."

"Lawyers? What will they do? Go to court. And what will the courts do? Come today, come tomorrow, adjourn till next week, adjourn till next month, adjourn till next year."

"You talk about your lawyers, Zuba," Mrs Egbetuyi said. "Don't you know we can get a lawyer too? We could turn this into a long drawn-out fight if you want. You know our courts. The matter will probably not be finished in three years."

"And we'll still be here, doing whatever we want to do." Mr Egbetuyi showed his teeth in a crocodilian smile. "Believe me, Zuba, you do not want us here for a second longer, not after what you have just done. You have declared war."

Zuba stood up. His eyes were slits. "This talk is over. I advise you however, in your best interests, to comply with the letter."

Mr Egbetuyi looked Zuba up and down, then got up. As he passed Zuba, his wife following him, he paused.

"Don't be foolish. You just got the salaries paid. That means you're now in control of the accounts."

"Get out," Zuba said through clenched teeth.

"Don't be greedy. Share a little. You know the money does not really belong to your family anyway. It is money stolen by your father and his senator father when they were in government. Or do you think they acquired this estate from their salaries alone? If General Babangida had not overthrown Buhari and freed your father and all the other corrupt politicians, your family would be as poor as mine."

"I said get out!"

Mr Egbetuyi stood where he was, hulking, staring down at Zuba, long enough for Zuba to feel the physical presence of his menace.

"You'll pay the money, I assure you, otherwise my name is not Frank Egbetuyi."

Zuba steeled himself for the bang of the door being slammed off its hinges. But Mr Egbetuyi shut the door quietly behind him.

Zuba sat back on his chair, trembling, and began to rub his keloid.

Ballooning Problems

Zuba woke early on Monday morning. He lay in bed, listening to the cooing turtledoves and to the hoarse voices of the palm-wine tappers walking down to the stream. Was it only yesterday that he had dismissed Mrs Egbetuyi? He would take no chances. He would get in touch with Chigbo Chambers and have them write to the Egbetuyis. That should make them know he was serious, ensure compliance. Tanna's face rose in his mind – the perfect crescent of her smile – and he decided to visit the chambers again rather than make a phone call. He sprang up from the bed.

He nodded a greeting to Gandhi on the wall, humming as he picked out navy-blue trousers, a sky-blue shirt and a navy-blue tie from his wardrobe. He retrieved a novel from the top shelf and threw it on the bed. Then he walked across to Nonye's room, tapped on the door and entered. The smells of talcum and perfumed body creams enveloped him. Nonye was under the sheets. *One Night of Love*, said the Mills and Boon before her face.

"Nonye, do they look good together?" He held up the shirt, trousers and tie.

Nonye yawned and stretched, raising intertwined hands towards a poster of Snoop Dogg.

"Hmmmn. How come you're asking me about your dressing today. Where're you going?"

"Answer me first. Do they go well?"

"No, you answer me first. Otherwise I'm saying nothing."
She made to pick up her book.

Zuba grinned. "OK, iron lady. I'm going to the office."

"And then?"

"Why this interrogation? Just answer me."

"I need to know where you're going and what you'll be doing so I can match your dress appropriately."

"OK. You win. From the office I'll be going to Chigbo Chambers."

Nonye started laughing. "I knew it. I knew it. About time too."

"So do they match?"

"Emmmm... I think it looks too blue. Add a little contrast, character, heat. Wear the reddish tie I gave you on your last birthday."

After bathing, Zuba stood before the mirror in the bathroom and pulled on the strands of hair under his chin: *hairlings* that stubbornly refused to grow. As a child, he used to ask adults what they did to become hairy; following one's advice, he had sneaked into their father's room to rub gin on his chin, chest, arms, legs and pubic areas while his brother Chuu looked on. "Heyyy!" he would call out to Chuu days later as he examined his chin in the mirror. "It's coming out."

He considered his eyes. "Shut those beady, seedy, piggy eyes of yours," his English-language teacher had once snapped at him. The teacher had asked the whole class to "fly like an aeroplane" – to stand on one leg, leaning forwards with arms spread out horizontally and eyes closed – and had caught Zuba spying on him.

Finally, Zuba focused on his keloid. It looked smaller today, like a leech that had been on hunger strike. He massaged it, pressing it down into his skin.

He discovered he had spent too long in the bathroom, so he dressed up quickly.

"How do I look?" He stood in the open doorway of Nonye's room.

Nonye put aside her book and began chewing on an invisible burger.

"Thanks," he said, smiling.

As his black brogues *crup crup*-ed towards the main door of the house, he heard Nonye's call:

"Zuba. Zubaaa…"

"What is it?" he screamed back.

"I think she likes you."

"How would you know?"

"I can tell. We women can tell."

Zuba smiled as he stepped out of the house. He stopped after a few paces, returned and poked his head through the door.

"But you're still a girl," he shouted, and rushed away before she could reply.

He hurried through his commitments at the office: a lengthy discussion with the vice principal, Mr Nwandu, and then a staff meeting at which he announced the dismissal of Mrs Egbetuyi and the appointment of Mr Nwandu as acting principal.

He got to Chigbo Chambers after 3 p.m. His hand fiddled with his tie as he walked down the corridor to Tanna's office. Vestiges of floral and musk perfumes hung over the passage.

"Hey, Zuba, how are you," she said when she saw him in the doorway.

Did her eyes light up? Open wider? She looked fresh from court, smart in her black skirt suit and sparkling-white blouse. But she was standing before her desk, gathering her things, as if she was on her way out.

"Not bad at all," he said, adjusting his tie again, this time twisting it away from the centre of his throat. "And you?"

"I'm fine. Unfortunately I have to dash off now for an appointment."

"I came to see Barrister Chigbo, and brought you this." He held out the novel he had picked off his shelf that morning.

"Hey," she said, reaching for the book.

"It's the Coetzee I told you about. Just finished reading it. Excellent. Thought you might want to read it."

She caressed the book. Her fingers were long and slim. She read through the blurb, her eyes shining like the gloss on her fingernails.

"I'll go on to the barrister's office now, so you don't go late for your appointment." Zuba said. "Happy reading."

* * *

The following morning, he had the lawyer's letter delivered to Mrs Egbetuyi. He spent a few minutes trying to imagine their reaction. The legalese, the flourish of imperatives, the concluding paragraph would surely send them packing:

Be therefore warned that if within seven (7) days of your receipt of this letter, you fail to comply with our client's legitimate demands and vacate the school premises following your dismissal, we shall be left no alternative than to initiate the severest legal measures against your person. Be therefore advised and comply accordingly.

Two days later Zuba received an envelope. *Duru Chambers* was inscribed on its lower left corner. He tore it open. The

letter within had been typed on a manual typewriter and
had several Tipp-Ex smudges:

*Re: Termination of Mrs Adebisi Egbetuyi's Employ-
ment and Payment of Her Full Entitlements.*

Zuba lifted his face and stared at a landscape painting on
the office wall. He took a deep breath, then bent over the
letter again. The key sentences whipped into him:

*... Your letter terminating the appointment of my client
is an act of illegality of the highest order, predicated as
it is on a Power of Attorney of doubtful authenticity...*

*...If however you still wish my client to leave your father's
employ you should pay her her full entitlement, to wit...*

*...By this letter we hope it becomes clear that we are not
afraid of you and your solicitor's purported "severest
legal measures". On the contrary, we welcome it very
much, and are prepared to pursue the matter up to the
Supreme Court in our quest for justice for my client...*

The claims laid out totalled two hundred thousand naira.
   Zuba exhaled. Why did people have to prove so difficult?
He reached for the phone on the desk.
   An hour later, as he left the office, he dropped the letter
on the secretary's desk. "Make a copy of this letter and
have it sent to Chigbo Chambers." He walked out into the
scorching sun.
   "Something great happened in the hospital yesterday,"
Nonye said as he stepped into the house. "Dad spoke for
the first time."

"Really?" Zuba asked. His voice was still heavy with the strain from the office.

"He was staring around all day and suddenly said, 'Wha... Wha... Nonye?'" Nonye mimicked a husky voice. "It did not sound like him at all. It sounded so rusty. But it was the sweetest music to us. Aunty Chinwe sent me to fetch the doctor while she tried to get him talking the more. By the time I returned with the doctor, however, he was snoring. Aunty and I hugged ourselves after the doctor left. She began singing hymns, so softly, while I watched the rise and fall of Dad's tummy. He will be well, he will be well." Nonye nodded. She bit off a chunk from the bright-yellow mango in her hand. "I returned about an hour ago."

Zuba sat on a chair beside her. Her optimism and the good news worked their way into him.

Nonye gestured towards the porcelain saucer which she placed on the stool beside him. It bore two mangoes, green and wet. They looked different from the yellow-skinned mangoes on her saucer.

Zuba picked one. It was his favourite type of mango. They remained green even when ripe. He never understood why they were called German mangoes. He massaged the mango's thick skin with his fingers, bit a hole near the stalk, and began sucking out the sweet pulp.

"So how has it been? Any new developments between you and your friends?"

"New developments? Nonye, you won't believe this. The problem is ballooning. Can you imagine that they got someone Barrister Chigbo described as a 'well-known, anything-goes, charge-and-bail lawyer', to write to us, demanding two hundred thousand naira as entitlement for Mrs Egbetuyi, and calling her termination letter 'an act of illegality of the highest order'?"

"Sounds impressive."

"And this, despite the fact that Barrister Chigbo attached a copy of my Power of Attorney to the letter he wrote them. They say they are ready to challenge the Power of Attorney in court." He brought the mango to his lips again and squeezed the now wrinkled flesh. "Barrister Chigbo said we should still wait out the seven days he gave them in his letter, and that we might even decide to wait some more. Since the school will no longer be paying her, they will definitely have to move on to make money, get another job to sustain themselves."

"So, we shall continue to sleep with them in the same compound?"

"Well, Barrister Chigbo confirmed that even if we were to take the matter to court right away, the quickest possible result would take two weeks to a month. But it may take more. So, whichever way we approach it, we shall indeed be sleeping with the enemy for some time. But I feel they'll be leaving soon enough, sooner than we might expect, in pursuit of a new job."

Walkabouting

The Egbetuyis now made it a point of duty to sit out on their veranda every evening so Zuba could see them as he walked back from the office. And the more he saw them, staring towards the offices and dormitories, still and silent like birds of prey, the more uneasy he felt.

"Zuba, maybe you should hold your nose and give Mrs Egbetuyi her so-called entitlements so they can carry their trouble and go," Nonye said to him one night. "The money in Dad's Contingency Account can comfortably cover the costs."

Zuba was pacing back and forth on the veranda, bare-chested. He had just sighted Mr Egbetuyi, by the light of one of the security lamps, snooping around a hostel in which students slept.

Nonye sat on a cane chair following his movements. The dieffenbachia that stood in a pot beside her bore the brunt of her nervousness. She stroked the plant with her fingertips; her nails left wet vertical scars on the stem.

"The gateman confirmed he never used to take such nocturnal walks. I'm sure he's just trying to get under my skin," Zuba said. He sat beside Nonye and stared up at the insects flying around the light above them – moths, bugs, ants and beetles of different sizes. They kept buzzing and head-butting the ornate lampshade as if the bulb inside was a treasure they were trying to reach. A bug fell exhausted to the ground beside his foot. He stamped on it with undue force. A nauseating odour filled the air. He began to rub his keloid.

"Zuba, I'm beginning to have a bad feeling about this whole thing. With Dad in the hospital, we do not need this kind of pressure."

Zuba disliked the sadness in her voice. "But Dad says life is all about pressure." He laughed, hoping to draw at least a sympathetic chuckle from her.

"Zuba, this does not call for your politician's laughter. Why not just pay them their so-called entitlements and leave them to their conscience so we can get on with our lives?"

"Nonye, don't get yourself worked up over this. Let me be the one doing the worrying." He slapped the back of his neck and held his hand before his face. There was blood and a squashed mosquito on his palm. "Let's go in. These mosquitoes have started again." He rose from his seat. "I'll try to end this. I'll go to the police station first thing in the morning. The police boss there is my friend."

The local police boss seemed delighted to see Zuba again. After they had greeted each other in Igbo, he switched to English (a habit Zuba learnt was common with officers who had spent many years serving in parts of the country where they had no knowledge of the local language):

"Young man, what can I do for you this time?"

But Zuba stuck to Igbo in explaining his problem with the Egbetuyis.

The officer nodded and switched back to Igbo, "You did well by coming to report. I will fix this matter for you. I'll have them brought to the station and order them to restrict their movement to the immediate vicinity of their house in your school compound. And if they give you any trouble again, just let me know. I have taken a good look at you and see that you are a responsible person."

"Thank you very much, officer," Zuba said, confused at how easy it seemed. "I am grateful." He made to stand up, and his trousers caught on a splinter on the shaky wooden chair. He sat back on the chair and pulled his trousers free. Then he got up. He twisted back from his waist to look at the long loop of frilled black thread now dangling from the seat of his trousers.

"Sorry o," the officer switched back to English. "That's what we see here everyday. Gov'ment won't give us better chairs. They use Dunlop in their offices and give us *pako*, hard wood. Even my own uniforms have tear-tear finish." He stretched on his chair, pushing out his legs under the desk. He got up and moved to the louvre-less window, spat through the security bars, then returned to his seat. "Shuo! It's after two already," he said, glancing at his watch. "No wonder my stomach is biting me like this. You know, I have not even had breakfast. I rushed out of my house by five this morning. This police job! Protecting you people. And I forgot my wallet."

Zuba straightened up from staring at the hole at the seat of his trousers through which his underwear was visible. A frown sat on his brow. The trousers were new ones; he was wearing them for the second time.

"My young man, I said hungry is worrying me and I forgot my wallet at home."

"Oh," Zuba said. He reached into his pocket and handed some money to the officer.

The officer's eyes bulged from their sockets. "Thank you sir," he said.

Zuba looked up, surprised at how a handful of money could wring "sir" from the lips of an elder man.

"In fact, if you had come to me at the very beginning when you wanted to sack the woman, everything would have been solved since. They would have packed and gone. But you people always prefer to follow lawyer, and lawyer will continue to eat your money, and make a simple matter last long and long so they can continue to eat and eat your money. That's all they do."

By the time Zuba stepped out of the station, the picture of a barrister stuffing naira, dollar and pound notes into his mouth accompanied him. The sun was blazing. Heat spirals rose from the cracked, rusty roofs of the wrecked vehicles in the compound. Lizards sheltered underneath. He raised his hand to shield his eyes as he headed for his car.

The following day Zuba was on the lookout for Mr Egbetuyi. But he caught no sight of him in the compound. He saw Mrs Egbetuyi once as she hurried past the gates. Zuba relaxed, dismissing Mr Egbetuyi's threat as an empty one, until one Friday afternoon a parent drove into the school. It was after office hours, but Zuba was still in his father's office. Since the acting principal was in the dining hall with the students, he went out to meet the parent.

The parent, from the oil city of Port Harcourt in the Niger Delta, had two children in the school: a son in Junior Secondary 3 and a daughter in Junior Secondary 1. While they walked back to the office, he expressed regret that one of his children would be leaving for another school in Port Harcourt. .

"You know, I want them to be together. It's more convenient, especially during visiting days," he said.

On further questioning, he revealed that the principal had advised him to enrol his son in another school where he could take the Junior Secondary School Certificate

Examinations, since the school was having problems registering her students for the exams.

Zuba was shocked at the distortion of facts. He quickened his pace to his father's office.

"There," he said, placing documentary evidence of the school's registration for the exams before the parent. "It is true that the pioneer set of the school is ordinarily too small for the school to be used as a centre for the exam, but the school has agreed to pay extra costs to have the exams here nevertheless. It's a matter of prestige too. Why should our students be attached to another school for the exams?"

"Sorry. There must have been a misunderstanding."

"It's no misunderstanding at all. It was done in bad faith. That principal is no longer in our employ. And the info is going to be in our end-of-term bulletin."

Zuba sent for Ike immediately the man left. They drove to the local police station.

The police boss welcomed them with a huge smile. "Ah, my young man. Hope no trouble again?"

Zuba sat carefully on the edge of the chair. Ike sat next to him. "Good afternoon officer," he said. "Unfortunately, there is." He launched into an account of the recent event.

The officer bit off a piece of bitter kola. He chewed gently as Zuba spoke, his gaze never leaving Zuba's face.

"Have you contacted your lawyer about this?" he asked when Zuba finished.

"No. I felt like coming to you first."

"I can see that you learn fast, young man." He paused, then asked, "I'm sure you never saw them walkabouting your compound again after you came here last time."

"Not at all," Zuba said. "Thanks again for that. That's why I have come back. They need to be cautioned further, restrained from making any kind of contact with parents whose kids are in the school."

"I told you, these things won't be happening if you had come to me first. The man is a troublemaker. I took a good look at him. I know his type. You know some of these military men: they feel they're above the law, the alcohol of having ruled us for thirty out of our forty years of independence is still in their blood, they understand only force." He paused, then switched to Igbo. "The main thing is that you want them out of your compound, isn't it? You want their trouble to end?"

Zuba nodded.

The officer's gaze rested on Ike. "And who is this your friend here? Have I seen him before?"

"No. He's Ike, a member of staff. I came with him so I can send him to you any other time I am unable to come on my own."

"So you trust him."

"Completely."

"Then it's a simple matter. Come with one or two witnesses – he's already one," he nodded at Ike, "and report that the man and his wife are planning to do something terrible in the school. Something like…" – his eyes narrowed – "poisoning the students' food. And I will send my men to carry them out of that place with the evidence and lock them up."

Zuba felt his head spinning.

"Or you can simply say they were selling hemp to the students," the officer added, when he saw the look on Zuba's face. "It will only cost you something small for our mobilization."

Ike nodded. "Yes, Zuba. They deserve no better. You know, I sometimes get so maddened by all the trouble they are causing and wish I could punish them for it, give them a good hiding with my horsewhip. Your father is in hospital now because of them. Let's do it."

But Zuba inched his head from side to side. He would rather wait it out with the Egbetuyis; they could not remain for long without a source of income. His hand rose to his keloid and he smiled as he said, "Thank you, officer. I'll get back to you when I'm ready."

One evening, a week after the visit to the police, Zuba was in the house, lounging on a sofa, watching TV, when Ike burst in.

"They're leaving! The Egbetuyis are leaving. Mrs Egbetuyi has just asked if you would allow me to use the school bus to drop them with their belongings at the Lagos bus park by 5 a.m. tomorrow."

Zuba sprang up. "Yes! Of course. I'll allow you to use a limo so long as we'll be rid of them and their trouble." Then he hesitated. Why were they getting the news to him this late? So that the school housing officer didn't have time to inspect their apartment to ensure they were leaving it in good order? "Ike, make sure you don't load any school property into the bus along with their belongings."

When Zuba retired that night, he chuckled in his bed as he remembered the now lame-sounding threat: *You'll pay the money, I assure you, otherwise my name is not Frank Egbetuyi.* He wished Nonye were around; they would have talked and laughed far into the night. But she was spending the night in the hospital with their father and would only return in the morning.

111

When he eventually slept, he had the strangest dream: armed plain-clothes policemen from the central station, headed by a tribesman of the Egbetuyis in the capital, Awka, about thirty miles away, had appeared in the morning. The policemen arrested him and Ike on a charge of threatening violence and stealing, claiming he and Ike had hired armed thugs who harassed the Egbetuyis with horsewhips and machetes, bundled the woman and her husband with their belongings into the school bus, drove them to Onitsha and threw them out at the Lagos bus station, then drove off with some of the Egbetuyi's money and electronics before the items could be offloaded.

It happened that way.

The Middle World

Include Me in Your Budget O Lord

"My leg, oh my leg! My leg is killing me. Officer, I will die here o. You people don't want to treat me, eh?"

Zuba stirred. His skin felt sore in a thousand places; the mosquitoes had drunk their fill and gone. He opened his eyes. Beside him, Chemist had sat up and was squeezing his right leg, just above the bullet wound on his ankle. In the dim light of early dawn that stole into the cell, he saw Chemist's silhouetted shoulders shaking. He glanced to his left. Ike stared back, his eyes luminous with insomnia.

"Officer! Officer! Police! Idem! My leg is killing me!" Chemist screamed. "O Lord, is this what my life will come to? Will I be reduced to a cripple?" He broke into a lamentation that churned Zuba's stomach.

Zuba had never heard a man cry. Really cry. Sob. A lump formed in his throat. He sat up. Other inmates began to stir. He remembered how his mum used to lift his leg or arm with a pillow whenever he had a painful sore or boil, and how that used to alleviate the pain.

"Chemist, Chemist," he called. He wondered if Chemist was ignoring his call, or if he had not heard him. "Chemist," he called again, tapping him on the arm.

Chemist reined in his sobbing and faced Zuba.

"If you turn around and prop your leg up against the wall, the pain might go down a little."

Chemist stared at him for a while. The morning light was still too dim for Zuba to make out the expression in his eyes. Chemist turned and laid his head between Zuba and the ball-grabber's feet. He raised his leg and rested the swollen foot gently against the wall, beside Zuba's head.

The foot stank like putrefying meat. Zuba lay down, increasing the distance between his head and the foot.

"Thank you," Chemist said to Zuba thirty seconds later.

Peace descended over the cell. Some of the inmates sighed with relief, and Zuba felt it as a further thank you. He shut his eyes, listening to the cocks crowing in the distance, and to the twitter of the birds. He tried to grab more sleep. The dew-laden air, trickling in from the window above, settled on his face, soothing, against the tender skin of his eyelids.

The smells were worse in the morning, as people took turns to visit the slop bucket. Fresh faeces plopped into stale urine, creating a mixture of smells that defied description. A cloud of halitosis rose and hung in the air as people yawned in relay, and sneezed, expelling droplets of saliva that floated about like tiny capsules of the smelliest garlic.

Saliva oozed into Zuba's mouth. He felt the tang of gastric juice in his cheeks and tasted vomit on his tongue. He swallowed, and kept swallowing, willing his heaving stomach and rippling oesophagus to be still.

The prefect handed the matchbox to Mike and turned away, pressing his face back against the bars, his nose poked out to the corridor.

Mike rose and stood before the white cords of tissue on the wall. He struck a match and lit one of the cords, then stubbed the flame out with his thumb and forefinger, leaving the cord glowing like a cigarette. The cord smouldered, burning slowly, releasing a coil of smoke that spread through the cell to weaken the smells.

Mike cursed as his gaze fell on the mosquitoes bursting with stolen blood on the wall. He began to slap at them. They made feeble attempts at flying but their dinner held them back. Splat! Splat! Fresh blood dots appeared on the wall.

Footsteps down the corridor. Idem appeared in the doorway. A rifle hung from his shoulder. He rattled the lock with his keys and opened the door. "Carry out your shit bucket."

Papa pushed himself up beside Ike. He lifted the bucket. "Centipede! Centipede!" he shouted, and hopped to one side.

The inmates leapt to their feet. Only Chemist was left sitting on the floor. Mike stepped forwards and stamped his heel on the centipede as it headed for the shelter of Chemist's body. The centipede squirmed and turned over, revealing a bright underbelly and wicked-looking stings. Mike kicked it out of the cell. Idem stamped on it until it became still.

"Oya, bring the bucket," Idem said. He threw his face to one side and pinched his nostrils as Papa passed.

"Wash it very well o," the prefect called after Papa.

Idem locked the bars and followed at a good distance behind the bucket bearer.

"Thank you o. Thank you," Chemist said to Mike. "As if the pains I have are not already too much."

Papa returned with the bucket all wet and smelly.

"Officer, my leg is killing me here o. You people no want treat me?" Chemist called out to Idem.

"I no fit do anything. Only the officer who bring you fit do something, and I tell am."

"OK, I beg, buy me Panadol and ampicillin," Chemist pleaded.

"Bring money."

Chemist remained silent.

Idem locked their cell door and turned to the opposite cell.

Zuba pressed some money into Chemist's hand.

Chemist passed the money to the prefect, who in turn called Idem and handed it to him.

Idem unlocked the opposite cell. "Oya, your bucket."

A woman in a grubby grey skirt and blouse carried out the bucket. Minutes later Idem escorted her back into the cell.

"Nwamaka, come sweep our office," he said, holding the cell door open.

Nwamaka pushed herself up. She shuffled out of the cell. There was resignation in her eyes, the kind that was born of stale sorrow. She looked beautiful despite the sleep cobwebs and snot on her face. Zuba remembered his father advising a friend: "If you want to know if that woman is truly pretty, take a look at her first thing in the morning when she gets up from bed."

Idem locked the cell door and followed behind Nwamaka. The scratch-scratch of a broom against the concrete floor filled the building, echoing in the silence of the morning.

Zuba readjusted his buttocks on the ground. His body ached.

The cell was still. The inmates looked like characters in a grim painting. The prefect and Mike had laid down again and appeared to be asleep. So had Papa at the end of the row. Chemist's pain seemed to have subsided and he was hunched contemplatively over his swollen foot. Ike was staring at the wall, at the Buga graffiti, as if at a movie screen. Zuba raised his hand to his keloid. He winced. It was beginning to feel raw. He lifted his right buttock and sat on his hand. Then he joined Ike in staring at Buga. Buga stared back, a mocking smile on his lips.

The scratch of the broom against the floor ceased. In the silence, a tinkling floated down, clear and pure like a church bell. Zuba recognized the sound. It was the same kind of tinkling made by his belt buckle when he undressed. Muted pants filtered down the corridor. The sounds ended abruptly. The tinkle again. A minute later Nwamaka walked past the cell doors. She held a chewing stick to her mouth with her right hand, scrubbing her teeth, while her left hand carried a bucket of water. Idem followed her. When she returned minutes later, a whiff of carbolic reached Zuba in the cell. She sat back in her position. Her neighbour muttered something to her and Nwamaka snapped the chewing stick in two and gave her one half. She put away her own half in a cellophane bag and lay on the floor.

Ike was still staring at Buga.

"You OK?" Zuba asked.

Ike looked at Zuba, then smiled. The smile was too big, like a man in undersized clothing. It seemed he was becoming detached, looking down, and discovering something amusing in their plight. "As OK as can be," he said.

There was something flickering in Ike's eyes, an emotion hiding behind his smile. But Zuba was unsure. He returned Ike's smile and said, "Hey, look at your face."

Ike raised his hand to his face.

"And your arms," Zuba added.

119

Zuba checked his own arms and saw bumps from mosquito bites there too. He felt his face. The bumps pricked his fingers.

"True," Ike said, still feeling his face. "I want to look younger, but not like a pimpled adolescent."

Zuba chuckled. He turned to Chemist. "Is there any way we can get mosquito coils here? And chewing sticks?"

"Yes," Chemist answered eagerly. "When Madam Food comes, she can help us buy."

Ike yawned and lay down on the floor. Zuba yawned and followed suit.

Chemist picked up the cell's Gideon's Bible. He began to read in a low hard voice:

Mine eye is consumed because of grief; it waxeth old because of all mine enemies...

Zuba awoke to the sound of singing from the opposite cell. A middle-aged woman was standing in the centre of the cell. Her breasts looked full, like those of a nursing mother, and jiggled inside her shirt with each movement she made. She was staring up at the tiny window on the wall, from where a beam of the afternoon light fell upon her, making the tears on her face sparkle. Her arms rose towards the light as she sang:

Include me in your budget O Lord
Include me in your budget
My suffering overwhelms me.

It was a common religious song that Zuba had heard many times before. But never so heartachingly rendered.

He shut his tear-filled eyes and prayed – something he had not done since Chapel, in his secondary school days.

Ike was still asleep, stretched out on his back with his arms by his sides in the perfect "royal posture". Chemist too was asleep, and his lips were parted, revealing well-shaped teeth. Mike, the ball-grabber, and Papa at the end of the row, were on their backs. While Mike gazed at the ceiling, Papa and the ball-grabber stared with longing at the patch of azure sky visible through the tiny cell window. The prefect was sitting up, watching as Nwamaka's hair was being plaited by her neighbour, casting only occasional glances at the singing woman.

The woman's voice climbed an agonized octave. The sound bounced off the impassive walls and ricocheted down the corridor. "Include me in your budget…"

"Hey! The person who dey sing there, reduce your voice," Idem barked from the front office.

The woman's voice rose higher. She began to clap and stamp her feet to the rhythm. "Include me in your budget…"

"Look, if you make me come in there I go hammer your face with slaps you go remember for the rest of your life."

The woman froze, then crumpled down at her post. Her body shook with her silent weeping, jiggling her swollen breasts.

Two Mouths and Five Hands

A car came to a halt outside. Two cars, it seemed. Doors slammed shut. The indistinct murmur of voices. Seconds later, the sounds of footsteps at the front office. Zuba shifted on the cell floor, tense and hopeful.

"Where Idem? IPO say make you allow them see their people," someone said.

"Thank you very much," said Barrister Chigbo, and Zuba nudged Ike awake.

The prefect turned to them. "Your people have come back."

Ike and Zuba leapt to their feet, smoothing their clothes. Freedom, at last. Zuba wiped his face with his palms. His palms became greasy, so he wiped them on his trousers.

A policeman in uniform appeared at the door. "You two, come out," he said as he unlocked the door.

In the office Nonye threw her arms around Zuba as Ike's wife rushed at her husband. Zuba squeezed her to his chest and nodded at Barrister Chigbo over her shoulder, his eyes widening in surprise to see Tanna standing behind the barrister. He released her, and they stood back to look at each other. Her eyes were red and swollen.

"You don't look like someone in cell," she said.

"What were you expecting to see after one night?"

"I heard they fight and beat people in there. I was terrified. I know you're not strong."

"Well, we paid our dues."

She ran a hand over his face, feeling the mosquito bumps.

"Nonye, you can't understand how glad I am that you people found us, how glad I am that Ike and I are leaving this place at last."

Ike extricated himself from his wife's arms. "Oby, my eyes almost saw my ears this past day. I feel—"

"I cried and prayed the good Lord to watch over you, to protect you." She held Ike's hand to her swollen belly and smiled. The puffiness of pregnancy made her face look sad despite the smile. She looked down and asked, "What happened to your shorts?"

"Don't worry about that now, Oby. We'll have time for stories when we get home."

Zuba pumped Barrister Chigbo's hand with both of his. "So great to see you, barrister."

The barrister smiled, looking formal in his dark suit. "Good to see that you're OK, Zuba."

Zuba shook Tanna's hand.

"Glad to see you're all right," she said.

"Your time dey run. It remain only two minutes o," the policeman said.

"Zuba, you two can be out by Monday," Tanna said.

"What did you just say? *Can* be out? Are we not going home now?"

"I'm sorry. My principal will explain."

"Yes, Zuba," Barrister Chigbo said. "The police have asked for twenty thousand naira, ten thousand for each of you, to release you two on bail. Yes, it is illegal, bail is supposed to be free. But it is the usual practice. I can however go to court to enforce your fundamental human rights, to obtain an injunction to compel them to release you, and you won't have to pay them anything. But that could take as long as—"

"I'll pay the money," Zuba cut in. Ike exhaled beside him.

"Actually, they demanded for fifty thousand – twenty-five thousand each. It took a lot of haggling to get it down to this amount. I wish I could get them to go lower."

"Time up," the policeman announced.

Quickly, Zuba called Nonye aside and instructed her on how to get the money. She gave him a tight hug. "It's OK, Zuba, we'll do everything to ensure you come out soonest." She squeezed some money into his hand, then showed him the cellophane bags containing the food packs, snacks and drinks she had brought. "I'll be back tomorrow, with Ike's wife. We won't let you spend Sunday here alone."

Zuba nodded. He picked up the bags.

"Hey, you! Wait," the policeman barked. "Drop the bags."

Zuba dropped them, startled.

"They must to taste the food first." The policeman leant forwards on the counter.

"It's to prevent people getting poisoned," Barrister Chigbo explained. "Nonye, go on, taste the food."

The aroma of restaurants, of dinners and buffets, spilt out when Nonye opened the containers one by one. She picked a fork and began to take a bit from each dish.

"Remove all fork, leave only spoon," the policeman said. He inspected the bags and nodded.

Zuba picked up the bags again. Ike made to take them from him as a mark of respect but Zuba gave him one and held on to the other. He moved to Tanna and the barrister. "Thanks very much," he said. "Nonye will provide the bail money."

"Tanna will be back on Monday to get you out," the barrister said.

"Be careful," Tanna whispered. "See you on Monday."

Zuba's sadness crowded in on him as he watched them leave. Tanna's arm was over Nonye's shoulders. Ike stood statue-still beside him.

"Oya, back to cell. Remember that your officer get mouth too o," the policeman said.

Zuba felt like hitting the policeman across the face with the bag of food, but he was too conscious of being in the policeman's power. He reached into the bag and placed a fruitcake and a chilled can of coke on the counter.

The officer's eyes lit up like a torch.

Back in the cell, Zuba and Ike dropped their bags of food and slumped down at their posts. Ike rested his head on his knees while Zuba stared at the Buga graffiti with pained eyes.

"That's how it is here o," Mike said. "Entrance is easy but exit is difficult. You people, however, know you will be going home soon, which is more than the rest of us can say."

Zuba pulled himself together; something in Mike's words had stung his conscience.

"Don't brood, keep busy, daydream or sleep – or, better still, eat, it will make the time go faster," Mike added, glancing at the bag of food.

Zuba heard Chemist swallowing saliva beside him, and became aware that the eyes of the other inmates were glued to the food bags. Tension was building up in the cell, the kind that preceded a feeding frenzy in the wild. He reached for the bags and passed round drinks and food. There were four packs of fried rice and chicken from Mr Bigg's. Zuba handed one to the prefect, one for Mike and the ball-grabber to share, and one for the other two.

"No, Okpu-uzu will cheat me. He will grow two mouths and five hands. Let me share with Chemist instead." Mike got up as the inmates laughed and sat opposite Chemist. Zuba placed the food between them. Papa got up and sat opposite the ball-grabber. Then Zuba kept one for Ike and himself.

"Hey... Hey... New-man," Nwamaka called out.

"His name is Zuba," the prefect said with his mouth full.

"Hey, Zuba remember us," Nwamaka said.

Zuba looked at Ike.

"It's OK. You can give her some," Ike said.

Zuba passed half of the food on to the prefect.

"Thank you, Zuba. You're a darling," Nwamaka said, as she received the food.

"And what about me?" the prefect asked.

"You, you're a pal," she said, and chuckled.

The ball-grabber and Papa were marking out boundaries in their pack of food. The aroma of the chicken rose in the cell, and the canned drinks squeaked as they were opened.

Mike gazed happily at Ike. "My man, how are you?" His voice was animated, as if he was speaking to an old friend after a long time, as if he was not the same person who, just the previous day, had led the assault against Ike.

Ike shrugged. "As long as there is life, we'll continue to live it." He sipped his drink, refusing to meet Mike's eyes.

"You've spoken the truth. Yes, you've spoken the truth." Mike switched his gaze to Zuba. "Like I said before, you two will be leaving soon – by Monday, I guess. You will surely have no problem with bail money. My people brought two thousand naira, but the IPO said they should make it up to five thousand. So they have been trying to raise another three thousand naira. I have resigned myself to a long stay here, praying the cell never gets too crowded." He motioned to the prefect with a jerk of his head. "Peter said whenever the cell gets too crowded, people get picked out, taken to court, and from there to prison to await trial. But ordinarily, the sooner you want to get out from here, the higher you'll have to pay for your bail; and the longer you stay, the lower you pay." Mike scooped more rice into his mouth.

"How long have you been here?" Zuba asked, and tore a piece off his chicken.

"Getting to a month. He has been here for about three months," he added, nodding towards the prefect.

"What are you being held for?"

He smiled with his eyes. "They said I did 419, that I duped someone of fifty thousand naira. But if I had that kind of money I would have paid for my bail since."

Zuba wondered if Mike would have smiled with his lips too if they had not been engaged in chewing and talking at the same time. He turned to Papa, who had been glancing at them while he chewed. Zuba lowered his voice respectfully. "Papa, what happened?"

"My child, it is a land matter. One Big Man in my village wants to build another big house. His land adjoins the land given to me by my father, and he wants me to sell part of it to him so he can have enough space. When I refused all the money he offered, he bribed some policemen and cooked up a case against me. They said they caught me burying juju in the man's land. I am a poor farmer, the land is the only thing I have to pass on to my children, the way my father passed it on to me. Money is like the morning fog.

It is here now and gone the next minute. But land remains for ever."

There was silence after Papa had spoken.

"Take heart, Papa," Zuba said. "It will all be well in the end." He wondered if his words sounded lame. But he knew nothing else to say.

For a while the only sounds were the smacking of lips and the cracking of chicken bones. Zuba leant forwards, "Okpu-uzu, what of you?"

"Mind your own business," the ball-grabber snapped.

Mike laughed. "Can't you tell from what we call him: Okpu-uzu?"

Blacksmith? What was he supposed to infer from that? He shook his head.

"They said he was making Awka-made for robbers."

"Awka-made?"

"Homemade pistols."

"OK," Zuba said. Then he nodded towards the prefect.

Mike whispered, "They say he's one of those okada riders who snatch bags from pedestrians. And she," Mike continued, following Zuba's gaze, which had settled on Nwamaka in the opposite cell, "was arrested in a hotel at Onitsha with her boyfriend, who they say is a notorious armed robber. She had followed him from Lagos. Nobody knows his whereabouts now. Her poor, illiterate parents had come to beg for her freedom. But the police said they cannot release her until they complete their investigations."

"Awhhhhhh," the prefect yawned. He pushed his empty dish aside and lay down. Papa got up and shuffled to the bucket. He unzipped his shorts and sat down. The bucket grated against the floor. A fresh stench rose in the cell.

"Ooooooooh! You this man! Why now?" the ball-grabber shouted.

"Shit is a red-cap chief whose summons must be answered," Papa said in a voice squeaky with exertion.

"Can't you, at least, try to hold it till morning? Why do you like stirring this hornet's nest of smells twenty times a day?" the ball-grabber continued. He screwed up his face and pinched his nostrils.

Zuba turned away. He could hear the frenzied buzzing of flies echoing in the bucket. He lay on his side, staring with envy at the prefect, whose face was pressed against the bars, nose poked out to the corridor.

The bucket scraped against the floor again. Zuba turned back and bumped into Ike who, eyes shut, had maintained his royal posture despite the smell. But Papa was still seated on the bucket, calm and easy, as if he was taking a rest in a delightful garden, watching butterflies.

Zuba looked away, reflecting on the different toilet manners of the cell inmates: when the prefect sat on the bucket, his eyes blazed around, daring anyone to look at him; Mike didn't give a damn; the ball-grabber's eyes actively sought those of other inmates, his lips pursed and ready to bark "haven't you seen a man shitting before?" while Chemist looked down or up, avoiding everyone's eyes.

Papa rose from the bucket, covered it, and pulled up his shorts without wiping himself.

Mike sprang up with the matches. He lit the fourth cord of tissue on the wall.

A barefooted boy appeared outside the bars. He held out two small nylon bags.

"Please collect for me," Chemist said.

Mike collected the bags and swung them over to Chemist.

129

"Thank you," Chemist said, delving into them. He handed Zuba some mosquito coils and chewing sticks. Then he picked out a capsule from the other bag, uncovered it, bent over his foot and tapped the contents into his wound.

Voices at the front office. A baby's cry. More voices.

Minutes later, the door of the opposite cell clanged open.

"Who be Mrs Igbokwe?" the policeman asked. "Come out. You dey go. Your husband have turn himself in."

The woman that had been singing for a share in the Lord's budget scrambled up. She re-tied her wrapper and hurried out with light steps.

* * *

When Zuba woke up on Sunday morning, his nostrils were clogged with the astringent smell of mosquito coil. He heard Chemist's voice beside him. But this time Chemist was not moaning in pain. He was clutching the Gideon's Bible before his nose:

Arise, O LORD; save me, O my God: for Thou hast smitten all mine enemies upon the cheekbone; Thou hast broken the teeth of the ungodly...

Even when he took his turn on the bucket later on, Chemist's lips still moved with his recitations while he gazed on the wall above everyone's head. He hopped back to his position when he was through, picked up the Bible, and continued:

Let all mine enemies be ashamed and sore vexed: let them return and be ashamed suddenly...

130

Zuba could recall from his days at secondary school that the book of Psalms was abundant in praise and contrition. He was therefore surprised as he listened to Chemist, and had to peer at the open page to convince himself.

"Please can I empty the bucket this time," Ike asked as footsteps approached the door. "I will like to stretch my legs and take some outside breeze."

The prefect shrugged.

Ike got up and made for the bucket.

Zuba was touched. He knew Ike detested seeing an elderly man being made to empty the common slop bucket.

Ike returned minutes later, sat down, and wiped his wet hands on his shorts-turned-skirt.

"Ike-power!" Zuba said, in admiration. He wanted to say more, but that would mean talking to everyone in the cell. He transferred his frustration to his keloid, winced, and sat on his hand again.

Papa laid a hand on Ike's thigh: "My child, it shall be well with you. You will live till an abundance of grey hair covers your head; and may your children, your children's children, and others' children, show you tenfold the goodness you have shown me."

The bulb came on, bright with full current. An Igbo gospel music blared from a radio in the office:

Prayer is my spell
Cast in the Lord
Prayer is my juju
I will invoke it again.

Zuba lay down and again sought escape in sleep. He discovered he was repeating some of Chemist's psalms

131

in his mind while picturing the Egbetuyis: the man with shrewd yellow eyes and a jaunty cock of the head, the woman with a mean-spirited smile on her lips. They were nodding: "We've got you! We've got you!" He remembered his police friend's advice: "*It's a simple matter. Come with one or two witnesses and report that the man and his wife are planning to do something terrible in the school. Something like poisoning the students' food or selling hemp to the students. And I will send my men to carry them out of that place with the evidence and lock them up. It will only cost you something small for our mobilization.*" He was sure some other policeman had given the Egbetuyis a similar advice: *It's a simple matter. Just bring some evidence and report that they threw you out and stole some of your things in the process. You and your wife are already witnesses. Then I will send my men to arrest and lock them up. It will only cost you a share of the settlement.*

He tried to imagine what would have happened had he gone along with the "selling marijuana to the students" scheme. The Egbetuyis would have been arrested, some Indian hemp probably recovered among their possessions. Then they would have been blackmailed into packing out immediately in exchange for his not pressing charges against them. Why hadn't he gone along with it?

From the office, the radio blared the seven-o'clock news. Something was being said about book piracy and the Nigerian Copyright Commission. Thoughts of Tanna rose in Zuba's mind and the hate-feelings rushed out of him like air from a punctured balloon. "I researched into the copyright laws protecting books for my final-year project," he heard Tanna say again in that Niger Delta lilt he found so exotic – that Niger Delta accent that occupied

132

the ground between the accents of the major ethnic groups: Igbo, Yoruba and Hausa. He saw Tanna again in her office looking down at a document, the tip of her pen resting on her lip, a slight frown on her brow. The soft, yet firm feel of her handshake. The sad and... yes, caring look in her eyes. "Be careful," he heard her say again. He looked through the bottle-lined shelves in his mind till he found the bottle with the label he was searching for. He unscrewed it, and Tanna's laughter leapt out. He saw her braids jiggling.

The clanking of the opposite cell door jarred Zuba out of his reveries. Nwamaka was stepping back into the cell. Her body was moist. She was now wearing a pink T-shirt over a black skirt, holding the bottom of the shirt up in a hammock that carried some fruits, exposing her taut stomach and slit-like navel. She began handing out ripe guavas.

"Give to Zuba and his brother," she said, throwing several across to the prefect.

Zuba recalled having seen a guava tree standing outside the station as he and Ike were being led in. He wanted no guavas. But he did not want to spurn the goodwill.

"Nwamaka, thank you," he said.

"You did more," she replied.

The guavas felt cool in his palm – luscious, without any blemish on their soft yellow skin – the kind he would have loved to dig his teeth into. He could feel hunger on his tongue: the bitter aftertaste of chloroquine. Yet he held back and decided to pass the fruits on to Papa. The guavas, he knew, could destabilize the delicate equilibrium in his stomach. Trigger a bowel movement. Even a runny tummy.

I Don't Understand Computer Language

Monday morning at last. Zuba woke with the first cockcrow and sat up, staring at the lightening sky through the tiny window, counting the minutes and clinging to the promise that this was going to be his and Ike's last morning in cell. Beside him, Ike sat rigid, his gaze directed at the sky too, his lips moving silently. The other inmates of the cell were just beginning to stir and awaken on the concrete floor.

After the slop buckets had been emptied, Zuba and Ike were led out to the reception. They found a plain-clothes policeman waiting.

"Wear your clothes quick-quick and come," the policeman said. "Your lawyer woman dey outside." Short and slight of build, he had a boyish face. A thick scar sat on his right forearm.

A hypertrophic scar – keloid's cousin, Zuba thought, and warmed towards him.

Idem had placed their clothes on the counter. Zuba and Ike dressed quickly.

"My watch and money?" Zuba asked after he had tucked in his shirt and belted up.

"You people no go yet. You go come back," Idem said, puncturing their elation.

Zuba and Ike followed the policeman outside, throwing Tanna a look as soon as they saw her.

"They won't even tell me what they're up to," Tanna said when she saw the bewildered expression on Zuba's face. "But they say it's something they have to do before you two can be released on bail. So I believe we're on course."

The albino policeman who had brought Zuba and Ike to the cell waited beside a red Toyota Starlet, his rifle clutched to his side. He smiled at Zuba, revealing teeth as yellow as his skin. Zuba looked past the man to the clear horizon, at the kites circling in the distance, and at the sun climbing higher. The air smelt of fruits and grass. He breathed rapidly, hoping to wash out the cell smell that clung to his nostrils.

"Bayo, make I bring handcuff?" the albino asked. He sniffled and reached for the cuffs on his belt.

Bayo, the boyish-faced officer, hesitated. "OK," he said.

"Hey, chairman! Why?" Tanna asked. "You know they won't run away. They've not been handcuffed since the beginning of this matter. Why do it now that the whole thing is about to end?" Tanna sweetened her words with a smile.

Bayo looked unsure.

"Chairman, look at them, just look at them," Tanna continued. "They're gentlemen. They're gentlemen, and you know it."

Bayo glanced at Zuba and Ike, who stared back with blank faces, unsure what expression would tip the scale.

"OK," Bayo said.

The albino sniffled. His jaws tightened.

Idem appeared in the doorway of the station. "Bayo, *abeg* come, make I give you message."

Bayo hurried towards Idem.

Tanna turned to the albino. "Honourable, thank you very much for your understanding. You people are a good example of that new friendly police force government is talking about on radio."

"OK," he said, and broke into a cough. He sniffled and took three steps towards the nearby guava tree. Pressing one nostril shut, he blew his nose.

Zuba turned to Tanna. "You surprise me. Chairman? Honourable? What title will you use next?"

Tanna chuckled. "It's a trick I learnt from my principal. You need to see how he uses it on their top brass."

Bayo returned to the car. "Enter, enter." He held open the back door for Zuba and Ike.

"Where are we going?" Zuba asked.

"You'll soon know," Bayo said. He slotted a cassette into the car stereo. Tina Turner's *Simply the Best* filtered through the speakers.

The familiar music softened the edge of the unfamiliar experience. They drove through backcountry roads, avoiding the usual Monday morning Awka township bustle. Farms and forests, stalls, houses, buses, cars, cyclists and load-bearing pedestrians flew past. Zuba's gaze was fixed on the scar on Bayo's arm as he made sharp turns on the steering wheel to avoid potholes. What could have caused it?

They slowed down as they approached a market. A red-black-green Biafran flag with the rising-sun insignia fluttered on a bamboo pole, near a billboard with pictures of men pissing and shitting blood beneath captions promising traditional cures for gonorrhoea, syphilis, herpes, piles, itching of private parts, worm-like movement in the body, and staphylococcus. Tied low across the billboard's legs was a white banner:

WE SAY YES TO BIAFRA! WE SAY NO TO NIGERIA!
MOVEMENT FOR THE ACTUALIZATION OF THE

SOVEREIGN STATE OF BIAFRA (MASSOB) NON-VIOLENT! NON-EXODUS!

A woman sat with her back to the banner, frying yam and bean cakes on the roadside. Firewood crackled under her pan, and smoke rose with the steam from the sizzling yam slices and bean-cake balls, wafting into Bayo's car through the wound-down windows. Zuba's mouth began to water. He heard Ike swallow beside him. "Please can you stop let me buy some fried yam and *akara*?" he said.

Bayo brought the car to a halt. A girl of about seven ran to them.

"Shall I bring it? Shall I bring it?" she asked. She was a miniature of the woman seated before the frying pan.

"How do you sell it?" Zuba asked.

"One, one naira."

Zuba glanced round the car before passing two green notes to the girl, "Bring forty naira's worth – twenty yam, twenty akara."

Ahead, battered commuter buses were double-parked on the roadside leaving only one lane open for traffic. They revved their engines and blared their horns. Conductors hung from the open doors screaming: "Onitsha! Upper Iweka! Leaving now-now!"

Touts scouted and hustled for passengers, grabbing passers-by by the arms and towing them towards buses.

The steaming wrap of yam and akara filled the car with a delicious aroma. The red pepper-and-tomato sauce sprinkled over it still sizzled.

"Pure water, buy pure water," hawkers called out, holding out small black-and-blue-lettered packs of water.

Zuba ignored them. "Let's eat," he said, placing the wrap between the front and back seats. He took a piece of yam and stuffed it into his mouth. The heat burnt his tongue and palate. He opened his mouth and breathed air through the squashed morsel before he swallowed. He felt the purifying heat inching down to his stomach. Ike chewed and swallowed likewise, smacking his lips. So did Bayo and the albino. Tanna said thank you and buried her face in an official-looking document after a piece. Zuba reached for the wrap again and again, hoping none of the others would grow two mouths and five hands.

It was the school that Bayo drove them to. He blared the horn before the school gate. "*Where your child wants to be*," he muttered, reading from the school signboard. The gateman emerged, buttoning his shirt and squinting at Bayo.

"It's all right. I'm the one. Open the gates," Zuba said.

"Heeeey! Good morning sah! Welcome sah." He stepped back and threw the gates open.

"Direct me to your house," Bayo said, driving slowly through the neem arches over the road, his head swinging from side to side. "This your school fine o," he said. "My child go fit come here so? He is twelve years and just finish secondary school. Or your school be only for Big Man children?"

"Sure, he can come here," Zuba said.

"How much be the fees?"

"Em… about one hundred and fifty thousand naira per annum."

"Haaa! That one pass my one-year salary o. You see, na school for only Big Man children."

"There are scholarships. Exams are conducted for scholarships."

"True?" Excitement sharpened Bayo's voice. "My child dey very bright. He go blaster your exam and get your scholarship. You go see. How I go get the form? The form free?"

"Usually from the office. It's not free but I'll help you get one."

"Haaa! Thank you very much."

"No, it's this way," Zuba said.

"I know. I just want look around."

"What is in that place?" Bayo pointed at a small enclosure hedged by red hibiscus flowers.

"It's a fish pond."

"You mean the children here get their own fish pond?" He shook his head.

Zuba smiled.

"This be your house?" Bayo asked, as he parked where Zuba indicated.

"No. My papa's house. I have my room there."

"I hear say your papa sick?"

"Yes. He's in hospital."

"Sorry o. But we have to search your room for the stolen items: the electronics and money," Bayo said when they got to the veranda. "And after, we will search your driver's house."

Tanna blocked his way. "You have a warrant, I suppose?"

"You this woman!" Bayo brought out a folded sheet from his pocket and handed it to her.

The housemaid opened the door when Zuba rapped on it.

"Hah! Broda Zuba! Welcome," she said.

"Thank you," Zuba said. He led the way into the house. "You're back. Hope your sister's marriage went well. How are your people?"

"They are all fine, Broda. They send their greetings."

"What of Nonye?"

"She went to relieve Aunty Chinwe at the hospital yesterday evening. She will be back this afternoon."

"What of my wife?" Ike asked.

"She's inside. She's not feeling well."

"It's OK," Zuba said after a glance at Bayo. "You can go on in and see her. I'll let you know when they're finished with me."

"No run away o," Bayo said. "Otherwise we go carry your wife go."

Zuba had left his room in a hurry on Friday morning. His bathroom slippers were kicked apart on the carpet and his towel was heaped on the bed beside his pyjamas. The stale smell of poorly dried laundry rose from the towel. On the desk, beside his computer, was a half-finished glass of juice.

"OK. Declare any money or electronics you have in your room before we commence with the search," Bayo stated.

Zuba noted the new officious tone, the flawless English. "I have just a little money and this computer here," he said.

"Declare them," Bayo said. His gaze roved round the room. An amused expression came upon his face when he saw the inscription beneath the Gandhi on the wall. Tanna too was looking at the picture, her brows furrowed in thought.

Zuba rummaged in his wardrobe and brought out a handful of money. He placed it on the desk, beside the computer. "Six thousand naira. This is all the money. And this computer is the only electronic equipment here."

Bayo's gaze lingered on the money, then on the computer. "Let me see the receipt for this computer."

Zuba sighed. "I'm sorry, I don't know where it is any more. I've had this computer since my second year in university."

"Then how do I know it is not stolen?"

"Of-fee-cerrr!" Tanna began in a light singsong. "Officer, make we take am easy o. We all know we no fit find receipts for everything for our houses." Her pidgin was smooth, accomplished, as Zuba had expected.

"That may be the case," Bayo cut back, still in perfect English. "But I am not the suspect here."

Tanna smiled. "But you know that no computer is listed among the complainant's alleged stolen items."

"My superiors will decide that when the computer gets to our station." He looked back and barked, "Corporal."

"Sir," Yellow answered, and sniffled.

"Carry this computer, and all its parts, to the car."

"No. Wait! Wait! I can show you that this computer is mine. If we turn it on you will see it is registered to me."

"My friend, I don't understand computer language," Bayo said.

"It is simple. If we turn it on, you will see my name. It will show you my name as the owner."

"I have told you, I do not understand computer language. If you want to talk to me, talk to me in a language I can understand."

"Officer," Tanna called. "Excuse us for a minute." She beckoned at Zuba and they stepped out of the room, into the corridor.

They brought their heads together and spoke in hushed tones. The spicy smell of akara was still in her breath,

141

perfumed with her femininity. He restrained himself
from moving his face closer still, from bridging the gap
between them, from smothering her words with his
lips.

"I can't allow them to remove my computer. I have a lot
in it. You know if it gets to their office it will cost more
money and time to get it out. Or, worse still, they may
break it or declare it missing."

"Well, you must have seen them ogling the cash. So
you either give them a share of the cash or allow them to
carry the computer."

In the bedroom Yellow was still squatting before the
desk, twisting the power cord of the computer in his
hand as he saw Zuba.

Zuba reached for the money on the desk. His lips moved
silently as he counted out some notes. At the periphery of
his sight, he saw Bayo's lips moving too as he watched. He
squeezed the notes into a ball, held it to the centre of his
palm with his thumb, and extended his hand. "I'm sure
you understand this language," he said.

Bayo chuckled. "Very well," he said as they shook
hands.

"Hmnnnh, Zuba. You surprise me. You seem quite
adept at this sort of thing," Tanna said.

"I see it done on road checkpoints," Zuba said.

"OK. Leave the computer," Bayo barked at his companion. "Search under the bed, let me check the wardrobes."

Zuba looked on, amused by the perfunctoriness of
the search. Bayo flung open the doors of his wardrobes,
staring into each of the shelves without touching anything.
Zuba's eyes caught Bayo's scar again and he wondered if
it ever itched. He pushed the thought away and glanced
at Tanna.

The light from the window traced her frame in a shimmering white, giving a surreal aspect to her. Her black jacket had assumed a sheen and contrasted with the floral curtains on both sides of her. She looked like an exquisite painting, the kind he heard fetched six-figure sums at auctions. He wanted to sweep her into his arms. Just to hold her close and feel her warmth.

"Hey! See this book," Bayo said as he peered into the last wardrobe, pulling out a green-and-white book. *General Studies: Government, Society and Economy*, said the title. "They tell us to buy this book for school for our general studies. You fit borrow me this book?"

"You studying?" Zuba asked, surprised.

"My friend, you think I want remain inspector for ever? I dey read psychology for one university satellite campus for Onitsha. I dey my third year now. When I finish, I go do my master in criminology. And one day I fit become Area Commander or even Commissioner of police, make my wife and children happy-happy."

Zuba smiled, amused more by Bayo's switch back to pidgin than by his words. "How I wish that day was now," he said. "The book is yours."

"OK, make I look at your driver's house sharp-sharp, and if nothing-nothing, I go drive you straight to my boss and he go release you quick-quick."

"Ike, where are you?" Zuba called out. "Come on, it's your turn."

There's Enough in It to Nail You

Bayo handed his report on the search to his boss and stepped out of the office. Zuba and Ike were sitting in there with the Egbetuyis. The officer tossed the report aside and continued haranguing Zuba:

"...the evidence before us shows you wanted them out of your school compound. They refused to go, questioning your Power of Attorney, and demanding you first pay them their full entitlement. They even got their lawyer to write you with the same demand." The officer brandished a letter from the open file before him. "Now tell me, who will believe your story, that they suddenly woke up one morning and decided to pack and leave without collecting the said entitlement and—"

Zuba cut in: "All you have to do is—"

"Mister man, I don't like being interrupted. Don't add rudeness to the chain of your offences."

Zuba shut his mouth, growing tighter in the face. He glowered at the Egbetuyis seated beside him. Mr Egbetuyi's hand was resting in her wife's lap, and she was gripping it with both hands. They had barely glanced up as he and Ike were led in.

"The evidence shows you had motive to throw them out. And you have the resources to hire your gun, machete and axe thugs that the complainants said harassed them before bundling them and their belongings into your school bus before dawn." The officer poked his hair with a biro. It had a grey patch the shape of a horseshoe. His face looked shiny, as if smeared with Vaseline. He retrieved a handkerchief and wiped his brows. "Then your thugs and your driver drove them to the bus park and threw them and their things out." He flashed a photo that showed bags and belongings scattered on a roadside. "Unfortunately for you, your driver and the thugs decided to pull a fast one, to gain some loot from the operation. So they took their money, and their electronics: Kenwood 3-CD changer, 29-inch Sony colour television and all the rest. Mr and Mrs Egbetuyi have provided us with photocopies of the receipts of their missing electronics." Several receipts lying beside the file got two taps from his ringed index finger.

"They're all fake," Zuba blurted out. "Officer, I hired no thugs. And I tell you, they never had a Kenwood CD player or Sony television."

"Shut up your mouth. Quit lying," roared Mr Egbetuyi. "You did it to punish us because we refused to leave. You're lucky I cannot lay my hands on you."

Shocked, Zuba turned to Mrs Egbetuyi. "Madam, how can you lie so? How can you?" He spoke in a low voice aimed at her conscience.

Mrs Egbetuyi said nothing. She refused to meet his eyes. Her husband placed an arm around her shoulders. "Leave her alone. She is still too distressed by your wickedness to talk."

Zuba turned back to the officer. "Believe me, they're lying. I've been in their house many times; they never had any Kenwood CD player or Sony television."

"Is that so? If this matter gets to court with the receipts as evidence, you will have a hard time convincing the magistrate that a couple of their standing, after many years of work, do not have a television in their house."

Zuba rubbed his keloid.

"Now, I will continue. Don't interrupt me again. The officer picked up Zuba's statement. "In your own statement you deny everything. You say it is a set-up. But you admit motive. You admit you wanted them out. You say you had felt so relieved that they were finally packing out 'with their trouble' that you waived the usual packing-out procedures for them. You did not even get any of your staff to take inventory, inspect their apartment to confirm they were leaving it in good order. You say that your driver said all their belongings were offloaded and that he was only accompanied by his visiting cousin who was travelling that same morning." He paused and regarded Ike with contempt. "Drivers are all the same: crooks ever ready to stab their masters in the back. He has the money and goods of the complainants safely hidden somewhere, and after this whole matter, he will resign to go and start some small business with his own share of the loot."

Zuba explained the officer's words to Ike in Igbo. He felt Ike's leg vibrating against his. He took a deep breath, then whispered, "Is it true?"

"Of course not, Zuba. How can you even think so?" Ike looked as if he had been stabbed.

Zuba placed a hand on his thigh. "I'm sorry," he whispered. "I never thought so. I only asked because I am expected to." He turned to the officer. "He says it's not true."

"Of course, what else do you expect him to say? But curiously, he made very interesting and helpful revelations in his statement, contradicting you in some places."

Zuba explained the officer's words to Ike again.

"That's not true," Ike shouted. "Unless the policeman wrote something other than what I told him. And what I

146

told him was the same thing I told you: nothing happened; they loaded their things in the bus that morning and offloaded them when we got to the bus park. They even waved me goodbye as I drove off. Then I saw Mr Egbetuyi through the rear-view mirror scattering their things on the roadside. But I thought nothing serious of it. I thought maybe his wife had angered him and he was throwing a tantrum."

The officer laughed. "His statement is with the police and the prosecution, and I tell you, there's enough in it to nail you. If this your matter gets to court, your conviction and jailing is a sure banker, so you should thank your stars that the complainants here are ready for an out-of-court settlement. They have shown they are not the do-me-I-do-you kind. They want to put the whole incident behind them and continue with their lives, rather than being in court for years and years over the matter, and ruining your life at the end. They demand however that all their stolen items be returned. Or in the event that you are unable to do so," he cast a contemptuous glance at Ike, "that you provide the cash equivalent of... of..." he flicked through the file. "Yes, a cash settlement of two hundred and fifty-five thousand naira, being the one hundred and fifty thousand naira cash they were dispossessed of, and one hundred and five thousand naira being the current market value of their electronics. Isn't that it?" He turned to the Egbetuyis.

Mr Egbetuyi nodded, his lips turned down in reluctance.

"So, mister man, it's all up to you how we proceed. Do you prefer an out-of-court settlement or do I go ahead and charge you to court, issue an arraignment notice?"

Zuba's anger had seeped out steadily while the officer spoke, and consternation had crept into the vacated spaces. "I have already told you. This is a set-up. Clearly an attempt to extort the money he swore I would pay. There can be no talk of settlement for fictitious goods or money they never had in the first place." His voice was strained, like something a little breeze could have blown away.

The officer reclined into his seat. He tilted his head back, resting it on the black security bars of the window behind him.

"I see you have no idea what you have got yourself into. I will have your arraignment date set seven days from today. It should give you enough time to think this over well-well. If you then change your mind, you can call at my office with the settlement. The complainants will sign a document withdrawing all charges against you, your driver, and others still at large, and the arraignment will be cancelled. Just remember one thing: your lawyers will oppose your settling out of court because they will thereby lose whatever income they would have made from the case going to court and remaining in court month after month, year after year. So I advise that you think this over yourself and not involve your lawyers. It is your neck."

"Like I have already said, there's no way I'm going to pay a settlement for a crime that never happened, for fictitious goods and money they never possessed in the first place," Zuba said.

The officer studied Zuba's face. He shook his head. "Bayo."

"Sir." Bayo appeared in the doorway.

"Issue arraignment notice to the suspects; threatening violence and stealing. Fix the court appearance for the 24th, next week."

"Yes sir," Bayo said.

Mr Egbetuyi sprang up and stood rigid before the desk. "Permission to fall out, sir."

"Permission granted," the officer replied.

Mr Egbetuyi saluted.

Mrs Egbetuyi arose. "Thank you, sir," she said.

The officer nodded.

Zuba pulled his hand out of his pocket and ran it over his face. He stared at his glistening palm. He placed his elbow on the desk and began to rub his keloid.

Bayo came in with a small white sheet, which he handed to Zuba.

Outside, the Egbetuyis were standing under an almond tree at the centre of the station. Fresh and rotting fruits littered the ground around them. Mrs Egbetuyi's boubou rustled in the breeze as she muttered something to her husband. A young woman knelt at their feet, heaping cups of groundnut and popcorn from her tray onto an old newspaper. They looked up as Zuba and Ike emerged from the office. Zuba was taken aback by the animosity in Mrs Egbetuyi's eyes. There was neither anger nor hate in Mr Egbetuyi's face. There was a glow of triumph, and a muted grin of multiple meanings that reminded Zuba of the Buga graffiti on the police-cell wall.

Wrong Parking

"Crooks! Perverts! Idiots!" Barrister Chigbo's voice boomed, rattling the cream blinds in his office. "They're hand in glove with Mrs Egeb... Mrs Ebge... with that your sacked principal with the unpronounceable name. And her crook of a husband." He began pacing his office, clutching the arraignment notice so tightly that Zuba feared his fingers would puncture the sheet.

Opposite Zuba, Tanna's gaze followed her boss. The grin on her face showed she was used to such outbursts.

"Money! It's all about money. They want to frighten you into a settlement, so they can share it among themselves. You did the right thing. You did the right thing, Zuba, in turning down their offer. We'll meet them in court. Yes, in court, if they have the nerve to go that far. And if I get that crooked woman and her twisted rogue of a husband on the witness stand, I'll tear them to shreds. To tatters." He made a tearing motion with his hands. "They told you lawyers oppose settlement because they do not want to lose their litigation fees, eh? Well, you'll tell them when next you see them that I'll be handling this matter pro bono..."

"Pro bono?" Zuba asked in a whisper.

"Free of charge," Tanna whispered back.

"Is this his courtroom voice?"

Tanna rolled her eyes and nodded.

"I surely will not want to be interrogated by him."

They smiled, conspiratorially. Zuba felt the ache in his belly again.

"...and I'll be there at each hearing. It's the least I can do for you and your father in the present circumstance. How is he anyway?"

"He's improving. I'll be going to see him tomorrow."

"Ask the doctor when you get there if he can now receive visitors. I'd like to see him myself."

"I'll do so and get back to you."

"Sir, we have to talk about the sureties for his bail against the arraignment," Tanna said.

"Yes, thank you my dear. Sometimes I wish I had you for a son instead of my basketballer boy." The barrister came round to his seat, rubbing his bald patch.

Barrister Chigbo lowered his bulk onto his seat and reached for his diary. "Hmmmmmmnh... on the twenty-fourth, Tanna will be in Lagos and I will be at the Court of Appeal in Enugu. I will send Greg for your arraignment. Nothing much will happen that day. You and er" – he glanced at the arraignment sheet – "Ike will be called into the dock. The charges will be read out to you and you'll be asked 'Guilty or not guilty?' You plead 'Not guilty' and Greg will apply for your bail. The magistrate will grant bail. A date will be chosen to begin the hearing. Your sureties will sign the bail papers and you can return home. Just make sure you appear in court with two of your uncles. Each of them must have landed property, and have their Certificates of Occupancy, and three years' tax-clearance certificates with them."

"Barrister, what can I say? Thanks so much."

"You're welcome."

Zuba glanced at Tanna, then at his watch. "Guess I'll have to be leaving."

"Don't forget to send me news about your father," the barrister said, pushing the arraignment sheet towards Zuba. "Tanna will make a copy of it for our file before you leave."

"OK. Thanks again," Zuba said.

Tanna looked at her watch. "Sir, I'll be leaving too after making the copies."

"That's all right. Have a pleasant evening."

Zuba rose and followed Tanna to the door.

"Feeling much better about the whole matter now," Zuba said as they walked down the corridor. "My fears have been laid to rest. I only wish I had brought Nonye along. You should have seen the scene she put up when I returned from the station and told her what had happened: 'You've started again, Zuba! This is not a matter of right or wrong. It's a matter of saving your neck. You should settle and leave them to their conscience so that we can put this whole thing behind us.'"

"She has such fierce love for you. She was on our necks throughout the time you were in the police cell. Crying most times."

Tanna finished making the copy and they faced each other. He thrust his hand into his pocket. "Em... Your Lordship, I was wondering if you would allow me to give you a ride home?"

Tanna chuckled. "Since when did you begin to talk that way?"

"It's a trick I learnt from one lovely lady I'm getting to know. She uses it only on policemen."

Tanna was laughing by the time he finished.

As they left the office, walking between croton hedges to the car, Zuba castigated himself. Why hadn't he asked her straight to dinner as he had intended? Now he had to find a way to introduce the idea during the ride.

The car filled with her perfume and the windscreen reflected the whiteness of her blouse. Zuba became aware of how close they were in the confined space. His hand rose towards his keloid but stopped midway. He glanced at her, then went on to rub the keloid anyway.

Tanna smiled. "Does that scar itch?"

"It's not a scar. It's a keloid." He steered the car out of the compound and headed towards the dense Oguta Road rush-hour traffic.

"Does it itch?"

"Sometimes. But even when it doesn't I often feel this urge to rub it."

"I have noticed how you stuff your hand in your pocket sometimes to keep yourself from rubbing it."

"You have?" Zuba cast a wide-eyed glance at her. "You know what they used to call me in school because of it?"

She shook her head.

"Scarface."

They smiled at each other.

"And there's no real cure for it. You cut it out – it grows back with a vengeance, probably twice as big. It has a life of its own, I tell you. But research is on towards finding a cure. And I want to be part of it in any way I can."

"Hmmm. The lab rat, eh?"

"Yeah. I'll be pursuing a master's degree in medical biochemistry."

"Great. But why didn't you go straight for medicine in your first degree?"

"I couldn't make the cut-off mark for the admission. I wasn't bright enough."

Tanna began to laugh.

"What?"

"Your candour. It is unusual, especially in a man."

The commuter bus ahead of them stopped suddenly in the middle of the road. Zuba stamped on the brakes to avoid hitting it. The conductor jumped down. "Upper Iweka Road! Are you going? Come on in. Quick-quick." He beckoned at two men running down by the roadside. The men squeezed into the bus. The bus moved on with the conductor hanging from the open door.

Zuba drove on. He had to ask her to dinner soon. He looked around for any good-looking restaurant they could try out together. Shops and stalls lined both sides of the road: a clothing shop displaying an array of old clothes with new labels, a cement shop with the bags heaped in neat pyramids, a video store with life-size photos of local stars beneath crimson titles, a smoked fish stall with fishes laid out on trays, black and stiff like embalmed bodies, a building-materials store, a beer and palm-wine parlour, motor spare-parts store, a patent-medicine store, mechanic's workshop, and a medley of other stores stretched as far as his gaze could reach. The town's main market, located miles away, was spreading out like a wild creeper, overgrowing every space, every crack and crevice, and transforming the city into one big field of buying and selling.

"It must have been a long day at work for you," he said.

"Doesn't feel that way at all. I enjoy the challenge of standing up for something, of defending someone you believe in. It's often demanding. Like when a policeman told me once: 'I have someone like you at home cooking my food, washing my uniform and warming my bed.' But I'm glad my principal got me involved in your case. It is giving me insights in more ways than I had anticipated." She flashed a smile at him.

"Yes. It has been insightful for me too. And I'm not talking about the cell alone."

"Aha. I had wanted to ask, if you would not mind. How was the cell?"

Zuba grinned. "Incredibly interesting. But it's not a story to be told on an empty stomach. There's still time. Maybe we should find a place to grab a bite, then we can talk about it while we eat."

"Sure."

Zuba's grin widened. He came to the DMGS roundabout and turned into the Old Market Road.

The red and yellow colours of Mr Bigg's appeared ahead. The small road that ran beside the fast-food house, where he usually parked whenever the parking lot was full, was filled with cars. He sighed and drove further down the Old Market Road, parking in front of a metallic-blue Volvo. "Yeah, this will do," he said. He rubbed his hands together, smiled across at Tanna, then opened his door.

He had just set one foot on the ground when he saw three men heading his way. They had dried wiry features, the kind associated with men who began their day by downing shots of *kai-kai*, the super-strong locally brewed gin. Their bloodshot eyes glinted with triumph as they approached.

"Wrong parking," one of the men said. He blocked Zuba's way and flashed a grimy identity card that said Onitsha Road Decongestion Task Force. "You'll have to pay a fine of two thousand naira." He dug out a dog-eared receipt booklet from the back pocket of his jeans. It had the insignia of the state government under the heading: Anambra State Internally Generated Revenue.

"Rubbish," Zuba said in English. "There's no sign prohibiting parking here—"

"If you like you can speak all the grammar in the dictionary."

"…and there's another car parked here."

"Yes. We missed the driver. But he won't leave without seeing us." The man stepped back so that Zuba could lean out and look at the car. One of the car's rear wheels was missing. The axle rested on a block of wood.

"Pay up, collect your receipt and we'll allow you to go and park elsewhere. Otherwise we'll take you to our office, and there you'll not only pay for your wrong parking, you'll also pay to get your car released."

Zuba became aware of Tanna's eyes on him. "Stop all this nonsense," he shouted. "Just show me a sign on this road saying 'No Parking'."

"Can't you use your common sense? I can see you want it the hard way." He nodded at his companion stationed behind the car, who sprang the boot open and lifted out the spare wheel and jack.

Zuba cursed the central locking on the car.

"When you're ready to pay your fine you'll get your tyre and jack back," the man said. "You think I have the time to stand here and look at that ugly wart on your face?"

"Look…" Tanna began.

Zuba placed a hand on her thigh to stop her. His voice was low as he said, "All right, all right. Return my tyre and jack. Let's go to your office. I want to talk to your superiors."

The tyre and jack were popped back into the boot. Two of the men got into the back seat, crowding out Tanna's scent with their tobacco and alcohol smells.

Zuba realized that his hand was still resting on Tanna's thigh and snatched it off. He flexed the arm as if it had a cramp when Tanna glanced at him.

"OK. Head for our office. At Upper Iweka Road," the man said. He gripped the headrest of Zuba's seat.

"Where in Upper Iweka?"

"Beside NITEL."

Zuba started the car. Further down the road, a crowd had gathered, narrowing the drive lane. Their white vests bore the inscription: MASSOB. Non-Violent. Non-Exodus – and the banner they carried read: Movement for the Actualization of the Sovereign State of Biafra (MASSOB). The red-black-green Biafran flag with the rising-sun insignia fluttered in their midst as it was hoisted on a bamboo pole in front of the General Post Office. Zuba took a bypass to the New Market Road. He joined the traffic at Awka Road and snailed on. Silence hung in the car, punctuated only by the occasional cough from the back seat. He avoided glancing at Tanna, though she had looked his way several times. His heart raced as he wondered if his scheme would work.

When they got to the Zik Roundabout, he turned and sped towards the army residential area.

"Where are you going? That's not the way," the man behind him shouted.

"I know," Zuba said. "First, I have to inform the owner that you are impounding his car."

"And who is the owner of the car?"

"Lieutenant Colonel Maduekwe."

"It's lie," the man blurted in English. His voice had climbed an octave. "Why is there no army sticker on the car?" He switched back to Igbo.

"You can ask him when we get to his flat."

"OK. Let me see the papers of the car."

"Tanna, please can you check in the pigeonhole. You will see a brown envelope. Kindly give the vehicle registration paper in it to the man."

Tanna opened the pigeonhole. She retrieved a sheet from the envelope and handed it to the man.

"There is no Lieutenant Colonel before the owner's name," the man said.

"That's no business of mine. When you meet him, you can put it to him."

"And his address here states Ojoto." There was a triumphant note in the man's voice.

"Of course, what is stated there is his hometown, his permanent address," Zuba said as he turned into the area and stepped hard on the accelerator.

The man's companion, seated behind Tanna, bent forwards and made signs at the man.

"OK. Stop. Stop," the man said. "Stop!"

"Why? What's your problem?" Zuba stepped harder on the accelerator.

"Please stop. Stop. Please. I don't want to get into trouble with my bosses. Police and army don't disturb us, and we don't disturb them."

Zuba ignored him. He drove past the Mammy Market. There had to be some good-looking bungalows or duplexes somewhere.

"OK. Please, stop. I don't want to get into trouble with these army men. You know how they behave…"

"Mister, I beg stop," his companion said. "You want us to keep begging you? My man here has told you it was a mistake."

Zuba slowed down and made a U-turn. "I'll drop you at the bus stop," he said.

The men couldn't jump down quickly enough. One of them knocked his head against the top doorframe as they scrambled out.

"Thank you, thank you," they said as they banged the

door. They dashed over to the bus waiting at the other side of the road.

"The killjoys!" Zuba cursed under his breath, glaring after the men while rubbing his keloid.

Tanna began to laugh.

"Don't worry. We'll still have the dinner," she said. "But not today any more. It's already getting late. I have another idea: will you be free the weekend after your arraignment – say, Sunday?"

"Yes."

"Then can you pick me for lunch at about 2 p.m.?"

"Sure, sure."

"Great. So you too can see where I stay. I don't decorate my walls with Gandhi though."

Zuba eased the car back into the traffic.

"My place is not far from here. You know Omagba Estate?"

"Yeah."

"I stay with my aunt in her bungalow. She's an air hostess. Not a bad job for someone who hates remaining in a place for too long."

After several minutes on the road she pointed at a building.

"Here," she said.

Zuba could only see the silvery aluminium roof of a bungalow peering over a high, unpainted fence. He parked before the gates.

"Now I too know your place." He turned to her as she gathered her handbag and files.

There was amusement in her eyes. Once again Zuba had the feeling that she could see through him, read him like one of her novels.

She leant over and gave him a kiss on the cheek.

"See you next Saturday, Director. Thanks for the ride," she said.

Zuba cleared his throat. "All right, Solicitor-General. Have a good night. And a nice trip to Lagos."

Tanna shut the car door and walked towards the gate. Zuba's gaze followed her back, her narrow shoulders and slender arms. She disappeared behind the gates. His head felt like a balloon floating above his body on a long string. He touched his cheek. Then he started the car and drove slowly out of the estate.

Call a Spade a Spade

Professor Chukwueloka Maduekwe half-opened his eyes. His children were on the three-sitter conversing in muted tones, but their whispers had floated into his dream and their presence had soothed away his medicine-induced grogginess.

Nonye was in a bright yellow dress with a rash of deep blue dots. Her hands rested on her lap. She wore her hair differently from the way he last remembered. It was relaxed and pulled back, accentuating her forehead and heart-shaped face. He was sure there was a clasp at her nape holding the hair together, keeping it stretched tight, smooth and shiny. He studied her face. Her eye pencil, mascara and rosy lipstick were applied with artistic precision. He still disapproved. Make-up was for adults: it made immature girls like her look prematurely ripe. And worldly wise. He had fought a losing battle to keep her from using it.

Her eyes were intense, squinted. Her lips were puckered. No doubt, she was in disagreement with whatever Zuba was saying, and couldn't wait for him to finish speaking. Professor Maduekwe knew that if he could stretch and look lower, he would find her right foot grinding her impatience into the ground, like her mother used to do. But she would eventually win the argument. The Professor's eyes narrowed in a smile.

Zuba's lips were moving rapidly, flashing the white of his teeth and the pink of his tongue. The top buttons of his shirt were open, showing a hairless chest and almost jutting breastbone. His hand kept flying up to his face – as a boy he'd been obsessed with his keloid, but then the scar had occupied a big part of his tiny face. Now his face had broadened, making the keloid look smaller, almost like a fighter's scar that lent a touch of ruggedness to his face.

There was a new strength in his eyes, a calmness that could only spring from conviction. No, Nonye would lose the argument.

He beckoned them. They shut their mouths instantly. Yes, startled. What could they be hiding from him as they rushed and stood before his bedside? He squeezed his son's hand and ran his hand up his arm.

"*Kedu?*" he asked. His voice was raspy; his speech, slurred.

"I'm fine," Zuba said. He searched his father's face. "And you?" he asked.

The Professor nodded.

Zuba pulled a straight-back chair to the bedside and sat down.

Professor Maduekwe grasped Nonye's arm. He pulled her close till she was bent over him. He caressed her face, running his hand over her cheeks, forehead and hair. A clasp came off her hair and fell on the bed. It was bright-yellow, like her dress. Professor Maduekwe inhaled deeply and patted the bed. The plastic sheet underneath the white bedding squelched as she sat beside him. She reached for some tissue on the bedside table and dabbed at the wetness on the side of his lips.

The Professor pointed at Zuba. "Wha... What has been happening... to your brother? Doesn't he look... radiant?"

"He's been keeping secrets, Dad. Even from me! He's been that way for the past two days. Singing in the bathroom, counting days on the calendar."

A lopsided smile appeared on the Professor's lips. "Is there something you'll like me to know, son?"

Zuba scratched his keloid. Under normal circumstances, he knew he would never tell his dad, no matter how much he asked. But it was hard to turn down the request when it came from a hospital bed.

He glanced at Nonye. "Dad, I'm seeing someone."

"Yes, I suspected," Nonye screamed, and began to laugh.

"Seeing... Seeing someone?"

"He means he's dating a girl. It's Tanna, isn't it?"

The Professor's smile widened. A wave of wetness streamed down one end of his lips. "W-who is Tanna?"

"One fine lawyer girl who... who works at Barrister Chigbo's chambers," and she just stopped herself from saying "who sprung him from cell", a line she had once used to tease him.

The Professor's eyes sparkled. He remained silent, his potbelly rising and falling with his breathing. He remembered how he too had whistled while taking a bucket bath before his first date with their mother.

The doctor came in with Aunty Chinwe. He walked to the bedside and touched Zuba's arm. "He should rest now," he said. "He looks as if he has had enough excitement for several days."

"Aha. Dad. Barrister Chigbo wants to come and see you," Zuba said as he rose from his seat.

The Professor nodded. "How is my school?"

"All is going on well." Zuba stopped himself from going further. His gaze fell on the *softsell* magazines lying on the bedside table and he changed the subject. "Will you like to have the latest Stephen King? Or are there any other books or magazines you'll like to read? I can have them sent down tomorrow."

Professor Maduekwe nodded. He uttered two words in reply.

"What?" Zuba stepped closer.

"Bank statement," the Professor repeated.

Zuba straightened up. There was a new smile on his face. His father was recovering.

* * *

"This is it." Zuba pointed at the open gates beside a signboard that proclaimed the Anambra State High and Magistrate Courts in Ogidi.

Ike signalled left and turned into the gates. The road from the gates sloped downwards, past the offices of the local government. Erosion had eaten away chunks of the tar on the road to expose reddish, oily earth. The car weaved between the craters, past the clumps of bushy flowers in the lawns, and the cars parked at the premises, many of which bore the green-yellow-black Nigerian Bar Association sticker.

The courtrooms were housed in a long, yellow, colonial-style building. A stairway, shaped somewhat like an inverted Y, stood in front of it. People milled around in dignified attire, feet weary, faces marked with anticipation or dread. Others gathered in small groups, conferring with men who looked as at ease in the surroundings as they did in their dark suits.

Zuba waved in relief at his two sureties waiting for him in their cars. They all greeted each other as they got out.

One was the family doctor who had first treated Professor Maduekwe after the stroke. The other had the red cap of a titled man on his head. Zuba called him Uncle Arinze, although he had little idea how they were related. It was one of those great grandfather's-father's-elder sister's-son's-son kinds of connection that his father's generation knew how to keep track of, but which always made him dizzy. "Ask him to be one of your sureties – he's your uncle," Aunt Chinwe had said.

As Zuba was allowing Uncle Arinze to pat him on the back, he saw a man in a black suit checking his licence plate, and at the same time he noticed the albino policeman heading towards them from another part of the compound. He glanced at his watch: 8.50 a.m.

"Good morning," said the man in black suit. "I'm Barrister Greg Amazu, from Chigbo Chambers. You must be Zuba, here for an arraignment in a matter involving—"

"Mister man, good morning," the albino policeman interjected. "They send me to tell you say your arraignment no go take place today again. They say make you come to station come take another date."

"Why? What's the problem?" Zuba asked.

"I no know. When you get to station you go know."

"You say the arraignment will no longer take place today?" the barrister asked.

"Yes. They say make you come to station come take another date," the policeman repeated.

"Please excuse us for a minute," the barrister said.

The policeman took several steps away.

"Can you see your complainants anywhere here?" The barrister asked.

Zuba scanned the court premises. Beside him, Ike did the same. He shook his head.

165

"Did you look well?" Uncle Arinze said.

Zuba looked around again. "Yes, they're nowhere out here. Unless they're inside."

"No, they won't be inside. I won't be surprised if they have fled. Let's hope they and their accomplices have seen they cannot scare you into settlement with an arraignment, and have now dropped the fictitious charges against you two. You should thank the Lord."

Zuba smiled and slapped Ike on the back. Ike grinned.

Uncle Arinze threw up his hands. "O Lord thank you o. Court is trouble, and no one likes trouble."

"So what now?" the doctor asked.

"I will go on with Zuba and Ike to the police station. I don't think there's any need for you two to come with us. You may leave now if you wish."

Zuba shook hands with the doctor and thanked him. He hugged Uncle Arinze. "Take care, my son," Uncle Arinze said.

"Officer, officer," the barrister called to the albino. "Let's go."

They drove through off-roads and backstreets till they got to the station. Mr and Mrs Egbetuyi were seated on a bench under the almond tree, staring towards the office block with a smugness that riled Zuba.

"There they are," Zuba muttered to Ike as they walked towards the office. "Our complainants."

"Yes, come in, come in," Bayo's boss said when they appeared at the door. He dismissed the policeman with him.

"Barrister Amazu, from Chigbo Chambers," the barrister said, extending his hand.

"ASP Ajah," the officer said. "Sit down, sit down. Good of you to come with them." He tapped his biro on the file before him as they arranged themselves on the bench before his desk. "I don't have much time. So I will go straight to the point," the officer began, turning to Zuba. "Our legal department have finished going through your case file. They discovered an error."

A smile waited to grow on Zuba's face.

"They say the charge against you, your driver and others at large should not read threatening violence and stealing. But armed robbery – defined in law as 'stealing with violence or threat of violence', and that we should call a spade a spade, not a digging implement…"

"But superintendent, you know this is outrageous. Far-fetched. You know such a charge cannot stand."

"That will be for the court to decide—"

"And even if—"

The officer held up a hand. "Barrister, be a gentleman and allow me to finish. You'll have your own time to talk." He looked towards the door. "Bayo."

"Sir." Bayo appeared in the doorway.

"Issue them with a new arraignment notice for the charge of armed robbery. Today is Monday, eh?"

"Yes sir."

"Set the arraignment date for Thursday. I'm tired of this their case and want to wash my hands of it. When they get to court they can bail themselves and continue the case with their lawyers."

"Superintendent," the barrister began again, his voice harsh and rising. "You know as well as I do that armed robbery is not a bailable offence in this country – that once you arraign them in court for armed robbery they are bound to be remanded in prison."

"Me, I no know o. I am not a lawyer. I am only a policeman, and all I'm doing is my job." The officer looked at Zuba. There was a hint of amusement in his eyes, despite his grave bearing.

The implication of the change in the charge had left Zuba stunned for some seconds. He recovered with a jerk. "Wait, officer…"

"Yes?" The officer leant forwards, but Barrister Amazu tapped Zuba on the thigh to keep him quiet, and the officer frowned.

"OK, OK, I don't want to hear anything more on this matter. In view of the seriousness of the charge against your clients, we shall be keeping them in custody, in our cell. We shall take them to court from here for their arraignment. We don't want anybody running away. Bayo."

"Sir." Bayo came into the office. He placed a sheet on the desk before Zuba.

The barrister picked up the arraignment notice and skimmed through it. He shook his head. "Superintendent, we should never forget when carrying out our duties that there is One greater, the Boss of all the worlds, Who we will have to account to in the end."

The officer's expression soured. "Bayo, send these suspects back to cell immediately."

"Yes sir." Bayo tapped Zuba on the shoulder. "Make we go."

"We shall be taking this up with your legal department – if indeed it came from them, and the commissioner," the barrister said as he rose from his seat.

The officer's expression soured further.

"Take heart, Zuba. I don't understand how people can act so without fear of the Lord. I'll be off to their legal department right away. We'll ensure the armed robbery charge is dropped. Even if it means seeing the commissioner or writing to Abuja. Everything will be OK. Take heart."

A numbness crept over Zuba. His mind began to distance itself from his body. He took the car keys from Ike and handed them to the barrister. Please take the car to my sister. Also, put these in the car." He removed his jacket and tie. Ike removed the gold chain on his neck and the brooch on the pocket of his caftan.

"Yellow," Bayo shouted. "Yellow, where you?"

The albino policeman appeared in the doorway. A rifle now hung from his shoulder.

"Make we go." Bayo led the way outside.

Zuba, Ike and Yellow followed. Somehow the stench of the cell already filled Zuba's nostrils.

The smugness vanished from the Egbetuyis faces when they saw Zuba and Ike being followed to Bayo's car by a gun-toting policeman. Mr Egbetuyi's mouth hung open in mid-sentence. Zuba wasn't going to settle?

Zuba was too dazed to give them more than a vague glance. His thinking had slowed down under shock as the implications of the sudden change in their circumstances percolated further. He and Ike got into the back seat of Bayo's car.

"You this man, what is wrong with you?" Bayo screamed as he drove out of the police station. "What is wrong with you, eh? Why you be so stubborn? You want prove say you tough? Or is it that *yeye* hopeless lawyer you want follow? Why they even send you this nonsense born-again lawyer anyway? Why they no send that fine woman? Anyway, this no be lawyer matter again o. This na your life. Make you save yourself now. We all know you get the money. My boss no too care about your complainants again; he and his own boss want chop money from this your case too. So if you no want settle your complainants, just find something for my boss make he change your charge back to threatening violence and stealing. If you no do this, and you go court with this armed robbery charge, na straight to ATM you go go o. And I tell you, you go hate yourself if you go there. They go beat the life out of you; they go use broken bottle shave this your fine hairstyle. Hmmmnnh! Na terrible place. It no be like cell o." He kept glancing at Zuba from the rear-view mirror as he spoke.

Zuba felt Bayo's words prodding him like many tiny electric rods. He stared at the back of his head. Could he trust him? Or was Bayo trying to railroad him to a pre-planned end?

"Look, make you no follow lawyer," Bayo continued. "I sure say as we dey drive you go cell now, that your lawyer dey handle another person case. As you dey suffer now, him dey enjoy, dey make him money from another person. You know how vultures go leave meat make it die and rotten before them begin eat? Na so some lawyers dey do. Them go leave case make it bad well-well first. For this my job, I see lawyers delay so their clients go enter ATM first so they go fit charge more money. You better save yourself. If you want, I go turn around now and drive you back to station to see my boss and settle with him."

"What is ATM?" Zuba asked.

"ATM na Awaiting Trial Men, prison where they keep people awaiting trial for serious offences. Na terrible place."

"Please give me time to think about the whole thing," Zuba said. But in his mind he had taken a decision: he would give his lawyers some time to reverse the situation. The arraignment was slated for Thursday; if by Wednesday morning he and Ike were still in cell with an armed robbery charge hanging round their necks, he would send a message to Bayo's boss, settle with him, do whatever was required. The decision made him feel better. He wanted to communicate his decision to Ike in Igbo so that Bayo would not understand. But Yellow would understand, and he didn't trust Yellow.

They drove for miles in silence. The car began to descend a hill, at the bottom of which the police station and cell stood. Thick cumulus clouds were gathering above, dimming the blaze of the late-afternoon sun. Bayo began again: "My friend, you know you lucky? My boss no want punish you. Otherwise he for send you to State CID Cell, where they keep the *ogbologbo*, the original hardened criminals. Where them dey stay naked in cell, where you no go escape beating and sleeping in toilet. You lucky. That's why you fit say you need time to think. Time to think about what? Because you know say na better cell you dey go. You know say we dey go lock you up for the GRA of cells."

The same yam and maize farms framed the compound, and the same wild wire grass surrounded the building. A man in black shorts was bent over, whipping the grass down with a cutlass. The swish-swish of his blade kept time with his singing. Sweat streamed down his body. His trousers and shirt hung from a low branch of the nearby guava tree. Ripe, rotting and bat-eaten guava fruits littered the ground. A fruity scent hung in the air.

Zuba and Ike followed Bayo on the foot-worn red-earth path that led into the station.

"Idem, lock them up," Bayo said, placing a detention order on the counter.

"Hah! Zuba. You again?" Idem said.

"Good afternoon, Idem," Zuba said. "I don't understand what is happening. But it will be over soon."

"Zuba, is it you? Is it really you?" Nwamaka's soprano rang out from the corridor.

Zuba hesitated. "Yes, Nwamaka. It's me."

"It seems you've gotten yourself a girlfriend here," Ike tried, but neither of them could smile at the joke, and Zuba got the feeling that Ike had said it only to keep something else hidden.

"Zuba, what happened?" Mike called out.

"Enough of talk," Idem said as Zuba made to answer. "Undress and go meet them. Then you fit talk all you like."

They kept their trousers on this time. Zuba stripped to his vest and Ike went bare-chested.

"Zuba," Nwamaka called as he walked past her cell.

"Nwamaka, how are you?"

She shrugged. "I'm still where I am."

Zuba felt the embrace of familiar smells as the bars clanged shut behind them. The smells curled around the hair in his nostrils, wove themselves into the hair on his head, wriggled into his ears, bored into his pores, and latched onto his clothing.

The prefect and Papa were no longer in the cell. Mike was now in prime position, seated by the door, followed by the ball-grabber, Chemist and two new young men.

Mike and Chemist greeted Zuba and Ike warmly.

"What happened?" Mike asked.

"Don't mind this police people," Zuba said. "They're trying to extort money from us."

Mike looked down the line of seated inmates. "Make space for them there," he motioned between Chemist and the two new inmates.

The two young men shifted. Their faces were impassive, although their new position placed them opposite the slop bucket.

Zuba and Ike sat on the ground.

Chemist placed a hand on Zuba's thigh. "Truth is, I'm happy to see you again. Yet, I should not be happy that you are returning to this horrible place."

Chemist stank. Zuba drew back. He tried to change his sitting position, but stopped as he remembered Chemist's bad foot. He glanced down. The mouth of the wound was covered in pus. The surrounding skin, spreading out, was assuming the sickly whitish-yellow of the pus. Zuba felt like spitting. He forced himself to swallow the saliva. His eyes were glazing as he looked up at the opposite wall.

The Buga graffiti stared back. There was a wicked twist to the grin on his face. *Welcome back.*

You'll Be the One to Suffer It

Zuba woke to the sensation of water being sprinkled onto his body. The cell was pitch-dark, the smells were subdued, and the storm made a din outside. A gust of wind blew more rain through the narrow opening up on the wall. A drop landed in his left eye. It felt icy, and stung the sleepiness from his head. A streak of lightning, brilliant-blue, lit up the darkness. Zuba started and felt the hair on his body rise. Chemist was sitting up, deathly still, hunched over his bad foot. A rumble of thunder rose above the clatter of the rain. Zuba sighed and turned away. Ike stirred beside him.

He had been dreaming before the raindrops roused him. Their arraignment in court had gone on as scheduled, and sparks, red-orange and blue-yellow, had shot out from the magistrate's mouth as she berated the police prosecutor. The prosecutor had twisted and turned to avoid the sparks; he writhed with a grimace on his face each time the sparks burnt through his black uniform to singe his flesh.

Ike stirred again. He tried to curl up, and his elbow dug into Zuba's ribs. Zuba noticed that Ike was shivering. He sat up, pulled off his vest and draped it over Ike's bare torso. Ike murmured and curled up further. His knees pushed into the warm space just vacated by Zuba.

Zuba felt the warmth of Chemist's shoulder against his. The lightning flashed again, and Zuba glimpsed Buga staring down at him from the wall. There was a gloating expression on his lips, and his eyes seemed to be saying: *You don't know what is coming to you, do you?*

A thunderclap shook the building, chilling Zuba to his bones.

* * *

In the morning, an hour after the slop bucket had been emptied, Idem appeared at the doorway. Keys jingled in his hands, drowning the psalms being murmured by Chemist.

"Zuba, you and your partner, come out. You people dey go."

Zuba pushed himself up. The news made him light-headed. He nudged Ike. "Ike, Ike, wake up. We're going."

Ike leapt to his feet.

They said hurried goodbyes to Mike and Chemist.

"Zuba, bye-bye. Zuba's brother, bye-bye." Nwamaka pressed her face against the bars. Her left hand, wrapped round one of the rods, displayed bitten fingernails. Staring into the twinkle in her eyes and at the whiteness of her smile, it struck Zuba that she was genuinely happy for them. Whereas Mike and Chemist's goodbyes had a veiled sullenness. He hesitated before the door of her cell.

"Make we go, make we go," Idem said.

Zuba followed Idem and Ike to the office. Bayo was standing by the door. "Quick, collect your belongings, let's get going."

Zuba stifled a smile. Bayo's brusque expression showed he was annoyed. The other side had lost out. Zuba collected his shirt, watch and money from Idem. He patted his pocket. "My handkerchief, I left it in the cell. I'll ask them to hand it to me," he said, and hurried down the corridor.

"No waste time there o," Idem called after him.

Zuba squatted before Nwamaka's cell. "Nwamaka, would you like to send a message to anyone, your people?"

She shook her head. "They know I'm here. They've tried, but there's nothing they can do. I'm not to be allowed visitors till the police finish their investigations."

"OK. Tell me your name, your full name."

"You never get your handkerchief? Wetin you dey do there?" Idem shouted from the reception.

"Nwamaka Ezeh."

Zuba sprang up. "I don get am. I dey come."

Outside, Yellow was waiting for them. His rifle hung from his shoulder, and he gestured to Bayo's car with it.

"Where are we going?" Zuba asked when they hit the road. "You want to search our houses again?"

"I told you. I warned you, didn't I?" Bayo said.

Zuba and Ike were thrown forwards as Bayo stepped hard on the brakes. A commuter bus had stopped suddenly. NO FOOD FOR LAZY MAN was written in red across its rear. The conductor beckoned at a pedestrian.

Bayo drove into the oncoming traffic and eased the car to the driver's side of the bus. "Break him mirror," he said.

Yellow poked the muzzle of his gun out of the car and jabbed at the bus's side-view mirror, spilling shards of glass onto the road. The driver's lips parted in a scream, but he caught sight of Yellow's police uniform.

Bayo drove on. "I warned you," he continued. "I told you: you'll be the one to suffer it."

"Tell me. Where are we going?"

"We're taking you people to court for your arraignment."

Zuba sat back. It could not be. He had seen the arraignment notice himself. It was for Thursday. This was Tuesday morning. "What about my lawyers? Do they know I'm being arraigned today?"

"Look at this man! You're still asking about your lawyer."

The oncoming traffic had snagged up in a jam, and now their own lane came to a standstill.

"Kill him! Kill him!" Shouts rose from a crowd at the nearby junction. Drivers were turning off their engines; passengers were scrambling out to join the crowd.

"What's happening?" Bayo muttered.

"Looks like Bakassi Boys. Seems they have catch another robber," Yellow said.

Zuba poked his head out of the window. An electric crackle of voices rose from the crowd. The bodies of pedestrians, artisans, farmers, hawkers, students and children, adorned in a variety of styles, pressed together in riotous colours, forming an impenetrable curtain around a raised machete. The broad blade glinted in the daylight. Silence fell over the crowd as the blade descended. A heartrending cry, shrill and intense, turned into a glottal gurgle as hot blood spouted up. The crowd shifted back. Zuba caught sight of a headless body whirling on the ground, the legs kicking in a race for its life while the arms jerked against its handcuffs.

A man in a red scarf doused the quivering body with fuel. He struck a match, dropped it in the pool near his feet, then drew back as flames engulfed the corpse.

Zuba felt the rush of nausea. But only a long stream of gastric juice-tainted saliva exited from his mouth. He wiped his lips with his handkerchief.

The smell of roasting flesh rose in the air. Passengers ran back to their vehicles. Cars began to clear from the road, driving pedestrians further into the shrubbery bordering the highway. Ahead, a bus driver and his passengers stuck out their hands and waved. "The Bakassi Boys are coming. Up Bakassi!"

"Those Bakassi people dey come," Yellow said to Bayo. "Clear! Clear!"

Bayo turned the steering and stepped on the gas pedal. The car lurched off the road, joining others in the shrubbery.

More screams rose from pedestrians and from the parked vehicles: "Up Bakassi! Bakassi anti-robbery squad! Bakassi, thank you-ooooo! We can now sleep at night! Thank you-ooo! Massacre the robbers! Bakassi for ever!"

A bus, gleaming white and new, appeared ahead. It blared its horn like a siren as it drove against traffic. A man sat on the roof, all in black except for the blood-spattered red bandana wound round his head. The glasses that covered his eyes were as black as the rest of his attire. A single leaf from a palm frond, young and yellow-green, hung from his lips. His legs were spread out wide, as if the bus was a horse he was straddling. A machete, still crimson, lay across his thighs. More machetes, and rifles, stuck out from the windows of the bus.

After the Bakassi Boys had passed by, tyres squealed as cars rushed back to the road. Bayo pushed hard on the accelerator. Yellow spat out of the window as they drove by the corpse, cursing as he studied the mound of burning limbs, torso and skull.

"Aha," Zuba said at last. "Do my lawyers know you are arraigning us today?"

"This man! Your lawyers, they will be in some court after a sweet hearty breakfast, busy making money from some other people's troubles. While you, your troubles are now beginning. I pity you. After all the advice I gave you, after I stuck out my neck for you."

* * *

The Egbetuyis were seated on the visitors' benches of the courtroom, his caftan and her boubou cut from the same blue brocade. They returned Zuba and Ike's stares with blank faces.

A wooden dock stood in the centre of the courtroom, between the visitors' benches and the pews where black-robed, blond-wigged men and women sat before long tables strewn with red-ribboned files and fat volumes.

Bayo pointed to a bench against the wall, facing the dock and its present female occupant. Zuba and Ike sat down. Beside them was a man whose leg, arm and head were swathed in bandages. Dirty yellow fluid had soaked through, spreading a foul smell in the stuffiness of the courtroom that reminded Zuba of Chemist. Bayo signalled to one of the two women sitting below the magistrate's desk, and she followed him out of the courtroom. They stood in the passage outside the doorway and conferred in hushed tones. Bayo handed a sheet to her. She glanced at it, nodded, then they returned to the courtroom.

Zuba's breathing became laboured. The magistrate's voice sounded garbled, and the bar morphed into a collage of black and white paint. He forced himself to take deep breaths. He tapped Bayo on the thigh when the room stopped spinning.

"What is it?" Bayo whispered.

"Will something like fifty thousand naira do it?"

"Haaa! Stubborn man! What took you so long? Why you no talk so before?"

"OK, stop the arraignment," Zuba said.

Bayo looked up. Mr Egbetuyi's eyes were on them. "Come make we all go talk outside," he said. "See if you want settle them too."

Bayo stood up. He bowed and walked out of the room. Zuba followed. At the door, Bayo beckoned at Mr Egbetuyi, then turned right into the passage.

Mr Egbctuyi emerged from the courtroom with his hands clasped in front of him. He wore the beaten-down expression of an oppressed man.

"Hello, Mr Egbetuyi." Zuba stretched out his hand.

Mr Egbetuyi's handshake was limp, and his expression remained unchanged.

"I need to confirm certain things from you quickly. I believe we can resolve our differences once we talk honestly, man to man. I was not there when the school bus conveyed you and your belongings to the Lagos Bus Station. So I don't know what happened. But tell me, truly, honestly, were you robbed of one hundred and fifty thousand naira as you claim? And if yes, how did you come about such a sum?" Zuba rubbed his keloid as he spoke.

Mr Egbetuyi sighed. "Zuba, I don't know how else to prove it to you that we were dispossessed of our money. Believe me, you don't know what Ike and his accomplices did to us. At least he had to admit that some other person accompanied him, since the gateman saw one of them. If you truly don't know anything about it, then Ike is taking you for a ride. But we have no other choice than to believe you planned it, or at least were in the know as a way to punish us for whatever trouble we might have caused you—"

"And the money?" Zuba cut in. He already knew he was going to agree to settle. He just needed an excuse to make his volte-face believable.

"Yes. We could not remain waiting endlessly for you to agree to pay us my wife's entitlements. Our logistics were running low. So we took the little money we had, borrowed some from friends to make it up to two hundred and fifty thousand naira, and decided to redeploy back to Lagos, where my wife would get a new commission in another school. We spent one hundred thousand to buy the Kenwood CD player, Sony TV and a few other electronics on the day before our departure, since they are cheaper here and we could sell them for a good profit when we get to Lagos. We decided to leave you to your conscience. We are a poor struggling couple. Struggling for everything, even to have our own children..."

Zuba turned away. Doubt gnawed at the edge of his mind: could they really have been robbed? And by Ike? "OK, we have spoken. I'll settle with them too," he said to Bayo. "Stop the arraignment."

He went with Bayo to the doorway of the court, where Bayo tried catching the lady's eye. Zuba suspected she was the court clerk. The lady looked up, saw Bayo raising a finger, and a frown crossed her face.

Bayo and Zuba returned to join Mr Egbetuyi.

The lady appeared, still frowning, fear in her eyes. "What is it now? You want to put me in trouble? Her Worship does not like people walking up and down in her court."

"Sorry. I beg, please withdraw our matter. We cannot continue with it now. There's new development," Bayo said.

The lady turned and withdrew into the court.

"Truly, we never wanted this court case. We don't want to punish you or anybody. We just want our money back so we can leave and continue with our lives," Mr Egbetuyi said.

Minutes later, Zuba returned with Bayo to the doorway.
The lady shook her head at them. She scribbled on a sheet
of paper and passed it on through the police prosecutor
seated against the wall to her left. The paper passed from
hand to hand, heading to the rear of the court. Bayo took
a few steps in, collected it and came out again. Zuba
rushed to his side. The inscription on the paper read: *Too
late. Your matter is already before Her Worship. Come in
and sit down. It's about to be called up.*

Bayo slipped the paper into his pocket and stared at his
feet. When he raised his head and turned to Mr Egbetuyi,
an iciness had crept into his eyes.

"What's the matter? Are we no longer settling?" Mr
Egbetuyi asked.

"No. It's over," Bayo snapped. "Get back inside. The
case is continuing."

"Is there no way we can stop it?" Mr Egbetuyi said.

"No, it's out of our hands. It is court matter now. It can
only be stopped by judicial process now."

"Sure there's no way? No way at all?" Mr Egbetuyi
pressed.

"Yes, go in and snatch the charge sheet from the magistrate's hand," Bayo snapped.

Mr Egbetuyi snorted and turned away. He began
wringing his hands.

Bayo's expression turned to pity as he placed a hand on
Zuba's shoulder to steer him towards the courtroom.

Zuba shrugged off his hand. He followed him back into
the court, bowed and sat down. Then he turned to Ike.

"Ike, I must ask you again." Zuba's voice was a hoarse
whisper. "Did you... I mean, were the Egbetuyis assaulted
or robbed of any of their belongings that morning you
drove them to the bus station?"

182

Ike's eyes widened. "Zuba, I have already told you: nothing of such a kind happened. I would have told you otherwise, you know that. They are lying, they are lying."

Zuba looked into Ike's eyes and saw the deep hurt his question had inflicted. "Ike, I'm sorry. I just had to ask. I believe you, I believe you."

But Zuba also saw something else in Ike's gaze. It was the same thing he had seen flicker once or twice in Ike's eyes while they were in cell, something Ike had been hiding: *If only you had agreed to the Ojoto police boss's suggestion, the Egbetuyis would have been the ones in this situation, not us.* But he knew that, out of deference, Ike would never voice it.

"Did anything come out of your talk with them?" Ike asked.

Zuba shook his head and gave Ike's knee a squeeze. A wet smudge remained on the knee of Ike's trousers after he removed his sweaty palm. Ike's lids lowered over his eyes.

Zuba began to take deep breaths, staring at everything from a great distance. He focused on the object before him. It was the dock. The bandaged man who had been seated beside Ike was now standing in it. The court registrar's voice rang out as she read from a charge sheet. From his haven outside his body, Zuba heard the word "murder" several times. He heard "driver", "oil tanker", "run into", "bus", "kill", "passengers".

The registrar began reading out a list of names. Zuba remembered that the driver of the tanker that killed his mum and brother was never caught. The man had bolted. He wondered if his father had pursued the matter. He took a good look at the fellow in the dock. He looked pathetic and pitiable in his bandages, with the blood spots in his eyes and the sprinkling of white hair on his chin.

The magistrate ordered his remand in prison. His lawyer objected and pointed to his injuries: the man should be allowed to complete his treatment before being remanded in prison. The magistrate refused. The man should arrange with prison authorities to continue his treatment while the lawyer applied for his bail at the high court.

Prison. Prison. Prison. That was all that stuck in Zuba's mind from the exchange between magistrate and lawyer.

"As court pleases," chanted the bar at the end of the magistrate's pronouncement.

The man's cane tapped on the wooden floor of the dock as he limped out.

The registrar read out some codes and announced, "Commissioner of Police versus Zuba Maduekwe, Ike Okoye, and others at large."

Bayo tapped Zuba on the thigh and pointed to the dock.

Zuba stood up. His body walked to the dock while he followed a few paces behind it. Ike brought up the rear, occasionally stepping into him. In the dock they stood facing the magistrate and court officials. The magistrate looked pretty and magisterial. She regarded them through the lens of her rimless glasses. Expressionless. The clerk's eyes were wide open. Lidless. Zuba was oblivious of what emotion was pushing them out from their sockets. Shock? Sadness? Incredulity? Regret?

The registrar continued:

That you Zuba Maduekwe and Ike Okoye on so so and so date did conspire with others at large to commit felony, to wit, armed robbery, an offence punishable under section blah blah blah of the Criminal Code...

That you Zuba Maduekwe, Ike Okoye and others at large on so so and so date did arm yourselves with dangerous weapons: guns, machetes, daggers and axes, and dispossessed the complainants, Mrs Adebisi Egbetuyi and Mr Frank Egbetuyi, of the following items: one hundred and fifty thousand naira cash, 29-inch Sony television, Kenwood CD player...

That you Zuba Maduekwe, Ike Okoye and others at large...

Eventually the question: guilty or not guilty?

"Not guilty," Zuba shouted through his body. The sound came out just above a whisper.

"Not guilty," Ike said.

The sight of a man who looked like Barrister Chigbo hurrying into the courtroom pulled Zuba back into his body. He looked closely. No, it was not the barrister. Words began tumbling out of his lips: "Your Worship, excuse me, please we're being wrongfully arraigned here..."

Alarm leapt into the court registrar's eyes. She pressed her finger to her lips and shook her head at Zuba.

Zuba's breath came in short gasps again. The sounds in the court came to him as if from a telephone receiver, and the sights seemed like scenes on a TV screen.

The magistrate began her pronouncements. Only two of her many sentences struck Zuba:

Bail is neither considered nor granted in a case of armed robbery. It is hereby ordered that the accused persons be remanded in prison custody.

And then the chorus:

As court pleases.

A man walked up to the dock to lead them out. He had protruding eyes and a pallid face which, coupled with his mournfully black police uniform, made him look like an undertaker. A pair of handcuffs flashed silver in his hands. One hoop was clamped around Zuba's wrist while the other snapped shut around Ike's.

Bayo rose, bowed and walked out of the court without a backwards glance.

The magistrate rose.

The court scrambled to its feet. The room erupted in noise after the magistrate's exit. Banters and shuffling feet, the scrape of furniture against the ground, barristers pulling off or adjusting their robes, visitors filing out.

The Egbetuyis now stood alone at the aisle beside the visitors' benches. Mr Egbetuyi fiddled with his hands. His lips hung apart. Zuba was certain that what he saw in Mr Egbetuyi's eyes was remorse. But he was unsure if it was remorse over the fate that had befallen him and Ike, or remorse at having lost the "settlement" at the last moment. His wife's lips were pursed, like those of a child sucking on a particularly sweet candy.

Zuba looked away and began to rub his keloid. The undertaker-policeman collected a sheet from the clerk, folded and slipped it into his pocket, then headed back to Zuba and Ike. The handcuff bit into Zuba's wrist. "It will be all right," he said to Ike.

"I know…" Ike said. His face was swollen, his eyes were red. Zuba was sure his own face looked the same. He looked again into Ike's eyes. Ike too was trying to find something to say, something to lighten the terrible weight that made breathing difficult.

"You remember what Mama Bedbug said to her children when hot water was poured on the mattress they called home?" Ike finally said. "'Hold tight, children. What is hot will later grow cold.'"

They both could not manage a smile.

"Let's go," the undertaker-policeman said.

The Inside World

African-Style

The taxi groaned uphill. Children with sun-blackened faces and adults in jaded dresses lined the road like citizens welcoming a beloved leader. They displayed their wares like gifts. Trays of fruits: oranges, mangoes and avocados, heaped in neat pyramids, stood on rickety weather-beaten tables. Biscuits, sweets and cakes in colourful wrappings gleamed in the evening sun. Fragrant smoke rose from sooty cooking pots. Vultures circled above.

The undertaker-policeman coughed in the passenger seat. Zuba stared out of the car window, rubbing his keloid with the index finger of his left hand. He looked past the hawkers, at the dark waters of the Niger flowing some distance behind them. The sight of the river had a soothing effect. He watched the birds that swooped upon the waters and came up with squiggling silver fishes in their talons. The vehicle shuddered into a pothole and the handcuff chafed against his wrist. He joined Ike in staring at the towering fence that loomed ahead. Jagged shards of broken glass and rows of barbed wire sat on its head like a crown of thorns. Dread grew in his heart as he wondered what lay behind the walls. He struggled to shake it off. You survived the police cell – this cannot be much worse. You will survive it too.

The car turned before a set of gates and clattered to a halt.

"Come down," the policeman said.

Zuba and Ike inched their way out of the car. They held their wrists rigid together to prevent further chafing by the handcuff.

Two guards observed them, nursing their guns on their laps under a nearby mango tree. The tree's branches were gnarled and stunted, its leaves scant and scraggy. Only one of the guards waved back when the policeman waved at them. The other stared with red eyes while smoke spiralled out of his nostrils.

The policeman rapped on the gate. A window slid open and a face appeared. It slid shut again. Keys jingled and bolts clacked. A door in the gates opened noiselessly. They stepped in. The bolts clacked home.

They were in a small forecourt. The walls were a dirty light green. Rooms and offices stood on both sides, their doors ajar. Warders in brownish-green uniforms moved about. A group of young men sat on the bare floor outside the offices. MASSOB. Non-Violent. Non-Exodus, said the vests on their chests.

The men paid no attention to Zuba and Ike. They stared through the gates at the other end of the forecourt, at the flash of naked sweaty chests and rugged hairy legs jostling after a football, and at the crowd of faded men in faded clothes clapping and cheering within the prison yard.

The policeman led Zuba and Ike into one of the offices. He unlocked their handcuffs and walked across to the opposite office, clutching a white sheet in his hand.

Zuba lifted his arm to examine his bruised wrist.

"Your name?" the warder asked, staring at Ike. He noted Ike's particulars on the open page before him. "Your name?" he asked again, this time staring at Zuba.

"Zuba Maduekwe."

"Maduekwe? Is that the Maduekwe of Chukwueloka Maduekwe?"

Zuba nodded.

"Dr Maduekwe! The former commissioner of education whose father was senator?"

Zuba kept silent.

"OK, you two, undress quick-quick. Bring all your valuables too. Remember, I will search you after."

Zuba and Ike undressed and stood before the warder in their undergarments.

"Spread your arms and legs," the warder said, coming round to them. He frisked them from head to toe and returned to his desk.

A roar rose from the prison yard: "Gooooooooooo-ooal!"

Zuba and Ike started. They looked at each other. Then their eyes darted about the room, jumpy as their nerves. They took in the pile of belongings of new inmates behind the warder, the brand-new fan spinning above him, the thickness of the bars on the louvre-less window looking into the prison yard, and the dreariness on the warder's face as he filled in the logbook. The sight of a horsewhip and a small dagger lying on the floor jolted Zuba.

"Please, is there any way you can help us? I don't want us to be beaten," he said.

"Nobody beats anybody here," the warder snapped.

"OK. Thank you. Please can you put us in the same cell?" Zuba asked.

"No. People on the same charge are kept separate. To avoid conspiracy. You can now wait in the passage with those other men," the warder added, as he saw Zuba's lips parting again.

They stood beside the seated MASSOB men and stared into the prison yard. A young man in blue prison uniform waited on the other side of the gate. He glanced occasionally into the courtyard. His cheeks and jaws were covered with a profusion of pus-tipped razor bumps, the worst Zuba had ever seen.

The warder called out: "Maduekwe, come back in."

Zuba returned to the office.

The warder was perched on his desk. He kicked his legs in the air as he studied Zuba. After a minute or so, he began in a low voice: "Maduekwe, I have decided to help you. For your stay here to be smooth, there is a clique in here that every new moneyed inmate must do cell-show for. Collect five thousand naira from your people when they come and give me to pass on to them. They will never collect anything directly from you, because they don't want their cover to be blown. Beating may have been outlawed here but, if you fail to settle them, there are other terrible ways they can use to get their dues."

Zuba remembered what had happened at the police cell. The policeman, Idem, had likewise offered to help. But he had pocketed most of the money and the pittance he passed on to the cell prefect had only angered the prefect. He and Ike would have been pulverized had he not given more money to the prefect for their cell-show. The thought got Zuba growing tight in the face. He looked away and said nothing.

The warder's eyes narrowed. "Well, have it your way. I'll still be here when you change your mind."

Zuba stepped out of the office and stood beside Ike.

"OK, Okwu, go take the new inmates in. The game go end soon. Superintendent want talk to them." The words came from the opposite office. A green curtain, aged to transparency, hung over the door. Okwu parted the curtain and stepped into the courtyard. He regarded Zuba and the other inmates with the laughing eyes of one who took nothing seriously. "Attention! All of you. Massobians. Stand up. You're going in now."

His voice was squeaky: the screech of a throttled man pleading for his life. Zuba thought it affected.

Okwu unlocked the gates leading into the yard. "Amaechi, take them to the front of the superintendent's office," he said.

"OK," the prisoner with the razor bumps said. "You people, follow me."

Zuba was last in the line of inmates walking behind Amaechi. He hated the sight of Ike's naked torso as it moved in front of him. It made Ike look powerless, stripped naked of his personality.

The football match was still raging, and hardly anyone in the yard spared them a glance. Amaechi led them along a sandy walkway between the playing field and a row of offices. A church building stood ahead; yellow, white and bright.

"What's you people's case?" Amaechi asked, looking back at them.

For the moment, Zuba welcomed the assumption that he and Ike were part of a group. He was too embarrassed to say it was a case of armed robbery that brought him and Ike there.

"We did nothing," the man closest to Amaechi said. He seemed like the leader. "They arrested us from Post Office, where we were demonstrating peacefully and carried us to cell, then to court, then to this place." He ran a hand through his rebel beard. "We are not bothered anyway. Throughout history, freedom fighters have always been persecuted. What about you? What is your case?"

"Robbery and murder," Amaechi said.

The ease with which he answered, as if he was giving his date of birth, silenced further discussion.

"We'll wait here till the game ends," he said.

They sat down on the raised concrete platform that formed part of the foundation of the church. The church cast its shadow over them, soothing, in the late afternoon heat.

Zuba looked around. Apart from the church and the green-painted offices to their left, the other blocks framing the yard looked greyed. The broken-bottle- and barbed-wire-topped fence, which blocked his view whenever his eyes sought the horizon, was the same burnt-out-ash grey. Sand, desert-brown and sterile, covered the whole grounds. Not a single mellowing bit of greenery sprouted in the stark environment.

"It will only be for a short while," he murmured to himself. "Yes!" He turned to Ike. "Ike, it will only be for a short while. Nonye and the barrister will find us soon and we will be out of here. Let's adjust, flow along and keep safe the best we can. Let's imagine it's some... some... Yes! Some school excursion."

"You forget I never went to school," Ike mumbled. His gaze was set on the shards of glass and barbed wire of the fence at the other end of the field.

"You can call it an adventure then."

"My wife will be due any day from now. I am stuck here without having made any arrangements, and you're saying..."

"Ike, don't dwell on that. She will be OK. Nonye will take care of her. Like the last time. She will—"

"Mr Non-violent-non-exodus, where are you going?" Amaechi called out.

The leader of the MASSOB men had risen and was walking towards the fence at the back of the church.

"Excuse me, I want to ease myself."

"You can't piss there," Amaechi said.

"No, I just want to gas."

"Do you have to go all the way to Jericho because you want to fart?"

"I respect myself. I like to respect myself," the man said.

"There's nothing like that here," Amaechi cut in. "You're now in prison. You fart where you like. Or will it knock us out?"

Zuba forced himself to laugh with the others. His laugh was loudest, and he bumped into Ike, hoping to cajole him into joining. He turned to Amaechi. "Anyway, I agree with the man. Like Gandhi said, nobody can take your self-respect from you unless you yourself surrender it."

Amaechi laughed long and hysterically. "I'd like to know what you think about that after you've spent just two weeks in this hole."

The Massobian patted Zuba on the thigh. There was warmth in his eyes. "You know, it's people like you we need. You should join our Movement," he muttered.

"That's the least of my problems now," Zuba said. "Besides, I can't swallow some of the things you people believe. I've seen your posters and handbills."

The Massobian shook his head.

The referee's final whistle sounded, and the supporters of the winning team clapped and jumped up and down in front of their cell block. The team, bare-chested in contrast to their red-vested opponents, hugged one another. They leapt into the air and danced about the field raising a cloud of dust. One of them began somersaulting. It was all unrestrained and free, and soothed the fears Zuba had been struggling to suppress.

A golden trophy stood on a stool at the fringe of the playground. Beside it sat a prison official. The crisp newness of his uniform, and the epaulettes on his shoulders, proclaimed him the superintendent. A few paces to his right, two female warders ushered a handful of gaunt women in haggard mufti off the playground. They disappeared into an adjoining compound through a gate at the other side of the church.

The superintendent lifted his diminutive frame from his seat and made for the office block. A prisoner carried the trophy and followed behind him, struggling to keep up with his energetic strides.

"Get up! Get up!" Amaechi said, and he hustled them over to the steps in front of the superintendent's office.

"I have asked to see you, to talk to you before you are led into your cells," the superintendent began. His accent was clear, his English impeccable. "You are now in prison, what Fela Kuti called 'The Inside World'. You have no rights here. You just do as you are told. Even President Obasanjo, when he was in Yola prison, had no rights.

"I am not concerned with your guilt or innocence. That is for the courts to decide. I am only concerned that you comport yourselves as good inmates during your time here. You people have been charged with treason, so you are likely to be here for a long long time. I have been asked to take special note of you. And I want to warn you: do not cause any trouble in my prison, otherwise the consequences will be grave. As you have seen this evening, we are a happy family. Everyone here – the warders, the two hundred and sixty convicted prisoners, and the nine hundred awaiting-trial inmates – enjoy a cordial relationship. Do not try to continue your campaign for the rebirth of Biafra in my prison. Do not try to convert, or incite other inmates with your ideas. You are free to hold your beliefs, but keep them to yourselves. I look at the caricatures of Fidel Castro's beards on your cheeks, at the vulnerable youthfulness of your faces, at your starry eyes, and just shake my head. If Biafra is to come about, it is not through people such as you. I have warned you, and will have my people watching you." He turned, parted the curtain that hung over the door and stepped into his office.

"Let's go," Amaechi said. He led Zuba, Ike and the other new inmates across the football field.

"MASSOB! MASSOB! Non-violent, non-exodus," some prisoners on the field hailed, raising clenched fists in the air. Several warders ordered them to shut up. A smile played on the lips of the leader of the group.

Most of the cell blocks were shut tight. The windows were crowded with bare-bodied men, making it impossible to see what was inside. Zuba eventually saw a block with open doors. Black double-bunk beds were arranged closely along the wall. Towels hung on the foot rails while browned mosquito nets were bunched up above some of them. Not so unlike boarding school.

"Where's your cell? Enter your cell." Okwu's screech sounded in the distance. He was chasing prisoners about. They laughed at each screech of his voice as they ran to their cells. Zuba thought Okwu looked like a teacher on duty chasing errant students into their dormitories to observe siesta, swinging a baton instead of a cane. Yes, it was like a boarding school. Even his boarding school had been surrounded by a high wall with shards of glass at the top.

197

A clang resounded as Okwu slammed a cell door shut.

"Aaaaahhh! My hand," somebody screamed.

Amaechi led them on, towards the other end of the field. Bright Chimezie's *African Style* began blaring from the prison forecourt. Amaechi sang along, snapping his fingers and moving his arms to the rhythm: "African styyyyyyyle."

A group of men waited for them at the other end of the field. Unlike Amaechi, they were all well dressed in mufti. Amaechi walked up to a man in jeans and a black tank top with the inscription: *Public Enemy No. 1.*

"Philip, here they are," he said. "I have to run off now."

"OK," Philip said.

Amaechi jogged off.

The men looked the new inmates over.

"OK," Philip said. "Let's begin."

The five men spread out to different positions.

Zuba suddenly knew what was coming. He had seen it done many times in his school days from his position at the fringes. Team captains spread out on the football field, selecting players for their team from a pool of students who stared expectantly at them.

"You! You! Wartface!" Philip called, pointing at Zuba. "Come this way."

Zuba started. There was no laughter. The name was not going to stick.

"I knew you would pick him first, he looks like someone who'll do a good *cell-sho*," one of the men said to Philip. "Who is his partner? Come this way."

When it got to Philip's turn again, he pointed to a sturdy-legged new inmate. "What's your name?"

"Nasa."

"You have the legs of a footballer. Can you play? Can you help my cell win the superintendent's cup?"

Nasa nodded.

"All right. Come this way."

The last person Philip picked was the bearded MASSOB leader. "Massobian, come this way. I hope you won't give me trouble in my cell," he said.

"Let's go." Philip led them to the back of one of the cell blocks. Several old inmates waited there. They were dressed in faded shorts, bare-chested, all bones and tendons. Black spots dotted their bodies, and their complexions looked friable, as if their skin could rub off. Their scalps shone in the waning sunlight.

The old inmates lined Zuba and his fellow new inmates against the cell wall.

"Sit down all of you," a voice called out.

One of the old inmates stared down at Zuba. His pupils stood out in his eyes. "Remove your vest," he said.

Zuba pulled off his vest and stared up at him again, wondering what next. The old inmate had removed a razor from its packet. He muttered along with the music playing in the background as he snapped the blade in two and began to fit one half into an improvised shaving stick: a scalpel-shaped piece of aluminium folded at one end to hold a blade.

A haircut. Prison-style! Zuba looked to his right and his heart sank. A quarter of the hair on Nasa's head was gone. His scalp, clean as his face, blinked a whitish grey at the unaccustomed exposure; and his face was assuming the forlorn prison look of the man sweeping the blade through his hair. Zuba held up his hand:

"I'm sorry. You cannot scrape my hair to the scalp. I have a sensitive fontanel from recurrent bouts of meningitis, and it should not be exposed." He delivered the last sentence in English, patting the top front part of his head.

A power failure cut the music blaring from the forecourt and made the light bulb flicker off.

The barber's lips hung apart in mid-song. He turned and looked past his equally baffled companions. "Sir Boss-man," he called.

Philip took a few steps towards them. "What is it?"

"Say what you said again," the barber said to Zuba.

"I asked him not to expose my scalp because I have a history of meningitis and my fontanel is sensitive," he patted the top front part of his head again.

The first peal of laughter burst out of Philip like an exploding fizzy drink. He bent over, but all his mirth had vanished by the time he straightened up. "Does this boy know where he is?" he barked. "Someone should give him a slap to remind him."

The two inmates beside the barber jostled for Zuba's cheek before the slap came in.

The barber's blade descended. Zuba felt the rush of air against the scalp above his right ear.

Philip approached and stood beside the barber. "What's your name? And your occupation?" he asked in clear English.

"My name is Zuba. I just finished from school. About to proceed with further studies."

"Which school is that? What course?"

"University of Benin. Biochemistry."

"So, of course, you wouldn't know that only babies have fontanels." Philip chuckled. "I was at the University of Calabar myself, studying medicine. But had to switch to physiology after I failed my MB twice. That was about ten years ago." He tapped the barber on the shoulder. "Leave a little hair on top of his head."

The new inmates were given a bath after their haircut,

and handed fresh mufti. Zuba had to fold the shorts he was given to keep them from slipping down.

"All right, all right. IG, take them in. Put Zuba in GRA," Philip said.

IG led them round to the front of the cell. They waited before the door. It was made of sturdy rust-coloured iron and had a small square window at eye level. Above it was the inscription: *Cell B3: 17 Units*. Zuba wondered if he would be assigned to a top or lower bunk. A warder approached with jingling keys. He unlocked the door.

"OK, get inside," the warder said.

"Clean your feet of sand first," IG said.

Zuba took one step over the threshold and stopped.

"Move on, move on."

He felt a push from behind. The bare outstretched legs in his path folded up. Inmates seated on the floor hugged their knees to their chests, creating a narrow walkway. Scores of eyes looked up. Zuba took two strides to the centre of the cell, careful to avoid stepping on the toes poking into the path. The ground was warm and prickly against his bare feet. The smell of distant soakaways, stale sweat, rotten spittle and rotting bodies enveloped him. He felt the dankness of exhaled air on his face.

Zuba stood in the centre of the cell, directly under a naked sixty-watt bulb. The other new inmates bunched up behind him, stomach to back. He refused to meet the eyes boring into him, and focused instead on the lone double bunk that stood like a throne amidst the bodies on the ground. The lower bunk was bare, but the top had a fat mattress and pillow dressed in matching purple sheets. It stood at the right end of the cell, its head touching the wall, its foot pointing to the centre of

the cell. It was equidistant to the large windows on the
walls, dividing that end of the cell into two equal halves.
A crucifix hung on the wall, beneath the sparkling-white
mosquito net furled up over it.

"You others will wait here in Corrordor," IG said. "You,
Mister Grammar, come this way to GRA, the Government
Reserved Area." He had stepped in between the bodies to
get to Zuba. "Wait here," he said, placing Zuba at the
right side of the double bunk, before the window. Then
he retraced his steps to the opposite end of the cell, sat
down between two inmates and rested his back against
the wall.

Zuba remained standing. Only two inmates were seated
on the ground here, on the two three-inch mattresses spread
like a carpet on the right side of the double bunk where he
stood, their backs against the dirt-blackened walls. Unlike
the rest of the cell, which had people sitting tight all along
the walls, cups, jerry cans and small sacks of belongings
wedged between them. Their legs were stretched out into
what IG had called "Corrordor". Two rows of inmates
occupied Corrordor, sitting back to back, their scapulas
grinding together. Skinny arms embraced folded-up legs.
Chins rested on bulbous knees, with feet sticking into the
narrow aisle, ready to retract further to grant passage.
Their faces were angular, with the skin lapping over the
bones like the thinnest of nylon wrappings. Zuba looked
across at the other side of the double bunk. In much more
space, men were seated around a Ludo board. The crisp
happy tinkle of the rolling dice sounded surreal in the
environment.

A key clanked in the door lock. Two inmates came in
bearing a large wooden tray. Plates of battered aluminium
were stacked on top of each other. A whiff of something

edible spread through the cell. Several Corrordor inmates stood up to make space, and the tray was placed on the ground. IG poured three portions into a plate and covered it. "Madubuchi, take and keep for Boss-man," he said.

One of the men seated at Zuba's feet at the right side of the double bunk rose and received the plate. He placed it on the empty lower bunk of the bed.

IG passed several plates to the other end of the cell, where he had been sitting. Then he declared in English: "Collect your plates for your ration." He stood watching as the other plates were shared out.

"Who no see food?" IG asked.

"*Onye afuro* ration *ya?*" the cell chorused, repeating his question in Igbo.

IG looked around. "Carry chop," he said.

Sounds of slurping, smacking and chewing rose in the cell.

"Shift there," IG said, pointing to some inmates in Corrordor. "All right, new men, sit down."

Nasa and the Massobian slid their way down between the bodies.

IG signalled Zuba to sit, then he returned to his post.

Madubuchi shifted. "Sit here," he said to Zuba, patting the space to his left, at the fringe of the GRA space.

Zuba was glad to sit down, to duck away from the resentment of some of the other inmates. He placed the aluminium plate on his lap. The countable brown beans in the bowl were dry and covered in black spots and holes. He wanted to pass his food on to Madubuchi. But he was aware of the eyes staring at him. He collected a spoon from Madubuchi, scooped some of the food into his mouth and forced himself to chew. The beans were saltless and hard, as if they had only been soaked in water instead of being cooked. Lifeless weevils crunched between his teeth. He swallowed.

"No, wait," Madubuchi said. He retrieved small bottles of palm oil, pepper, curry, Maggi cubes and salt from a cellophane bag beside him, poured Zuba's share into his, and began to transform the dish. He sliced some onions in. The pungent smell stung Zuba's eyes. When he finished, he dished some back into Zuba's plate. He conjured half a loaf of bread from under the bed, tore off a portion and handed it to Zuba. He looked on like a proud chef.

Zuba took half a spoonful of the beans. The hard rawness eclipsed the taste of the condiments.

"How is it now?" Madubuchi asked.

Zuba nodded. "It has a unique taste of its own."

Madubuchi beamed.

Zuba bit off some bread and forced himself to take another scoop from his plate. He became aware of other inmates staring at him again. But this time they stared with hunger. Plates, licked clean, lay on their laps.

"I'm sorry, I cannot eat any more," he said to Madubuchi.

"It's OK," Madubuchi said. "You can pass it on to anybody you want."

Zuba turned to the man on his left. "I can't eat any more," he muttered.

"Hey, bring, bring," the man gushed. He collected the plate and, with one sweep of his palm, left it gleaming in the fading light. He licked his fingers, brought out a small jerry can tucked beside him and poured a little water on his hand, and some into his mouth. He looked around furtively, then held out his hand, low, to Zuba. "I'm Aboki," he said. The hand Zuba shook was scaly and blistered with scabies, especially around the knuckles.

IG stood up at his post at the other end of the cell. He looked around, then bawled in English, "Packing pan?"

"Sweeping cell," the cell chorused in English too.

Three inmates got up and began collecting the used dishes. They heaped them on the wooden tray. Two other inmates went round with tiny brooms and flat pieces of plastic cut from the side of a water keg, which served as dustpans. The Corrordor inmates had to stand to enable the sweepers to scoop up the sand and stray squashed beans on the floor.

The superintendent's microphonic voice sounded nearby. IG peered through the window, then called to the cell inmates: "Philip's Angels!"

"Boys!" the cell answered.

"Greet the prison head," he said in Igbo.

"Good evening, sir!" the cell bellowed.

A warder opened the door, and the empty plates were removed.

Minutes later keys sounded in the lock again. The plate packers hurried back in. Behind them were Philip and a warder. Philip stepped in.

"Philip's order iiii-is…" IG called out in English.

"Final!" the cell chorused.

"Yo-ooooooo," IG continued.

"Ho-oooooo," the cell answered.

"Philip is a leader?"

"He's a leader!"

"*Cho!*" IG and the men beside him at the other end of the cell saluted.

The warder was standing by the door. He held a piece of paper in his left hand, while he used the biro in his right as a pointer in counting the inmates.

"No discharge. Three new admitted, making us fifty-seven now," IG said.

The warder nodded. He made notes on the sheet and left, locking the door behind him.

Philip removed his slippers before stepping on the mattress on the floor beside his bed. He walked past Zuba without a glance and dropped a fruitcake under the bed, among tins of milk, sardines, cocoa and other provisions. He pushed his plate of food aside.

"You people can have it," he said. Madubuchi pounced on the food with the inmate on his right.

Philip stripped to his under shorts and climbed up the double bunk. He sat cross-legged like a Buddha. "Philip's Angels," he called.

"Boys!" the inmates answered.

"IG, I wonder if we should still proceed with the induction tonight?" he said.

"Sir Boss-man, let's do it tomorrow," IG answered.

"OK then," Philip said. "Let's have thirty minutes' praise singing instead."

Inmates shuffled up to their feet. Zuba joined them. Percussion instruments appeared in several hands. A high-pitched voice began in Igbo:

O Lord You are good
O Lord You are good
Thou who walked upon the sea
O Lord You are good
Thou who snap iron as if it is wood
O Lord You are good.

The song was taken up with clapping and dancing. The combined voices in the confined space soared beautifully. Hips gyrated and feet stamped to the beats. Zuba had no knowledge of the song, but he moved his lips. He clapped only lightly to keep his body from heating up. He already felt the heat rising from the mass of dancing bodies, smelt the sweat and the foul breath.

Philip sang along. After a few more songs, he unfurled the mosquito net above him. Madubuchi and an inmate at the other side of the bed tucked it under the mattress. Philip knelt with his back to the cell, hands clasped before him, face lifted towards the crucifix on the wall, lips parted in supplication.

Zuba felt a tingle in his head. There was something saintly about the kneeling figure of Philip seen through the etherizing whiteness of the net, elevated on the double bunk amidst the dirty brown walls and dirty brown bodies of the cell. It was like gazing at an apparition at a shrine. Zuba's eyes misted. He squeezed them shut. "O Lord, please help me!" In those few words, he packed in his dearest wish in the world: that Nonye, Tanna, Ike's wife and Barrister Chigbo would have discovered his and Ike's whereabouts and come to visit tomorrow.

Philip crossed himself and sat back. "Let someone give us the last song for the night," he said.

A deep voice began in thickly accented Igbo:

> With tears and grief, I call upon Thee Father
> With a broken heart, I call upon Thee Jehovah
> If Thou shall mark all our misdeeds
> If Thou shall count each of our sins
> O Lord, who shall stand?
> Who shall stand before Thy face?

"Come, let's go and piss for the night," Madubuchi tapped Zuba on the arm after the singing. They joined a queue before the dwarf door into a tiny room opposite the cell door. A dustbin, made of a half-cut keg, stood beside the door. Zuba began taking deep breaths, preparing to hold his breath when it got to his turn, listening to the praise songs still ringing in the yard from other cells.

"Who's wasting time in there? If you want to shit, wait for those who want to piss to piss first," a voice barked.

"OK. I'm through. You can come and piss your gonor-rhoca."

When eventually Zuba stepped into the little room, he thought it better kept than his university hostel toilet. It was a bowl set in the floor, sloping towards a hole. The ceramic's whiteness sparkled through its urine-spattered surface. He caught the muted smell of distant soakaways rising from the hole as he peed, staring at the mouldy exfoliating walls, his toes turned up on the wet ground.

Philip was spread out on his bed by the time Zuba followed Madubuchi back to their corner. The net over his bed rippled under the breeze from the window. Zuba wished he could remain standing on the breeze's pathway, bathed by the glow of the security lights outside.

"Toshiba!" A tall thin man seated beside IG barked, pointing at a young man in Corrordor. Two other men beside him repeated the same calls. "You, Toshiba!"

Three men rose from Corrordor. Their glistening bodies reflected the light from the sixty-watt bulb. They picked their way to IG's end of the cell, collected flat pieces of plastic that had been cut from the sides of jerry cans and began to fan their summoners.

"Who no see post?" IG asked.

"*Onye afuro post ya?*" the cell chorused, repeating his question in Igbo.

IG looked around. "Good night cell members," he said.

"You, lie here, this is your post," Madubuchi said to Zuba, patting the space beside him. Zuba lay down at the fringe of the GRA. The mattress smelt of rancid sweat and drool. It was so thin that Zuba could have wound it round himself like a wrapper. Following Madubuchi's example, he stretched his legs out onto the bare floor under the double bunk. His neighbour outside the GRA lay on his back on a piece of cardboard, his knees up and his feet jammed against those of another inmate in Corrordor. Snores and the craw-craw of fingernails scratching against flesh filled the cell. Zuba looked through the inmates huddled together on the bare floor of Corrordor, right down to the toilet mouth, in search of Nasa and the Massobian, his fellow new inmates. Two cockroaches were crawling out from the toilet enclosure, descending towards the mass of bodies, stopping after every few steps to test the air with their antennae. One of them seemed headed straight for Nasa.

Nasa was already asleep. His head rested on the bare shoulder of the man seated to his left, wetting the man's shoulder with the spittle that dripped from his lips; his legs were folded up and leaning against the knees on his either side, and his toes were jammed against the soles of the feet of the inmate stretched out opposite him. The Massobian's head was bowed, resting on his folded arms, which in turn was supported by his propped-up knee. His scalp shone in the light of the bulb.

Zuba looked away, ashamed of his privilege. He no longer felt the ache of his elbows and head against the hard floor. He no longer heard the rattle of Madubuchi's snore in his ears. He pushed his legs against Madubuchi's under the bed, shifting Madubuchi's legs and creating a little more space. Madubuchi stopped snoring. Zuba tapped his neighbour outside the GRA and gestured to the extra space under the bed. "You can stretch your legs into this space so that the man opposite you in Corrordor will have a little more space." His neighbour cast a sleepy-eyed glance up at Philip's bunk and shook his head. He turned his face away from Zuba.

Madubuchi began snoring into Zuba's ear again. Zuba did not move, did not flinch. He stared at the concrete decking above the cell, and at the steel rods that peered through, wondering how Ike was faring. Was he stretched out or huddled up for the night? He tried to think about Nonye and Tanna, about his dad and Barrister Chigbo. But his mind refused to soar above his present surroundings, as if such thoughts were a luxury too shameful to indulge in at such a moment.

The mosquitoes came calling.

Zuba remained still. He refused to swat at them. Yes, bite me, stab me, puncture my skin and suck your fill, he wanted to shout. But he could not remain still when he began to feel on his bare back the pin-pricks from the bedbugs in the shadow of a mattress upon which he lay.

Man Pass Man

Zuba was awakened in the morning by a loud shout:

"Praiiiiiise the Lord!"

He opened his eyes and the smell of Nonye rose in his nostrils. She was going to be here this morning. She was on her way. He noticed a sheet on his chest and picked it up. *We are watching and waiting. If we don't hear from you after you get your first visit, you will hear from us!* was scrawled on it with a pencil. Zuba studied the paper. It was toilet-paper wrapping. He glanced at the window above him, his brows furrowed in thought.

The inmates by the walls were sitting up. Those on Corrordor were stretching their arms towards the ceiling, releasing cracks from their bodies. Zuba sat up. He winced as his back touched the wall. He slid the sheet into his pocket and kept yawning as someone said the morning prayers. His head was clearer when the hymn began:

Christ's a great provider
He will surely provide for you
And provide for me.

"Cell open," IG announced after the hymn. "DPP take over," he said, and sat down.

The man that had first shouted "Toshiba" the previous night moved forwards. He was extremely thin. Light-green rosary beads hung from his neck, bright against his bare trunk. He held a sheet of paper before him. "Duty roster for the day," he announced. He called out the names of some inmates, matching them against duties such as packing pans, sweeping cell, emptying dustbin and ragging water. "Felele, you will be cleaning the toilet today as punishment for abusing Nwa-Oyi's mother yesterday," he said.

"As coouuuurt pleases," the cell chorused at the end of his announcements.

Philip sat up on his bed. Madubuchi rose beside Zuba and picked his way to the toilet. He returned with a white plastic bottle, pulled aside part of the mosquito net and passed it in. Philip handed it out seconds later, yellow and heavy with urine. Someone at the other side of the bunk began folding up the mosquito net as Madubuchi returned to the toilet to empty it.

Philip yawned.

"Greet the leader," IG shouted.

"Good morning Sir Boss-man," the cell roared.

"*Kabiyesi Baba*! Man-pass-man Philippi! May you *waka jeje* and never stumble," a praise-singer chanted from the foot of Philip's bed.

"Good morning cell members," Philip said. "IG, begin with the induction."

IG stood up again. "All you new men stand up," he said.

Zuba stood up. The morning breeze pouring into the cell felt cool against his moist body. Through the window, he saw convicted prisoners in their blue uniforms assembled in the field in neat rows. Buckets and kegs of different colours lay at their feet. Several warders stood before them, one of whom was addressing them. Further to the left was the open door of a cell. The cell was empty save for the double bunks within it.

"Mr Grammar! Look here," IG raised his voice.

The cell inmates laughed.

Zuba turned away from the window. The name was going to stick.

"If you people had heard what he said yesterday when I wanted to shave his head," the barber explained. "He blew one powerful grammar and the lights went out."

There was more laughter. Philip continued to look down from his perch, a benign smile on his lips.

"He said the front part of his head is a *frontanel*," the barber continued. "IG, ask him to repeat what he said."

"After the induction you people can ask him if you want," IG said. "Move to the centre of the cell," he called to Zuba.

Zuba tiptoed through the bodies. He joined Nasa and the Massobian at the centre aisle, framed by scrunched-up legs. His heartbeat raced, and he felt naked and vulnerable. He avoided any eye-contact.

"Now you will introduce yourselves one by one, stating your occupation in the outside world and what brought you here. Starting with you, Mr Grammar."

"My... My name is Zuba. I am a student. I am here over a case of... stealing. It is a mix up that will be straightened up soon."

"So you're saying you did not do it?" DPP asked.

"His father is a Big Man. In fact, his family. They have been in government. Commissioner, senator," Philip said.

"Ooooh! That's good. So he'll bring us our own share of the national cake. Our own share of all the money they stole in government," DPP said.

"Are you expecting any visitors?" IG continued.

Better to deflect attention from my family, Zuba thought. His hand rose to his keloid. "Yes, my lawyers."

213

Philip's expression darkened. "Someone should give him a slap there," he barked.

There was a scramble among the Corrordor inmates seated on the floor around Zuba as they struggled to get to his cheek.

"Wait," DPP shouted. "His cheek is mine."

He picked his way through the mass of bodies like a stick insect and landed a bony slap on Zuba's cheek.

The morning staleness in Zuba's mouth was replaced by the warm saltiness of blood.

"You're expecting your lawyers?" DPP spat. "*Fa ga-eli ego gi rapu gi*! They'll eat your money and abandon you," he repeated in English. "We don't want to hear that word here, you hear that?"

Zuba nodded.

"Who are you expecting?" IG repeated the question.

"My people. Members of my family."

"Hope they will come with plenty money. Hope they will bring your *cell-sho*," DPP said.

"Read this." IG pointed at a chalked inscription on the wall.

Zuba squinted: CELL-SHOW = N5,000.

"Look around you," IG continued, "at all those people seated in Corrordor and toilet mouth. That is where those who don't do their *cell-sho* stay. Now look at the landlords relaxing against the walls. That is the position for those who do their *cell-sho*. Make sure you get your *cell-sho* from your people when they visit today, otherwise you'll be demoted to Corrordor."

"Sir Boss-man, Mr Grammar's *cell-sho* should be double," DPP said. "He should not pay the same thing others are paying. His family has been in government. They have stolen our money. They should refund some of it. To us."

214

Philip smiled and said nothing.

IG turned to Nasa and the Massobian. The Massobian said he was a trader at the Onitsha Main Market. His only crime, he said, was his involvement in a peaceful demonstration for the freedom of the Igbos and the rebirth of Biafra. He was expecting other Massobians and his family to visit. Nasa, on the other hand, said he was a driver. He was arrested on a robbery charge. He admitted guilt, and DPP shook his hand.

"I drove my master to the bank to withdraw some money and returned at night with my friends to withdraw it from him," he said, and giggled.

"You are welcome to B3 Cell," IG said. "The best awaiting-trial cell in this prison. You are lucky to be here. Our boss-man is Philip. Salute him and say: 'Good morning, Sir Boss-man.'"

Zuba and his fellow newcomers saluted and said, "Good morning, Sir Boss-man."

"Are you people women?" DPP barked. "Raise your voices like men and stamp your feet hard on the ground."

"Good morning, Sir Boss-man!" Zuba and the others repeated.

"I am Sir Boss-Man's assistant, the Inspector General of Police, the IG, while DPP is the Director of Public Prosecutions who handles the law here. DPP, over to you. Read them the laws of the cell." IG withdrew and sat back in his position.

DPP unhooked a small sheet of cardboard from the wall. He held it with both hands as if he was carrying Moses's stone tablets. "There are fifty-three laws in this cell," he began in English. "Anyone who breaks them again and again and again, showing he has no wish to conform, will be handed over to the warders for solitary confinement in

A Ward and eventual transfer to K Ward, the cell for crazy people." He raised the sheet to his face. Smiling, happy children above the caption *Standard Cabin Biscuit* stared at Zuba from the reverse side.

"The first law in this cell is: thou shalt do thy cell-show. Second, all cell members must obey Sir Boss-Man at all times, his order is final! Third, there shall be no 'instigation' – punishment: ragging water for one week. Fourth, there shall be no fighting or breach of peace. Fifth, there shall be no stealing – punishment for fourth and fifth: solitary confinement in toilet for three nights. Sixth, there shall be no homosexuality – punishment: the person will wish he had never been born..." DPP continued till he had read out the whole list. At the end he said, "But the most important law is 'Thou shalt do thy *cell-sho*'. If you keep it and break all the other laws, you have kept all the other laws. If you break it and keep all the other laws, you have broken all the other laws."

Zuba shifted as one of the Corrordor inmates at his feet leant against him, dozing. He scratched a burning itch on his thigh.

"All new inmates must entertain the cell for two nights each, with news from the outside world," DPP continued. "And, Mr Grammar, we shall be starting with you tonight."

The screech-voiced warder appeared outside the window facing Philip's bed.

"Philip's Angels," Philip called out.

"Boys."

"Greet Okwu."

"Okwu good morning."

"Eheeen. Thank you, thank you my people," Okwu screeched into the cell.

Some of the landlords began to laugh.

"Philip," Okwu continued. "Superintendent said you should gather other cell prefects and come and see him by eleven this morning." Okwu left.

"DPP, we'll continue in the evening. IG, my bathing water," Philip said.

Zuba returned to his position. Nasa and the Massobian sat back in Corrordor.

Philip hopped down from his bunk. Madubuchi squeezed Colgate onto his toothbrush, laid out his slippers, towel and soap dish, then returned to dress his bed.

Water seeped out from the toilet in steady streams as Philip bathed. The inmates seated in toilet mouth sprang to their feet. "Ragging water," one of them called. Two inmates rose from Corrordor clutching mucky rags in their hands.

A shaft of sunlight beamed into the cell. It fell upon Philip's praise-singer, who raised his face towards it and squeezed his eyes shut, as if he was receiving a painfully sweet massage.

A middle-aged man in Corrordor unravelled himself and stood on his feet. He stretched, pushing his hands towards the ceiling. Zuba heard the cracks made by his bones through the splashing of Philip's bathing. The man twisted his trunk, right and left, and began to mark time. He stopped after a while and picked his way to the foot of Philip's bunk. "Onye-owa, please I won't take much time today. Give me five minutes."

The praise-singer scowled.

"Onye-owa himself! Mr Speed! The fastest getaway driver on earth, who can speed on the darkest of nights with his headlamps off as if it is noon," the man began to praise the praise-singer.

"OK, two minutes," the praise-singer said, and got up. The seat of his shorts had worn away, displaying scaly black buttocks.

The middle-aged man planted his feet on the ground worn smooth by the praise-singer's bottom. He turned and positioned his bare back under the sunlight.

Zuba's skin crawled. A suppurating lawn of ringworm scabs and scabies covered the man's back. His scapula stood out like a triangular disc. The skin was stretched so tightly over it that Zuba feared the bone would cut through. "Ahhhhhhh..." the man exhaled, as the sunlight caressed his back.

Philip came out of the bathroom smelling of soap. He brought out a jar of lemon cream, a bottle of Sure roll-on deodorant, a hand mirror and a fresh set of clothing. The scent of lemon and musk filled the corner.

Zuba caught DPP scowling in his direction and inched his gaze higher up on the wall. When was Nonye going to arrive? Will they let her in? Surely. He and Ike were not being held incommunicado. He thought of Tanna, but the usual warm glow failed to rise and make him light-headed. Barrister Chigbo should also have heard the news. And the Egbetuyis. What would they be doing now? What would they be feeling? He clenched his fists as heat rose in his chest.

"Have some biscuits," Philip held out a packet of Digestives to Zuba.

Zuba hesitated, caught between Philip's stare and the glare from some of the other inmates. He rubbed his keloid. "I would love to, but my throat feels rather sore now. Thanks."

Philip raised his mug to his lips.

Zuba wondered if the mug hid a grin.

The cell door clanked open. A warder counted the inmates, pen and paper in hand. He stepped back when he was through. Philip rose and made for the door.

* * *

The long-awaited call finally came:

"Zuba Maduekwe and Ike Okoye of B3 and B2, come and receive your visitors. Maduekwe and Okoye…" Someone was shouting into the cell as he walked across the windows.

Zuba sprang to his feet.

"You can wear my slippers." Madubuchi handed him black flip-flops.

IG came forwards. He handed Zuba a green khaki tunic. "Wear this. And tell your people to bring the following for your use." He handed Zuba a list written on the inside of a toilet-paper wrapping.

Zuba threw the tunic on, trying not to think of the many other bodies it had clothed. He scanned the list: bathing soap, washing soap, toothpaste and brush, tissue paper, slippers, shorts, shirts, wrapper, Multivite, Novalgin, Tetracycline.

"Wait, bring it again." IG took the list, scribbled on it and handed it back to Zuba. He had struck out the Tetracycline and written Lincocin Upjohn. "It's better, stronger, though much more expensive. But you can afford it."

"What's it for?" Zuba asked.

"It's for use against all these boils, rashes and *nyam-anyama* that will soon begin to grow on your skin," IG answered. "Just go on straight to the forecourt. They'll show you to the visiting room. Don't forget to bring back your *cell-sho* o," he added as keys rattled in the cell door.

"No, let him forget and see what will happen to him," DPP called out from the toilet.

Zuba stepped outside and looked around for Ike. He took slow steps towards the forecourt. He looked back when he heard the squeal of a cell door being opened two blocks away.

Ike stepped out of his cell. He stood outside the door, blinking to get accustomed to the light. He ran a hand over his scalp; his other hand clutched a green tunic.

Zuba retraced his steps. He was hit by the stench of urine as Ike met him midway. "Ike, how are you?" he said, taking hold of Ike's arm.

Ike stared back at him with swollen eyes. Tiny capillaries fanned out, red and sore, around the irises. "I'm OK," he said. "Just tired. I have been unable to sleep. We, the newcomers, were squeezed together at toilet mouth. We were sitting and standing and taking turns in the toilet all night." He attempted a smile that brought tears to Zuba's eyes. "How was it with you?"

Zuba ignored the question. "We can't go to see them like this; it will break their hearts. I think the bathroom is this way..."

"Are you the Maduekwe that has a visitor, that came in yesterday?" A thin old man with a mat of grey hair stood before them.

Zuba nodded.

Shock made the man's eyes bulge from their sockets. "What are you doing here? I know your father. When me and some teachers were wrongfully laid off, he reinstated us, and met with us. He was commissioner—"

Zuba cut in: "Please help us. Our visitors are waiting and we need some water so that he can at least wash the smell off his legs..."

"What are you people still doing there?" The warder that let them out had returned. "Run to the visiting room now-now, otherwise I will lock you back in and send your visitors away."

"Booty himself! The eagled-eyed Booty himself," the elderly man greeted the warder in a praise-singer's voice. "Please, they're my children. Give them two minutes to freshen up. I'll bring them to the forecourt myself."

"Papa, you—"

"I'll prostrate for you if you say no o." Papa stooped to throw himself on the ground.

"OK, OK. But hurry up." Booty walked off, his oversized shoes giving his walk a millionaire's swagger.

"You heard him, we have to hurry." Papa led them through the back of the General Cell blocks to an open concrete flooring where several men stood, wet and soapy, before buckets of water. "Please, can you give us the remaining water?" He pointed at the little water in a bucket before an inmate towelling himself.

"Teacher, I'm saving it for my next bath."

"We'll buy you a full bucket when the prisoners return from the river," Papa said, and grabbed the bucket.

Ike rubbed soap on his legs and rinsed it off. He washed his face and arms, then rubbed soap all over his body like a lotion, as directed by Papa, before he put on his green tunic. They hurried off.

"Ike, did they give you a list of things to bring?" Zuba asked.

"List? No."

"Ask your people," Papa said, "to bring you twenty thousand naira tomorrow so you two can move to better cells where you can be coming out to the sun. Just do it. I'll explain later. I'll wait for you," he muttered as a warder let Zuba and Ike into the forecourt.

Zuba paused before the door into the visiting room. He exchanged glances with Ike. They understood each other. They pasted smiles onto their faces and stepped into the room.

Nonye and Ike's wife were seated beside other visitors on a bench in the narrow room. Nonye's back was rigid and clear of the wall behind her. Only the tip of her slippers touched the floor. Ike's wife was slumped against the wall as if her spine could not support her weight. Her hands rested on her swollen stomach. Her face had a sad world-weariness to it.

Zuba and Ike sat on the bench opposite them, beside other green-tuniced awaiting-trial detainees chatting with their visitors.

"Nonye-Nonye!" Zuba said.

"Oby *nkem*, my Oby," Ike murmured. "Don't mind the soap marks on my body. I did not bother finishing my bath. I couldn't wait to see you." He reached across the narrow aisle to take his wife's hand, speaking solemnly, as if he was trying to woo her afresh.

Two balls of tears, fat with grief, rolled down Nonye's cheeks. Her hands closed into fists on her lap.

Oby bit upon her lower lip in a doomed attempt at control. A sharp sob broke through and shook her whole body. Nonye joined her.

"What is this? We no want any cry-cry here. You no be the only women who get people for this prison. We go send you out," a warder shouted. He was stationed against the wall beside the door, tall, looking down on proceedings in the room.

A woman on the bench threw her arm over Nonye's shoulders and pulled her close. Nonye buried her face in the woman's bosom, stifling the sound of her sobbing. Ike rose and reached for his wife.

"Sit down there. Sit down," the warder barked.

Nonye straightened up. "Thank you," she said to the woman.

"Take heart, my daughter. Adversity is like the whirl-wind. It comes without warning, throwing up much dust. Be strong and hold it out. The dust will settle soon. You too, my sister." The woman squeezed the knee of Ike's wife.

"Your time is going o," the warder announced.

Nonye took a deep breath. "What happened? One policeman came to the house yesterday evening. He said he's your friend, that his name is Bayo. He said I should inform our lawyer that you two have been arraigned and taken to prison, and that I should quickly take some money and food to you. I thought you said you two were only going to put in an appearance in court, that you'll be bailed and be back?" Tears began to stream down her face again.

Zuba pulled his hand free from where it had been wedged between his buttock and the hard wood of the bench, and took his sister's hand. "Nonye, believe me, it's not my fault. They changed our charge to frighten us into settling. I would have settled, but the lawyer with us said they were going to handle the matter."

In Nonye's eyes was the answer that she was restraining herself from screaming: *Yes, it is your fault! If you had listened to me from the start, this would not have happened...*

"We brought some food. And money, three thousand." She whispered.

"Start rounding up," the warder announced.

"Thank you. Have you informed Barrister Chigbo?"

"Yes. He was mad. He swore he was going to use all his contacts to ensure the Egbetuyis and their accomplices were brought to book. He wished dad had still all his political contacts, as he did back in the '80s, so he could enlist their help to shake up the police and speed things up. He should be here with Tanna this afternoon, straight from court."

Zuba ran his hand over the tuft of hair on his scalp. Could he bear Tanna to see him in his present condition? He handed Nonye the list. "Please buy two of each item on the list and bring them to us tomorrow. You'll find money in my wardrobe." He lowered his voice. "Also we need twenty thousand naira. I will explain later. Bring me my cheque book."

"Don't worry. To avoid any delay, I will take the money from my account. Then you can *settle* me when you come out," she said.

"How about Dad?"

"He's OK. I was supposed to be there this morning to relieve Aunty Chinwe. But I sent the housemaid instead, with a letter."

Beside Nonye, Ike's wife wept silently as her husband spoke:

"Hold on, Oby, and be strong. We shall be out in no time. Just tell yourself we are on a short excursion, you know, like an adventure. How is Junior?"

"Fine. I thought of bringing him along."

"Oh, no, no. Don't bother bringing him. I will be out soon. Even you too. Though I will like to see you every day and every hour, I don't think you should be shuttling up and down to visit in your heavy condition, you hear?"

She nodded again.

"You need to rest. How is he?" Ike pointed at her stomach.

"*She* is fine," she answered.

Ike released her hand. He leant forwards and placed his hand on her tummy. "Let me see if *he* will talk to me. Hmmmmmnh. You know what he said?"

Oby shook her head.

"I'll only tell you if—"

"Time up," the warder announced. "Taste all food before handing them over. Now!"

Nonye opened the dishes and tasted from each of them. She passed the bag on to Zuba and squeezed his hand. "Be careful and take care. I'll try to make it back today before the end of the visiting time with all you requested and more. Otherwise, tomorrow morning."

"I hope it's not difficult getting in to visit."

"No. We were just made to write an application to visit first, and to wait for the visiting time – we were here much earlier. That's all." She rose to her feet.

Ike's wife pushed herself up. Nonye put an arm around her. "Ike, don't worry. I will take good care of her. She will be staying with me at our house again."

All visitors were ushered out.

"Sit down there," the warder barked as Zuba made to leave the room.

A loud clack announced the prison gate being opened. The visitors were filing out, taking their freedom and bright dresses with them. A line of convicted prisoners, in dull blue uniforms, began filing in after the last visitor had stepped out. Their heads were laden with buckets and kegs of water, and firewood. Two gun-wielding prison policemen followed behind them.

"Everybody, bring out all the money you received," the warder said. "Don't hide anything. We will search you, and if we find any hidden money we will seize it." Another warder had joined him. He fixed his eyes on the inmates while his tall colleague went from inmate to inmate. He searched the inmate thoroughly, then collected the money from him. He counted it, screwed up his face in calculation, removed some notes and returned the rest. When Zuba counted his money after it was handed back to him, he found that three hundred naira had been removed.

After all the inmates had been searched, the tall warder began to go through the food and edibles in the many cellophane bags. He opened a food container and grinned. A wad of notes, wrapped in nylon, lay on top of the rice and stew. He removed the wad and covered the container. The inmate beside Zuba glared at the warder with impotent rage.

"Hey, you. Maduekwe," the warder that had booked Zuba and Ike in when they arrived called out from the doorway of his office. "What are you doing in the General Cell? Go to welfare and apply for self-feeding. Pay the money and they will move you to the Big Man Cell. You can't survive in General Cell."

"Thank you," Zuba said.

He grabbed Zuba's arm and muttered: "Remember what I told you: I'm still waiting for you to bring it. Don't waste your money doing cell-show for your boss-man. Leave General Cell and bring me the money instead. This morning is your last chance. They'll get it from you anyhow."

Zuba remembered the note lying on his chest when he woke that morning. He thought it absurd that a man the warder's age could be involved in such a game. "Let go of me," he snapped, and wrenched his arm free.

Zuba and Ike were let out of the prison forecourt. Zuba gave Ike one half of the money. They stood midway down the steps that led to the prison yard, clutching their bags of food and scanning the prisoners and other awaiting-trial inmates milling about in the yard, looking for Papa.

Zuba saw DPP prancing around on his stilt legs, and he recognized Ike's cell prefect where he was stretched out on a mat under the sun; he saw Okwu, the screech-voiced warder, doing a slow march, mimicking a military president inspecting a guard of honour, while inmates bent over and laughed. He was so absorbed in his search for Papa that he did not hear the forecourt gates open behind him.

"Carry your *kwarikwata* come-o't," a woman said behind him.

He turned around. Ike had sprung away to a corner of the step. A female warder stood two steps above him; her face was wrinkled up. She had pulled her khaki skirt tightly around her like a pedestrian about to cross a mud-spattered bush path. "You no hear me?" she said. "I say take your lice and get out of my way, I no want catch your chinch."

Zuba stepped aside and the lady passed. She pulled her skirt tighter as she made her way past the inmates on the field, and only released it when she stepped into a neat-looking room that had *Clinic* written above the doorway.

"What are you people still doing there? Back to your cell," a warder shouted from the foot of the stairs.

"Well, we'll probably see Papa later to hear more about what he was saying and pay for the water," Zuba murmured to Ike as they hurried across the field. "Take care, Ike. With the money as part of your cell-show you will be treated better. We shall be out to better cells tomorrow. Just hang on."

After he and Ike had parted ways, he took a few quick strides to Ike's cell prefect. "Sir Boss-man," he said, squatting before him. "Please, he's my brother." He pointed at Ike's receding back. "Help me treat him well, take care of him." He glanced around and slid several notes under the mat. "Three hundred naira," he whispered.

The Boss-man smiled. He patted Zuba's arm. "Don't worry. He will be fine. As long as the rain continues to fall, the soil will continue to feed the plants, isn't it?"

Zuba stepped back into his cell. The door banged shut. His pupils dilated. The odours rushed at him, crowding out the fresher air from his lungs. A dozen legs retracted to give him passage to his corner. He sat down beside Madubuchi.

IG made his way to him. "Who was it?"

"My sister."

"What of your father? Your mother?"

"My father is ill, on admission in hospital. My mother is departed."

"Sorry. Mine too. Where's your *cell-sho*? What do you have there?"

Zuba handed him the bag of food and money. He scratched an itch on his thigh.

IG examined the contents. He frisked Zuba, then handed the bag back to him. "Keep it. Don't touch it. Hand it to Boss-man when he comes in." He counted the money. "One thousand and fifty naira?"

Zuba nodded. He kept the bag beside him, feeling its warmth. Its fragrance activated his taste buds, and he felt like chewing on his tongue. He kept expecting a jingling at the cell door, to see Philip step into the cell.

One of the landlords rose from his position. He scratched his side, then reached into his pocket and brought out a mouldy ball of money. "Wait," he said, as IG made his way back to his corner. "Please call the warder. I want to go out to stretch my legs and feel the sun today." He handed IG some money.

IG collected the money and continued to his corner. He pressed his face against the window bars and whistled.

"What?" A voice outside the window said.

"Someone wants to come out," IG said, and handed across the money through the bars.

"What of you? Don't you want to come out?" the voice asked.

"Not today," IG answered.

Seconds later the cell door swung open. It swung shut again after the landlord had stepped out.

There was silence in the cell. Zuba rested his back against the wall and listened to the sounds of feet shuffling past outside. The praise-singer was back to his position. The beam of light had disappeared from his corner. He was seated, resting his back against the foot of Philip's bed and staring at the opposite wall. Nasa's head rested in sleep against the Massobian's shoulder. The Massobian sat with arms wrapped around his knees, staring at the toilet door, a transcendent expression on his face. Around him, most of the other Corrordor inmates were nodding in sleep, huddled like roosting chickens. The scratch-scratch of fingernails against mould and rash-ridden flesh punctuated the air.

Madubuchi lay down beside Zuba. He covered the bored expression in his eyes with a Gideon's Bible. The Bible reminded Zuba of Chemist. A landlord stood up further down to Zuba's left and pulled off his shorts, exposing shrivelled genitals. Instinctively, Zuba looked away. But curiosity got the better of him and he turned back to stare. The landlord stood stark naked, unabashed, in his corner. He turned his shorts inside out and brought them close to his face. His eyes followed his fingers as they went through the fabric, slowly, as if he was counting the stitches. Two other landlords sprang up, pulled off their shorts and began to do the same.

Zuba tapped the landlord seated to his left. "What are they doing?" he murmured.

"Please, I don't want to be accused of instigation," he whispered. "Landlords are not supposed to tell new inmates anything. Ask him." He motioned at Madubuchi.

Madubuchi's eyes lit up when Zuba asked him. He grinned at the expression on Zuba's face.

"*Kwarikwata* checks," he said. He reached for Zuba's thigh, turned over the hem of his shorts and pulled down the seam.

Tiny, revolting, mean-looking, orange-black glassy-bodied lice were lodged along the seams. Zuba jumped up and yanked off his shorts. He picked out one of the lice from the seam and squeezed it between his thumb and forefinger. But it had no effect on the insect.

"Careful, don't let it fall on the bed." Madubuchi had stood up beside him. "No, it is not that way," he said, taking the shorts from Zuba. "You leave the *kwarikwata* on the dress, position it between your thumbnails and squeeze. There," he said, as a tiny crack sounded. He showed Zuba his blood-stained thumbnails. "Check at the seams of the waistband too. That's their favourite hiding place." Madubuchi pulled off his shorts. "See," he pointed at his waist.

Zuba looked. A blotchy black belt of bites was tattooed around Madubuchi's waist. He attacked the waistband of his shorts with vigour, feeling the dank air of the cell on his genitals.

Minutes later, Zuba and Madubuchi wiped their bloodied thumbnails on the underside of the mattress. They donned their shorts and sat down. The clink of rolling dice began from the other end of the cell.

"How long have you been here?" Zuba asked.

"Almost a month," Madubuchi answered.

"What brought you here?"

"It was an accident. Some cult members in my school attacked me. I broke a bottle and waved it at them to keep them off. One of them ran into it. He later died in hospital. My parents have been begging the deceased's parents for a settlement."

The cell door swung open. One landlord and one Corrordor inmate stepped in. They were both laden with goodies from a visit. The Corrordor inmate handed his goodies to IG while the landlord kept his. DPP walked into the cell with Philip on his heels.

"His order ii-is…"

"Final!"

"Yo-ooooooooo."

"Ho-oooooooooooo."

"Philip is a leader?"

"He's a leader."

Outside, Okwu's screech sounded: "Where's your cell? Get into your cell." Cell doors clanged shut.

"Maduekwe, where are you?" Papa called out from the window, peering into the cell. "Sorry I wasn't there when you people came back from visiting. I was teaching my students at the prison school. I hope you're fine. I'm going in now. Will check on you again. Philip, please help me take care of him, he's my child."

Zuba knelt up to the window. "Go to Ike's cell too. Talk to his boss-man."

"OK." Papa ran off.

Philip stood between Zuba and Madubuchi's legs and stared out of the window, up at the now sullen skies. "Philip's Angels," he called.

"Boys."

"Pray for a heavy rain," he said. "I have made arrangements to collect as much rain water so you can have general bathing tomorrow in the cell. I will buy plenty soap and Dettol too."

"Jah! Jehovah! Send down the rain," one landlord shouted.

"Amen," chorused the cell.

"Man-pass-man Philippi! We are tail-less cows. It is you that chases the flies off us. Because of you, our bodies will not forget the feel of water. *Kabiyesi Baba!*" the praise-singer chanted.

IG came forwards and handed the money Zuba had brought to Philip.

Philip counted the money. "How much *cell-sho* did you bring?" he asked, staring at Zuba.

Zuba glanced at IG. IG's face remained impassive, so he said, "One thousand and fifty naira."

Philip nodded. "A good start, a good start. Look, whenever you want anything – to take a bath, go out in the sun, eat better food or buy anything – just let me know."

Zuba said nothing. He held the bag of food out to him.

"Open it," Philip said.

Zuba uncovered the dish. The aroma made him want to bury his mouth in it like a dog.

Philip smiled as he took in the chicken chunks on top of the *jollof* rice. "Bring me a plate and spoon," he said.

Madubuchi handed him a stainless-steel plate and spoon.

Philip scooped a little of the yellow rice into his mouth. He nodded as he chewed. He bent over the dish again and scooped some rice and all the chicken chunks onto his plate, leaving only a small splinter piece of chicken for Zuba.

Zuba glared at him, unable to keep the resentment off his face.

"Surely your sore throat can't handle these heavy chunks," Philip muttered, and ascended his perch with his dish.

Madubuchi brought two spoons. Zuba turned till he was backing the rest of the cell, then began to eat. In no time, the dish was empty. His stomach groaned for more. The little rice had become a hunger-inducing drug, provoking maddening pangs. He stared down at his hands, listening to the sounds of Philip cracking chicken bones. The day's lunch was brought in and he pounced on his share. Even after Madubuchi had spruced it up, the *egusi* soup looked like water used to rinse out an empty soup pot. He picked out heat-baked maggots from the *garri* as he ate, and stopped eating when he discovered that the single floating piece of vegetable in his soup was a housefly. Madubuchi scooped out the fly and emptied Zuba's plate into his.

The heavens opened and the patter of raindrops drowned out the sounds of slurping in the cell.

Story *Kawai*!

"Zuba Maduekwe and Ike Okoye, come for your visitors."
The call again.

Zuba and Ike stepped out of their cells in their green
garb. Ike, too, now had slippers on. He no longer smelt
of urine and soakaways. The ground was wet, and their
flip-flops flung sand grains against their calves. The rain-
washed air felt cool. The clouds had shed their sullenness
and now sparkled a cheery silvery blue.

"No, not here. Go to the welfare office," a warder told
them at the gate to the forecourt, and pointed towards a
room next to the superintendent's office.

Zuba's spirits lifted when he saw, through the open
door, Barrister Chigbo pacing up and down. The prison
welfare officer sat behind his desk, watching the barrister
and nodding intermittently. Zuba smelt freedom. He
slapped Ike's back, and they stepped into the office. Tanna
was seated on a bench behind a long table, looking professional despite her sadness. A bookshelf stuffed with
Bibles, religious books and other dusty hardcovers stood
beside the table, its back against the wall like a landlord.

Barrister Chigbo stopped pacing when Zuba and Ike
walked in. His mouth remained open as he took two steps
to Zuba and placed a hand on his shoulder. "Terrible!
This is terrible. What kind of a country are we living in?
The beasts quickly arraigned you to cover their tracks, but
I'll do my utmost to get the culprits to pay. Are you OK?
You too, Ike?"

"Barrister, am I glad to see you!" Zuba stopped himself from hugging the man. "Are we OK? We can never be OK in this place." He noticed that the barrister's jacket was touching his green tunic and moved away, towards the table. "We are trying to manage the best we can. But we can *only* be OK when we are out of here."

Tanna was wearing a different hairstyle. No longer the Bob Marley braids. Her hair was a smooth sheen, rich, full, cascading down her nape and hugging her cheeks. She looked prettier than Zuba ever remembered. As he and Ike sat down opposite her, he reached across and squeezed her hand.

"Zuba..." she said.

A hint of scent... And that aching tenderness, scorched by the experiences of the past forty-eight hours, stirred within his midriff. "Great to see you," he whispered.

"I'm glad to see you two have not been battered," Barrister Chigbo said, coming round and taking a seat opposite Zuba.

"I told you so, didn't I?" the welfare officer said. "All that stopped since our new superintendent took over."

"Yes, you did. I'll make sure I meet your superintendent and let him know how much you're doing to project a good image of the Service," Barrister Chigbo replied.

The officer beamed.

The barrister focused on Zuba again. "Now, Zuba, I'll tell you what's going to happen..."

"Please excuse me sir," Tanna cut in. "I was wondering: could they be eating while we talk? They look a bit emaciated – maybe it's the haircut – but I think they may be better off eating this here..." She put a Mr Bigg's bag on the table.

Barrister Chigbo looked at the welfare officer, who

nodded vigorously, and Tanna pushed the bag towards Zuba and Ike.

Ike lifted out the food packs and handed one to Zuba. The label said *Spaghetti Bella and Chicken.* Zuba looked at the chicken, golden brown in the corned-beef sauce, and remembered Philip. He dug into the food, starting with the meat.

"What will happen is this," Barrister Chigbo repeated. "We'll get the police to send a copy of your case file to the DPP. They will take ages to do this, so I will deliver a petition to the DPP to request your case file. We will then follow up with the police to make sure they comply quickly. When your file gets to the DPP," the barrister continued, "they will examine the case and, hopefully, pronounce a *nolle prosequi.*"

Zuba looked at Tanna.

"A no-case submission," she said.

He looked back at the barrister. "Hopefully? You mean it's not certain? That we may not be released?"

"Zuba, I am always honest with your father, and now with you. No one can predict with certainty how a judge or a DPP might decide. But—"

Zuba cut in: "So it is possible that the DPP will say we have a case to answer?"

"Yes, Zuba. We're in a fight that could go either way. Your persecutors were advised and aided in putting together their case against you by law-enforcement agents, by policemen who understand very well how the law of evidence works."

Zuba's mind flashed back to the advice of his police "friend".

He took a sip from his can of Coke. If he had tried to settle with the Egbetuyis one minute earlier during the arraignment, he would be a free man. But now it was a judicial matter, and there was no settling with the courts.

A part of him wanted to play the ostrich, to look no further. But... "And what will happen if the DPP rules that we have a case to answer?"

"If that happens, then you and Ike will likely remain here until the matter is resolved in court. And that could take years."

Zuba felt cold as he saw the situation in a new light. Beside him, Ike was busy cleaning out his spaghetti bowl. He envied Ike his poor grasp of the English language.

The barrister reached out to touch Zuba's arm. "The good thing, however, is that I believe the odds are in our favour. The petition I will write, detailing the actual events, should help the DPP to see through the lies of your complainants. We could still improve the odds, yes. But they are currently in our favour. So we should be positive, think positive, project positive."

Yes! Be positive, think positive. The odds are in our favour, Zuba repeated in his mind. He forced himself to return the barrister's smile.

"Now, if the DPP pronounces a *nolle prosequi*, then they will send their advice to the magistrate, who will summon you two back to court and discharge you."

Ike chewed on his chicken bone, releasing a succession of cracks that sounded strangely like half-hearted applause. Zuba wiped his hand on a tissue, then took pains to wipe every trace of oil from his lips. Philip might not take kindly to having been cheated out of a juicy meal.

"Zuba, Ike," Barrister Chigbo continued, "we'll do our utmost to ensure that the DPP gives his verdict in three... four days at the most. So, just hang on, bravely, as you are doing. Keep out of trouble. Hopefully you'll be out soon."

All Zuba heard was "hopefully". "Thank you Barrister," he said.

"Thank you sir," Ike said.

"Sir, the self-feeding," Tanna muttered.

"Aha, the prison has self-feeding facilities. You can be moved to better cells where you feed yourselves. They say it will cost ten thousand naira each..."

"Yes, I have made arrangements," Zuba murmured. "Nonye will bring the money tomorrow, and we shall be moving."

"Good. Is there anything else you would like to know, or tell me?"

Zuba shook his head. He turned towards Tanna.

"In that case, I'll step outside for a cigarette."

Tanna laid a hand on Ike's forearm and spoke to him in Igbo. "How is your wife? Hope you have seen her?"

Her Igbo sounded strange to Zuba; it was the Niger Delta variant.

"Yes, she was here this morning."

"It shall all be well soon." She squeezed Ike's arm. Then she slid across on the bench till she was opposite Zuba.

She laid a hand on Zuba's arm. There was a vulnerability in her eyes that Zuba was seeing for the first time.

"I heard how it happened. I can't stop thinking that it would have gone differently if I had been there. I would have asked you to settle. To live to fight another day."

"Things must have gone the way they did for a reason. Like Gandhi said... said..." Zuba broke off. The thought that he and Ike could be caught in this prison for long still tormented his mind.

Tanna squeezed his arm. "If you lose hope now, what are we fighting for then?"

She spoke with such earnestness that Zuba felt a weight lifting off his chest. He intertwined his finger with hers on the table. "Thanks."

Tanna smiled.

"You're looking so lovely. Your hair, gorgeous," Zuba whispered.

"I did it in Lagos, specially for our lunch date."

"I was counting days too."

She smiled sadly.

"What happened? It's looking raw. Do I get you some ointment for it?" Tanna rose and leant closer to examine his keloid.

He drew back as her open jacket came close to touching the sleeve of his green tunic.

"Please don't come too close."

"Shhhhh!" She placed a finger on his lips. "Not a word. I understand."

Zuba wanted to say: *No, you could never understand. It is not just my itchy body, or the mattress's smell of decay that has papered itself all over my skin.* Instead, he tried to calm himself by savouring the cool feel of her finger against his lips.

* * *

Zuba explained the barrister's words to Ike as they went back to their cells.

"Ike, the Egbetuyis must have made at least one slip. We need to remember whatever we can and pass it on to Barrister Chigbo to improve the prospect of our getting out of here soon..."

239

"Hey! Ike-power!" A lanky inmate was jogging across the compound, his face split by the widest grin. "Is this you? What happened? When did you come in? I know you must have been wondering why I have not contacted you for my share of the booty. Now you know why. I am here over a different matter." He tried to pump Ike's hand.

Ike pulled his hand free. "Who... what... what are you talking about?" he stuttered. "Who are you?"

"Oh, sorry. Sorry. My mistake. I thought you were someone else. Forgive me," he said, and hurried off.

Zuba found it hard to breathe.

Ike turned and stared straight into his eyes. "Zuba, I've never met that man before in my life. I don't know who he is or what he was talking about."

Zuba fought a battle within himself. His heart resisted, but his head had to accept the evidence: only Ike's closest pals called him Ike-power. Zuba suddenly felt sick.

Two prisoners trudged past, bearing a stretcher towards the forecourt. The body on the stretcher was stiff, adorned in a pair of shorts, tattered and torn, that exposed the spongy ball of his scrotal sac. The belly was concave below ribs stark and countable under the rash-ridden, peeling ash-grey flesh. The grimy brown teeth were bared in a deathly grin; dried spittle marks streaked the cheek. The eyes stared blankly at the flies following the stretcher.

Zuba doubled up. A mess of spaghetti and chicken splattered on the desert-brown sand at his feet.

* * *

"Eloka, don't start again this morning," Aunty Chinwe said. "Open your mouth, let the nurse read your temperature."

Professor Chukwueloka Maduekwe shook his head. He looked at the buxom nurse on the other side of his bed. She held a thermometer suspended in mid air. The smile on her lips was as rigid as a plaster cast, while her eyes had narrowed with strained patience. He shook his head.

"Eunice," he said.

"But you heard the nurse say that Eunice is in another ward this morning, she's unavailable. Open your mouth, stop delaying the nurse. She has other patients to attend to," Aunty Chinwe said.

The Professor shook his head.

"OK, let me." Aunty Chinwe took the thermometer from the nurse. "Eloka, my brother – OK, open your mouth for me. You won't say no to your only sibling, would you?"

"Eunice," the Professor repeated.

Aunty Chinwe sighed. She handed the thermometer back to the nurse. "Is there any way you can get Eunice to attend to him? When he is this way, nothing will make him budge."

The nurse nodded without altering her smile. She placed the thermometer on a stainless-steel dish on the bedside table and left the room.

"Eloka, it is not good o. What has the poor nurse done to you? Don't you know what you have done might have hurt her deeply?"

Auntie Chinwe began a long chastisement as the Professor gaped at her. She was still complaining when the door swung open after a gentle knock. A light-skinned nurse walked in. Her uniform fitted her petite frame like a designer dress, and the cap sat on her permed hair like a tiara.

"Aunty, good morning. Hope you slept well." She moved to the bedside and smiled down at the Professor. "Prof, how are you this morning?"

The Professor nodded five times.

"Eunice, thank you," said Aunty Chinwe. "We woke up to another day by His grace. Now tell me, what potion have you given my brother that makes him insist on having only you attend to him?"

Eunice laughed. "Maybe my injections don't hurt."

"No, seriously. I don't like the way he treated the other nurse. I thought it quite rude."

Eunice looked down again at the Professor. She pursed her lips and shook her head, "Prof, you shouldn't do that."

The Professor nodded.

"We are all working towards the one goal of your recovery. That nurse taught me some of the tricks of our trade. She's London-trained. You should give her a chance."

The Professor nodded again.

"Now let's see exactly how you're doing this morning." The Professor's mouth was open and waiting for the thermometer. She made some notes on a pad, then wrapped the cuff of the blood-pressure device round his upper arm. She pumped the pressure ball.

The Professor watched her, taking in everything, from the tautness of her glossy lips as she concentrated, right down to the trim neatness of her fingernails.

On the settee on the other side of the bed, Aunty Chinwe held the *Daily Prayer Guide* before her face, and an open dog-eared Bible on her lap. The hospital-blue curtains on the window behind her rose and fell with the morning breeze.

Eunice leant forwards to study the mercury dial. Professor Maduekwe peered down her cleavage. Her breasts still looked firm after the two children she had had for her ex, and her stomach didn't bulge against her uniform. He remembered what he had heard somewhere

– that petite women had bodies like elastic bands, which snap back to place no matter how much they had been stretched.

Eunice lifted her face and made notes on her pad. "You're doing fine. Good. Hope you feel as good?"

The Professor nodded.

She smiled. "So you're hoarding your voice today? You don't want me to hear it, eh?"

"I'm feeling good," the Professor croaked, and grinned back.

Aunty Chinwe peered out from behind her book.

"You see, your voice is croaky because you've been neglecting it," Eunice said. "You should nod less and talk more."

The Professor began nodding. He stopped midway and said, "Yes."

Eunice moved to the other side of the bed. "He's making good progress," she said to Aunty Chinwe. She held his right hand. "Do you feel me touching you?"

The Professor nodded. "Yes."

"Can you try moving your fingers?"

The Professor's fingers twitched.

"Good," Eunice said. She moved to the foot of the bed and lifted the blanket off his right foot. The foot looked a bit swollen. She rubbed the instep, down to the toes. "You feel this?"

The Professor nodded. "Yes."

"Can you move your toes?"

Two of the Professor's toes wriggled slowly.

"Can you give me more than that? Can you move your foot?"

The Professor nodded. "Yes." He squeezed his eyes shut.

His foot inched from side to side.

"Hey!" Aunty Chinwe screamed. "Jesus, thank you!"

"Great, Professor. You're doing great," Eunice said.

"Urine," Professor Maduekwe said.

Aunty Chinwe beat Eunice to the bathroom and returned with a urine bottle for her brother.

The Professor pulled the bottle under the sheets with his left hand and fumbled with his groin. The sound of fluid trickling against plastic. He handed it back to Aunty Chinwe.

Eunice patted the Professor's arm. "Prof, you're doing great. I'm so happy. At this rate you should be up and discharged in the near future. OK, bye bye, I'll be seeing you again."

"Wait," the Professor said.

Eunice returned to his bedside. "What is it, my dear?"

"I'd like to ask you a favour."

Eunice smiled. "What is it, Professor?"

"I... I have a son," the Professor spoke slowly, as if he was counting his words. "A nice lad. He's been dating this girl, and will be bringing her soon to... to show me. I was wondering if you could be around to meet her too. I would like another opinion on the girl, a woman's opinion."

Eunice chuckled. "But Prof, Aunty Chinwe is here."

"I want a fresh set of eyes."

Eunice smiled. She glanced at Aunty Chinwe. She too was smiling. "OK, Prof. Just let me know when. And I'll come along wearing my freshest set of eyes."

The Professor grinned.

The housemaid stepped in as Eunice was leaving. She held a shopping bag smelling of food and fruits. "Aunty Chinwe, good afternoon."

"Thank you, my dear. How are you? What about Nonye?"

"She couldn't come. She gave me a letter for you."

* * *

Philip folded his legs into lotus position on his bed. "IG, proceed," he said.

"Story *kawai*!" IG called out.

"*Mbehhhhhhhh*!"

"Story *kawai*! *Kawai*!"

"*Mbehhhhhhhhhhhhh*!"

The thundering response wrenched Zuba from his grief. He swallowed saliva still tainted by the afternoon's vomit and sat up in his post. "What's happening? Story *kawai, mbehhhhh*? What does it mean?" he muttered to Madubuchi.

"Must everything have meaning?" DPP barked. "You book people. Story *kawai mbehhhhh* is story *kawai mbehhhhh*. Finish."

"I wasn't asking you," Zuba snapped.

Madubuchi shrank away from Zuba in horror, increasing the space between them. DPP's hand had risen high in the air. His knuckles landed on Zuba's scalp with a resounding crack.

A gasp escaped Zuba's lips as his hand flew up to massage the spot.

"Next time you talk back to me I'll make sure I give you another wound that will scar you for the rest of your life, and you'll sleep in the toilet in addition..."

"DPP, leave him," Philip said.

"Yes, Sir Boss-man." DPP glowered at Zuba, then turned away.

Philip looked down at Zuba. He switched to English. "Don't ever talk back to any of my officers again. You hear that? Ever."

Zuba nodded, still massaging the bump on his scalp.

"Story *kawai mbehhhhhh*?" Philip continued "A story is like a coconut. *Kawai* is the act, the sound of cracking open the coconut, and *mbehhhhh* is the gushing out of the contents, the coconut water, the story."

"So, who among the new cell members should we start with?" IG continued.

"Call Mr Grammar. Let him start," DPP said.

"Yes, yes," several other voices agreed.

"OK. You, move to the centre of the cell." IG pointed at Zuba.

Zuba stood up. The air from the window caressed his bare chest. The moon was a crescent outside, above the superintendent's office. He moved and stood under the glowing bulb, his feet wedged on every side by the bodies of the Corrordor inmates, his body pierced by fifty-six pairs of eyes. He focused on IG's warm face.

"We want to hear stories," IG said. "Give us news from the outside world."

Zuba continued to stare at IG.

"Have you grown dumb? Or you want us to beat the story out of you? If you don't give us good, long and entertaining news tonight, you'll be called out here every night for a whole week," DPP said.

"Go on, tell us stories, give us news," IG repeated.

Zuba's tongue felt heavy. What news should he relate? From where should he start? "Em... yes. No, no... OK... Aha..." he began.

"Stop dancing around like testicles," DPP barked. "Give us some news. And speak only in Igbo o. We don't want

246

grammar o." He looked towards Philip. "Sir Boss-man, what about a slap for each English word he uses?"

"DPP, you know that even you cannot speak without English words entering your speech," Philip said.

"The new inmate that came last week said something about Bakassi Boys. Let him start with that," one of the landlords said.

"What are you waiting for?" Philip said. "Go on, start."

"Em... yes. The government invited..."

"No, no. You must say story *kawai* before you start," IG said.

"Story *kawai*," Zuba said.

"*Mbehhhhhhhhhhhhhhhhhhhhhh.*"

"The state government invited the Bakassi Boys from Aba to check the growing incidents of armed robbery in the state. Before Bakassi came, things were so bad. The robbers were brazen. They would give advance notice of their visit. People kept money in their homes, for it was said that once you gave them money, they left you, otherwise they could kill you. In some areas of Onitsha, it was so bad that people left their homes at night to go and sleep together in cathedrals. But since the coming of the Bakassi Boys, people now sleep in their houses, even with their doors open at night, and nothing happens."

"You're yet to tell us how they catch the robbers," a landlord said.

"The general belief is that they have a powerful juju. That the juju not only makes bullets and machetes bounce off their bodies, but that it leads them to armed robbers and, especially, murderers. It is believed they have a special machete which turns a spiritual red when they hold it over anyone who has spilt the blood of another. They say people bring reports to them, and they judge suspects by holding that machete over them. And once they believe you are a robber or murderer, they tie you up, take you to a road junction, chop you up like firewood and set fire to your remains."

The silence in the cell was absolute.

"The president has asked the state governor to disband the outfit. But the governor has refused. He says the people of the state support it. He has been receiving awards as the most security-conscious governor, and our state has been described as the safest, the number one crime-free state in the country. The president is still mounting pressure, so the governor is now planning to forward the matter to the state House of Assembly so they can pass the Bakassi Boys into law and make it a legal outfit." Zuba stopped.

"*Na wah o!*" one landlord exclaimed. "Please, do the Bakassi Boys also pursue pickpockets? Because if they do, I might as well stop praying to be picked for release by the Attorney-General this year. After seven years here, I don't think one more will kill me."

"I'm not sure. I don't really know. But the general belief is that they are after all kinds of thieves and murderers."

"*Na wah o!*" the landlord exclaimed again. "And some of us whose case files have been declared missing by the police are hoping that the Attorney-General will release us during his visit this year."

"Of course," DPP said. "The river can't drown a person whose feet it has not seen. I'm still praying for my release, and once I am released, before I step out of the prison, I will arrange for a canoe to ferry me across the Niger outside the prison, straight to Asaba. They don't have Bakassi there, do they?"

"No," Zuba said. "But the Asaba people are planning to invite them down too," he lied.

DPP became downcast.

"You mean they actually chop robbers up when they catch them? Chop them up with machetes while they are still alive?" another landlord asked.

"Yes," Zuba said.

"Me, I have nothing to fear. I am not a robber," IG spoke right into DPP's ear.

"But you receive stolen goods," DPP snapped.

"How would I have known they're stolen?" IG snapped back. "Did you expect me as a busy car dealer to investigate every car brought to me? I was on my own and they brought me used cars at give-away prices. Did you expect me to reject them? Have you ever heard of a snake that refused to swallow the toad that ran into its mouth?"

"Well, that makes you a robber too then," DPP said.

"Even if we agree it makes me a robber, it does not make me a murderer, does it?"

DPP scowled. "If we kill people when we rob, it is to keep people like you supplied."

"Story *kawai*!" Philip said.

"*Mbehhhhhhhh*."

"Tell us more news," He said to Zuba.

"Em... yes. The federal government has announced a new minimum wage..."

"Tell us something more interesting."

Zuba racked his brain. No, he would not talk about the agitation for Biafra, he would leave that for the Massobian. Aha. "There were sharia riots in the country."

"Yes, yes. I heard something about this sharia. What is it all about?" DPP said.

"Sharia is a kind of law, old Islamic law. Some states in the north decided to start using it instead of our normal civil law. It is like the Old Testament's an-eye-for-an-eye kind of law. Punishments for breaking the law in those states range from stoning to death to flogging. Robbers, for example, will have one of their hands chopped off. The president disagreed with the governors and tried to stop them. But the governors went ahead and passed it into law in their states."

DPP sprang up. "That is why I like the military. Not this rubbish they call democracy. You want to tell me that if General Babangida or Abacha was president such things would have been happening? Such lawlessness? The governors would be falling over themselves to carry out their wishes. Lord! Why did Abacha have to die?" He spread out his hand before his face and flexed his fingers. "You mean they actually cut off a man's hand, just for stealing? Make sure you're telling us the truth here. Otherwise I'll get you ragging water for lying in this cell."

"Yes," Zuba said. "It was in the papers. In Zamfara state, a sharia judge sentenced a thief to have his hand amputated, and his hand was duly cut off."

"That judge is lucky that it is not to someone like me he gave such a sentence. I would have gathered my men and we too would pass a sharia judgement on him: that the tongue with which he pronounced that evil sentence be cut off too." DPP's voice shook with rage. He glowered at Zuba. Zuba glared back at him.

Half an hour later, Zuba was allowed to return to his post. His grief crowded over him again as he sat down. But the noise in the cell made it impossible for him to think.

The Massobian was asked to take the stand.

"Story *kawai*!" the Massobian called.

"*Mbehhhhhhhhhhh!*"

"Story *ka-ka-kawai-kawai*!" the Massobian called again. He looked happy, like a politician at a rally.

"*Mbehhhhhhhhhhhhhhhhhhhhhh!*"

"My brothers, I will not talk to you about Nigeria, because I am a Biafran, an Igbo, not a Nigerian." His Igbo was smooth, lyrical. "No right-thinking Igbo man will still consider himself a Nigerian today. For consider: it has been thirty years since the civil war ended, since we Igbos were brutally stopped from seceding and forced to remain in Nigeria, and Nigeria declared 'no victor, no vanquished' after it all. Yet no Igbo man has been allowed to occupy the seat of power in this country, or to head any of the sensitive ministries, like Defence or the police. For thirty years! For thirty years we're still being treated like those vanquished in a war. And this, despite the fact that we are one of the three major ethnic groups in this country, despite the fact that we were in the forefront in the fight for Nigeria's independence from the British. The other tribes distrust us and connive to keep us away from power. They victimize and marginalize us. Look at how the Muslims in the north massacre us at the flimsiest excuse. Look at how neglected and dilapidated our part of the country is. Look at our roads, for example; compare them with those in other parts of the country.

"But we members of MASSOB, the Movement for the Actualization of the Sovereign State of Biafra, have decided we will suffer in silence no more. *Mmegbu ndi Igbo*, the oppression of the Igbos, must stop. We are now demanding, through non-violent means, that we be allowed to rule ourselves in our own state. And, brothers, a lot has been happening in the outside world. With the support of the United Nations, we are now this close," he indicated a tiny space between his thumb and forefinger, "to gaining our independence from Nigeria and existing as the Republic of Biafra, as we did during the war. That is why the Nigerian government is now jittery, arresting we Massobians all around the country and clamping us in detention."

The Massobian claimed that Biafra had already been granted "Observer Status" at the UN, and now had only seven steps to the actualization of a fully independent Biafra; these steps included the hoisting of the Biafran flag and the introduction of the Biafran currency. Once these steps were completed, the Igbos would be granted nationhood as Biafra. MASSOB had already opened a Biafran Embassy in Washington.

The Massobian went on and on, and by the time he paused, there was excitement in the cell.

"Does Ojukwu support you people?" one of the landlords asked.

The Massobian smiled. "As the former Biafran leader, we believe he does. But he has to be tactful. That is why he speaks only of the 'Biafra of the mind'. He cannot be against us when the United Nations has already granted us Observer Status."

"This your… 'Observer Status', what does it mean?" another landlord asked.

The Massobian hesitated. "It means we now have the status to observe the United Nations. Only recognized countries can observe the United Nations. US, UK, France and other big countries all have Observer Status."

"All these things you're saying," the landlord continued, "the United Nations big grammar and embassies, how can we be sure they're true? How can we be sure they're not just propaganda that your learned leaders are feeding you and us to—"

Several voices shouted down the questioner. One voice rose above the rest: "Why must you think they are lies eh? Must you call him a liar? They are fighting for us. They're fighting for us and..."

A look of alarm crossed Philip's face. "Philip's Angels," he said.

"Boys!"

The power went off.

"Up NEPA!" Several inmates hailed the country's power-generating company.

A torchlight cleaved the darkness from the opposite end of the cell. "Clear! Clear! so I won't step on you," the voice behind the light said as it came forwards to Philip's corner. It was IG. He took a kerosene lamp from under the bed and lit it. A yellow glow spread through the cell, turning the inmates into silhouettes and chiaroscuros, casting impossible shadows on the walls. IG hung the lamp from the foot rail of the bed. He tucked the mosquito net around Philip and returned to his post.

The Massobian was still standing at the centre of the cell. His face looked oily in the dim light.

Philip cleared his throat. "United Nations granting Biafra recognition?" There was incredulity in his voice. "Biafran Embassy in Washington? Even if all you say is true, the Nigerian government will never allow us to secede peacefully. I hope you MASSOB people are not trying to lead us into another bloody civil war, another mass-sobbing?"

Mosquitoes whined and circled around Zuba's head. He slapped at them and hit his own face.

DPP took the cue from Philip and stood up. "What did you say your occupation is again?"

"I said I am a trader at the Main Market," the Massobian answered.

"Hmmnh. I was an apprentice trader at Main Market too, many many years ago. What did you sell at the market?"

"Inner wear."

"Men or ladies' inner wear?"

"Ladies'."

"What exactly is inner wear?"

"Panties, bras, petticoats and the like."

"Hmnnnnh. So you're very familiar with the feel of ladies' panties, eh?"

Giggles rose in the cell.

"I see," DPP continued. "You're a man, why did you choose to sell ladies' instead of your fellow men's underwear?"

"That's where the money is. Men can wear one pant for a week. Ladies can't." There was now a hard, cutting timbre in the Massobian's voice.

"You say you're a Massobian?"

"Yes, proudly."

"And your who-o-ole life is dedicated to preaching and selling MASSOB ideas?"

"Yes."

"And you sell ladies' underwear?"

"Yes."

"I therefore put it to you that MASSOB is about selling ladies' underwear."

The cell exploded with laughter, destroying the solemn, charged atmosphere that the Massobian's words had created. But some inmates refrained from the laughter. They glared at DPP and their laughing fellow inmates instead, their eyes shining, feline, in the shadows. The Massobian shook his head with gravitas.

"I rest my case," DPP said.

"As co-ooooooooourt pleases!"

"Who no see post?" IG shouted.

"*Onye afuro* post *ya*?"

"Goodnight cell members."

Vulture-king

Nonye was in the visiting room. Someone had made the announcement through the cell window. Zuba waited to be called, seated in his post, clutching a green tunic. The warder was slow in coming to let him out. A shaft of the morning sunlight beamed into the cell, resting on the praise-singer at the foot of Philip's bed.

Philip was sitting on the lower bunk of his bed, breakfasting on *okpa*. A dozen eyes followed every inch of the snack's journey to his mouth.

Zuba stared at the opposite wall, above everyone's head. His eyes were sore from insomnia. His heart still ached as if it had been stabbed. One thought went on and on in his mind: he had to find that lanky inmate and persuade him to open up in order to get conclusive proof of Ike's involvement.

Philip looked his way. "Will you like some *okpa*?"

Zuba's hand rose towards his keloid, but stopped midway at his chest. He shook his head.

"Your throat still sore?" A grin waited to grow on Philip's lips.

"No, thanks. I just don't want."

Philip's lips tightened.

The praise-singer glowered at Zuba. Zuba glared ferociously back at him. The praise-singer hissed and looked away.

Keys jangled at the cell door, and it swung open. Zuba sprang to his feet and made for the door.

"IG, tell him he's going for a qualifier match, if he fails to score well with this visit..." Philip left the rest of the sentence hanging.

Zuba stepped out of the cell and found Ike waiting.

"Zuba, good morning," Ike said. His eyes too looked sore.

Zuba's lower lip quivered, and he turned away. He strode towards the forecourt.

Ike hurried after him. "Zuba, please believe me, I do not know who that man is, I've never met him before in my life. I never robbed the Egbetuyis. It's all a lie. It never happened in the first place. At least you know the Egbetuyis never possessed all those bogus items they claim, and that you never went with me and some armed men to their apartment to assault them."

"They must have added that to punish me because they think I sent you to do what you did," Zuba snapped. "Too bad for you that we ran into your accomplice."

"No, Zuba, it's all lies. I don't know the man—"

"Then tell me, how come the man called you Ike-power? Did you not hear him? Only your close friends call you Ike-power."

"Did... did he call me Ike-power? I... I didn't notice..."

Zuba turned away and quickened his pace to the forecourt.

* * *

"I returned with the money and the other materials last evening, but I was not allowed in. I was told the visiting time was over." Nonye stared at the wall above Zuba's head as she spoke.

"You must have narrowly missed Tanna and Barrister Chigbo," Zuba said. "They met with us at the Welfare Office – guess it's lawyers' privilege."

"I'll be going to their chambers this afternoon," Nonye said.

Zuba cast a quick glance at Ike, who was staring down at his hands, a warder towering over him by the doorway. "Tell them *I* want to see them quick," he said to Nonye. Then asked, "Any news about the Egbetuyis?"

"No." Nonye said. Her eyes moistened.

"Please, Nonye, don't stress yourself too much. Barrister Chigbo will have everything under control soon. You look as if you've not been sleeping well."

Nonye nodded without meeting his eyes.

Ike straightened up, "How is my wife?"

"She is doing OK. She was watching TV when I left. She sends her love."

"And Junior?"

"He's fine too. A bundle of energy. Running all over the house." Nonye's gaze had shifted to Ike while she spoke, but her eyes were vague, without focus. Beside her, an old lady was shaking her head, tears streaming down her face as she clasped the hands of a skeletally thin inmate in green tunic.

"I have found you at last," she muttered. "After all these years, I have found you at last. O Lord thank you for answering my prayers, I have found my son at last."

"The police raided the bar and packed all of us off to the station claiming there had been a robbery in the area," the man was saying in a hoarse voice. "They demanded five thousand naira from each of us for our freedom, for our bail. I tried sending word to you, Mama, but everyone I asked said they could not travel the distance. Two of us were unable to pay, and when the cell became full, the police took us to court along with other men we did not know and arraigned us for armed robbery."

"Halleluiah! I've found you at last," the old woman said.

Zuba rummaged through the items of clothing and toiletries in the bag Nonye had brought. He brought out the A4 envelope containing a wad of notes. Nonye looked away as he straightened up. "Is there any problem?" he asked, placing the envelope on his lap.

"Start rounding up, other people are waiting," the warder said. His gaze penetrated the envelope on Zuba's lap.

"No, nothing. I'm just tired. I guess I need some rest."

Their eyes locked for a split second. Her eye pencil had been sloppily applied. Lines appeared on Zuba's brow: Nonye never stepped out of the house, even for a stroll within the school compound, without first finding a mirror. He tried to get behind the glassy vagueness of her eyes. She looked away.

A chill suddenly gripped Zuba. He hesitated, then asked, "How's Dad?"

She nodded. "He's fine. I sent the housemaid there yesterday. She returned this morning. He's been asking to see you."

"You're sure you're telling me the truth about Dad?"

Nonye nodded. "Yes. Dad is OK." She met his eyes briefly, reassuringly, and added: "In fact, he has started physiotherapy. The doctor said he is recovering well. In good time for you to still travel for your master's degree."

But a master's degree was the last thing on Zuba's mind. He studied her face again. She was lying, she was hiding something, something bad. He decided to try a different approach. He took her hand. "Nonye, everything will be all right soon. Now I want you to go home and rest, really rest. I don't want to see you here again before Sunday, you hear? We can manage with what you have brought till then. You hear?"

Nonye nodded.

More lines appeared on Zuba's brow. Nonye would ordinarily not have accepted without argument.

"Time up. Taste all food and get up," the warder announced.

Nonye reached into the food bag at her feet. She uncovered the dishes and began tasting. She seemed in a hurry to leave.

"Bye bye," she said as she made for the door.

"All right. Everybody, bring out all money. Remember, if you hide any, I will find and confiscate it." The warder began searching each inmate. When he got to Zuba, he dipped his hands into Zuba's short pockets, frisked him, and combed through the cellophane bag at his feet. His eyes lit up as he picked out a pamphlet from the bag of food. But they dimmed again after he unfolded the pamphlet and found nothing hidden within it.

"Let me see." Zuba collected the pamphlet from the warder. The title read 'Breaking the Yoke of Adversity'. He wondered how it had found its way into the bag. Had Nonye borrowed the bag from someone? He stuffed it into his pocket.

The warder collected the envelope of money on Zuba's lap.

"It's money for our self-feeding registration," Zuba said.

"True?" the warder asked.

Zuba nodded.

The warder counted the money. "There's extra five thousand on top," he said. He counted out five hundred naira and handed the rest back to Zuba. "Wait," he said. "I will take you to Welfare myself."

After he had searched all other inmates in the visiting room and done some more arithmetic, he led Zuba and Ike to the Welfare Office and left only after the registration money had changed hands.

"You know you can always come here to borrow books to read," the Welfare officer said as he browsed through the application letter duly signed by Zuba and Ike.

"Thank you," Zuba said. "Let me borrow a Bible, if I can."

The Welfare officer handed him a blue Gideon's Bible. "All right, lead them to their cell, prefects," the Welfare officer said to two other prisoners, "let them pick up their things, then take them to the head of the I Ward." One of the prisoners was Amaechi, the prisoner that had led them on arrival to meet the superintendent. His razor bumps looked septic as ever.

"What's wrong with you guys? Why the miserable faces?" Amaechi smiled at them as if at old friends as they left the office. "Best decision you could have taken. Those General Cells are hell-holes. In the VIP Cells you'll be freer, and I'll be seeing more of you. I hope to enjoy goodies from your hands, at least as your first friend here and as—"

"Zuba! I've got it! I've got it!" Ike called out suddenly.

"What?" Zuba asked.

"The induction! It's the induction. And the story *kawai*. They learnt my friends call me Ike-power during my induction and story *kawai*. I was asked all sorts of questions about myself and our case. And had to answer."

Zuba said nothing, but he was deep in thought. It sounded plausible, and he so desperately wanted to believe him. He feared however that it could be a false alibi, and he was wary of being fooled again. Amaechi burst out laughing. "Oh, so they've got to you people already? This should be a record. Well, I don't blame them. You're obviously birds of passage, so they have to hit fast if they want to get anything." Amaechi looked at Zuba's confused face and laughed again. "Forgive my laughter, but I just remembered your Gandhi quotation about self-respect. You've been here for only two days and you've already been reduced to the puppet of some prisoners. They'll be watching you and laughing their hearts out now."

Zuba was getting annoyed. "What do you mean? What are you talking about?"

"Someone outside your cell must have asked you for *cell-sho* or something and you refused?"

Zuba remembered the warder. He nodded.

"So they're manipulating you to get their *cell-sho* from you. They gather all they can about you people and your case, then someone drops some info that will make you think he's your partner's accomplice or something like that, and when you go to him for more info or proof, you'll gladly pay whatever he asks to get him to open up." Amaechi started laughing again. "Pardon me, but I've been in this prison now for more than two years, and watched new men being had, but I've never seen anyone fall as quickly and as hard as you have. You actually look bereaved—"

"Enough!" Zuba snapped. He was now angry.

"Sorry, Zuba," Ike muttered beside him.

Zuba held Ike's arm. "No, Ike. I should be the one apologizing. Please, forgive me."

"There's nothing to forgive, Zuba, it could have happened to anyone. I would have felt and acted the same way if the tables had been turned. Let's forget and never mention it again."

The other prisoner led Ike on towards his cell, while Zuba continued with Amaechi. Amaechi continued to chatter:

"That's why there's a law against 'instigation' in the General Cells. If landlords are allowed to talk to new inmates, some of them will forewarn the new inmates about the tricks here. Take the *cell-sho*, for instance: nobody is actually expected to pay the whole five thousand naira. You just pay something reasonable and get a post. But new inmates are made to believe that landlords paid up the whole amount and are fleeced for the whole amount…"

The sand of the yard was damp. Ant lions had bored tiny craters at the dry edge of the sandy field and waited, camouflaged, for straying ants. Zuba scanned the sand surface and the walls. It struck him that he was yet to see a single lizard in the yard. Few prisoners and fewer awaiting-trial inmates milled around. Most were seated on the concrete platforms that ran round each cell block, soaking in the mild morning sun.

They found Philip sitting outside his cell. The sunlight twinkled off the silver-thread design on his black shirt. His sturdy square face looked oblong, his eyes, profoundly sad, smouldering with secrets, as he stared at the iron gates of the forecourt. A change came over his face as he saw them approach.

"Philippi, he has registered for self-feeding. Welfare said he should collect his things and move to Big Man Cell," Amaechi said. He patted Zuba on the back and hurried back towards the office.

Philip shook his head. "You mean you paid them all that money? You know, with only a fraction of that money I could have made you live comfortably, come outside whenever you wish, have whatever you want."

"Thanks. But I'll rather be a free stray goat than a privileged cow, sore-tittied from being milked." The words tumbled out of Zuba's lips.

Philip remained silent.

Surprised by his own outburst, Zuba thrust his hand into his pocket.

Philip shrugged. His usual aloofness was gone when he said, "OK, you have anything in the cell?"

"No, Sir Boss-man," Zuba said respectfully.

"I'm no longer your boss-man, am I? Well, come let me help you get into my friend's cell. He's the president of the Big Man Cells, and his cell is the best."

Zuba hesitated. He gazed into Philip's eyes. Shorn of the fearsome aura that surrounded him inside the cell, Philip looked ordinary. A regular, average-sized Joe one could have beers with.

"Come on, come on."

Zuba followed him towards the back of the cell building.

"I even heard that one former governor and commissioner stayed in this my friend's cell after the military takeover of '83."

Zuba remembered his father. No, his father had been in Abakaliki prison.

"Man Philippi!" a prisoner they passed on the way hailed.

"How are you?" Philip answered.

Two rectangular blocks stretched to their left, behind Zuba's erstwhile cell. Their iron doors were locked fast,

their unpainted walls a dreary grey. To their right were
two other blocks, bright in their faded yellow painting.
The doors were gleefully open. Buckets and kegs of
different colours and sizes peered out from under the
double bunks spaced out in the cells. Next door was a
smaller building, the sounds of swishing brooms and
the pong of excrement rising from it. Two prisoners
stood before the door with buckets of water. They had
handkerchiefs tied over their noses, knotted behind their
heads, just the way Zuba remembered his mates doing
whenever they had to wash their boarding-school pit
latrine. The prison fence towered a few paces behind
the blocks. Several men, some in mufti, some in blue
uniform, peered out of a narrow space between the fence
and the toilet building. White smoke floated out, tainting
the morning air with the scent of marijuana. Sand, sand,
sand everywhere. Not a single bit of greenery, not even
a stray weed.

"Here you are," Philip said, as they approached a yellow
block with white patches.

But Zuba had paused and was staring across at a
new-looking building. Dove-eyed children stared at him
through the door and window bars, across the distance.
The sunshine washed over their faces and the skinny
arms they had stuck outside. A few paces to the left of the
building was another with the inscription *Clinic* above its
door.

"Come on, come on, you'll have the time to look around
later," Philip said.

Zuba hurried up to him.

A cracked concrete flooring stood at the foot of the
fence, five paces from the front of the cell Philip was
indicating. Inmates were stooped over buckets on the

flooring, splashing water upon their sud-covered bodies. The fragrance of toilet soaps and disinfectants swirled in the air.

Zuba ascended the steps into the Big Man Cells. He stood behind Philip at the head of a long passage. The walls were brown-black and rough at its mid-section, and displayed tiny granite chippings. Solid doors, with small windows at eye level, stood open opposite each other. A fresh breeze blew in from the door at the other end of the passage.

Philip turned into the first room. "Where's Vulture-king?"

"He's around here somewhere," a voice in the room answered.

"Vulture-king! Vulture-king!" Philip called into the passage.

"I'm coming, I'm coming." The voice was strained with exertion.

Minutes later a man emerged from a room in the middle of the passage, clutching a toilet roll in one hand and an empty bucket in the other. His skin was silky smooth, a lustrous light brown. He had thighs for arms and trunks for thighs. The buttons of his shirt looked asphyxiated by the effort of keeping the fabric on his immense chest.

He could snap someone in two, Zuba thought, as the man approached, splaying his legs out in his walk, moving his frame with ease. Nimble.

"Philippi, what's happening?"

"Seems you were giving birth in there," Philip said.

Vulture-king laughed. The sound was harsh, fitting for his broad chest.

"I brought you someone *good* for your cell."

Vulture-king led the way in and sat on the only spring bed in the square room. "Hang your bag on one of those nails," he said.

There were many nails studded in the dirty yellow walls. Bags and clothes hung from them, while rolled-up mattresses lay beneath them. "Please can my brother stay here too?" Zuba asked.

"He will stay in the opposite cell," Vulture-king said. "My nest can't be too tight. During afternoon lock-up, when everybody is around, we'll tell you what living here involves."

Ike appeared in the doorway. He held the bag of food Nonye had brought. Vulture-king rose and led him into the opposite cell. Zuba followed. There was no spring bed in the cell. Only mattresses rolled up, revealing the broken concrete flooring. Bags and clothing hung from the walls, and more bags huddled with bright plastic buckets and dishes in a corner of the floor, beneath the large window with forbidding bars.

Ike returned to Vulture-king's cell and sat beside Zuba. The shadow had lifted from his face, and light had returned to his eyes. He shared out the toiletries and clothing Nonye had brought, then uncovered the food container. A sweet aroma filled the room.

Zuba had no appetite, but he knew he had to eat. His head ached, and he was beginning to feel feverish. Nothing had passed through his lips since his vomiting the day before.

"Is there any kind of kitchenette, or some place where we could wash up these food containers," Zuba asked as Vulture-king made to leave the cell.

"You're now in Big Man Cell. Any of those prisoners will do your chores for you for some leftovers or occasional gift of some small money. Or better still, go to N Ward and get yourself a boy."

"N Ward?"

"The cell for juvenile offenders. Just pay for any child you like there to be let out for the day and he'll serve you."

Zuba picked up a spoon. Chunks of chicken lay atop the coconut rice, including a fat chicken rump. Traditionally, chicken rumps were never eaten by women and children, but only by the man in the house. All the time he had eaten with Ike in the police cell, Ike had always offered him the part out of deference. Now he pushed the rump towards Ike. "Why not eat it this time," he said.

He saw reluctance change to hesitation, then to acceptance in Ike's eyes. He watched as Ike smiled and scooped up the rump to take a bite. And as Ike's teeth bit into the juicy flesh, it struck him that Ike was actually the person giving while he was the person receiving.

"Mmmh," Ike said, and flashed another smile at him.

They had just finished eating when a prisoner appeared in the doorway.

"Who between you two is Zuba? There's a couple here to see you. They say they were sent by your lawyers."

Zuba and Ike exchanged glances.

"It must be the Egbetuyis," Ike said.

A frown darkened Zuba's face.

Seeing Is Believing

Mr and Mrs Egbetuyi were waiting on one of the benches. They looked up at Zuba and nodded a greeting. Their faces were long, blending well with those of other visitors in the room.

Zuba sat opposite them and looked them over. Mr Egbetuyi's face twitched. He was in blue denims under a red T-shirt that strained against his rippling muscles. Mrs Egbetuyi was in a loose-fitting grey dress. She seemed to have lost weight. Her eyes darted about through her glasses.

Their smells invaded Zuba's senses, and his mind dredged up his entire experience with them – from that first handshake one happy evening to the last wordless courtroom exchange – and compressed it into one vivid multilayered picture.

"What is it?" he snapped.

"Em... Zuba..." Mr Egbetuyi began. "I... we... em... believe me..."

Zuba felt like shouting: stop running around like testicles and state your crooked mission.

"...We're really sorry things turned out like this. It was never our target to harm you in any way. This was never supposed to get this far. But you... you were resistant, stubborn... and they decided to change your charge..." Mr Egbetuyi's voice trailed off.

Mrs Egbetuyi began: "Zuba, it is still not too late to end this now. The police prosecutor is baying for your blood. He wants to forge ahead with your case and is determined to oppose any application for your bail. We begged and pleaded with him that you be given one last chance for an out-of-court settlement so that we can kill the case and you become a free man again instead of rotting in here for years and years. He agreed grudgingly…"

"Everybody, start rounding up. This is a busy day," a middle-aged warder called out from his post beside the door.

Mrs Egbetuyi reached into her purse. She squeezed some money into a ball and held up her hand.

The warder stepped forwards and they shook hands. He returned to his post and stared outside.

"That's why we are here," she continued. "To offer you this last chance: pay us our entitlements and we'll kill the case."

"A win-win situation," Mr Egbetuyi said.

"This has already dragged on for too long," Mrs Egbetuyi continued.

"Oh, I see," Zuba said. "A last gambit. You're coming clean at last. It's not about any missing electronics or money, eh?"

"Zuba, you knew that all along," Mr Egbetuyi said. "I warned you at the beginning; all is fair in love and war. You started this thing, you declared this war."

Mrs Egbetuyi placed a hand on her husband's thigh. "Let's not go into that now." She turned back to Zuba. "I hope you realize, regardless of what your lawyer might have told you, that your situation is pretty hopeless without our cooperation. We're offering you this one last chance to end this matter and be released from here. We will not offer it again once we leave here."

Nonye's insomniac eyes, the strangled cry of Ike's pregnant wife, the profound sadness of Tanna's face, the outrage on Barrister Chigbo's brow, the shit bucket in the police cell, the eternally hungry mosquitoes, the loathsome *kwarikwata*, Ike staring with red-veined eyes, reeking of soakaways after a night in the toilet... Zuba tasted the blood from DPP's slap on his cheek, felt the trauma inflicted on him and Ike by some faceless prisoners. It was the same Egbetuyi-style deviousness which had landed him and Ike in prison that had landed his father on his hospital bed. Blood rushed to his face.

"Stuff your offer down your throat and choke on it. Get out! This audience is over. But if you think this is the end of this matter, you're greatly mistaken." He turned to the door. "Warder, I'm through with these visitors."

"Idiot! Is that how you talk to your father? You should call me with respect, not order me; I am not your servant," the warder barked.

Zuba's anger peaked into recklessness. "Warder, I said I am through with these visitors! I am through with these visitors! I am through..." he began to shout.

The warder almost jumped out of his skin. "Shhhhhhh! Shhhhhhh! OK, time up, time up. Everybody taste your food."

A prison officer appeared in the doorway. "What's going on here?"

"Nothing, sir. The man was just upset by some news. I have cautioned him. The visitors are leaving now-now. Everything is under control, sir."

The officer's stern eyes looked over everyone in the room, searching for any contradictory bit of evidence. The warder stood beside him, smiling apologetically at Zuba. Zuba took deep breaths to calm himself.

"OK, every visitor out," the warder said as soon as the officer left the doorway.

Mrs Egbetuyi sprang up, the animosity back in her eyes. Mr Egbetuyi shook his head. "I see you've grown crazy in here, and you've chosen to rot in here. Well, it's your choice." He rose and followed his wife out of the room.

* * *

The sun was overhead when Zuba stepped back into the prison yard. It left the cell blocks shrouded in their shadows. Waves of heat were beginning to uncoil from the sand in the field. Prisoners and awaiting-trial inmates trudged across, squint-eyed and sweaty, heading to or returning from the courtyard. Others clustered around the shadows of the buildings. Dark faces peered longingly into the yard from the windows of the awaiting-trial cells.

Ike was seated with Papa and Amaechi in the shadow of the church. Papa was talking, gesticulating, his torso bare, his shirt lying on his lap. The sight of Ike, bright in fresh jeans and T-shirt, legs stretched out fully and wide apart, reminded Zuba of their procured newfound freedom within the yard.

Amaechi sprang up when he sighted Zuba. He rushed ahead, placed an arm around Zuba's shoulders and led him aside. He smelt of fungus. Pus-tipped bumps peered out of the mat of hair on his cheeks. Zuba restrained himself from shrinking away.

"Zuba, I hear it is you people's complainants that came to visit. Is it true?"

"Yes," Zuba answered.

"Yeah! Yeah!" Amaechi cackled and slapped Zuba on the back. "You've got them! You've got your complainants by the balls. Oh no. No, don't tell me you'll let them go. No, no, you have to squeeze, squeeze with all your might."

Zuba felt excitement rising within him. "What do you mean?"

"I mean, I mean…" Amaechi cast a quick glance around, "that you can get them in here wearing the prisoner's blue, not the awaiting-trial green. You can have them in here for attempted murder. Signed, sealed and delivered!" Amaechi tightened his grip on Zuba's shoulders. He brought his head closer till Zuba could smell the beans in his breath. "My man, this is too good an opportunity to let pass. Can't you see the hand of the Lord in it? Don't you know that nothing happens by accident? The Lord wants to use you, use you to punish them for their sins. Complainants have no business visiting their accused in prison. Either they bribed their way in or told lies in their application-to-visit letter or both. All you have to do is bring money now-now." He glanced around again. Ike and Papa still stared with puzzlement towards them. He lowered his voice further. "I'll organize and buy some food and rat poison secretly. We add the rat poison to a part of the food, then you carry the food to your cell and, after swallowing a ball or two from the part of the food without the poison, you stir the food well-well and tell your cellmates that your complainants came to make peace and even brought you a meal. Your cellmates will scream and ask you not to eat it. Clutch your stomach a few minutes after, begin to moan and retch. They will rush you to the clinic. You stop the moaning after they have given you milk of magnesia, etc., etc., and cry out that you have been a fool, that your complainants tried to poison you, to kill you. The food will be kept as evidence. You have many witnesses. Your lawyer takes it up, your complainants are arrested, arraigned and brought here, while you become free."

Dainty fingers caressed Zuba's heart. He struggled against the alien smile breaking out on his lips.

Amaechi chuckled. He slapped and rubbed Zuba's arm. "Yeah! That's it. That's it, my man. Grab the opportunity. Squeeze their balls. Grab one in each hand and..." Amaechi squeezed his fist. Crack-crack-crack went the fingers in his hand.

Zuba stared deep into Amaechi's eyes. Behind the excitement they glinted with cunning. His hand rose towards his keloid but stopped midway at his chest.

"And what happens to my own balls afterwards?" he said.

"What?" Amaechi asked.

"In whose hands will my balls be afterwards to squeeze as hard and as often as he likes?"

"I don't understand." Amaechi left his lips hanging apart.

Zuba's eyes narrowed.

Amaechi burst into laughter. "My man! My main man! Was just checking you out. Hope no hard feelings?" He extended his hand.

Zuba ignored it. His mind had returned to Amaechi's words: *Complainants have no business visiting their accused in prison. Either they bribed their way in or told lies in their application-to-visit letter or both.* He regarded Amaechi thoughtfully – sometimes weasels can be useful.

Amaechi squeezed Zuba's arm. "Will have to hurry back to the office."

"No, wait," Zuba said. "Maybe we can still do business. I want you to get me something."

Amaechi smiled. "I'm sure you know that he who sends another to catch the smelly shrew must also provide him with water to wash his hands."

"Sure. That will be no problem. You say you work at the office?"

Amaechi nodded.

"And every visitor has to apply in writing before being let in to visit, eh?"

"Yes."

"Is there any way you could… you know, help me get my complainants' letter? I need it real quick."

Amaechi drew a sharp breath. "You don't know what you're asking? That is a different office. Okoro files and keeps the letters in his office."

"Okoro?"

"Yes, the most stuck-up warder in this prison. A fanatical born-again. He keeps to himself, smiles at no one, even other warders keep out of his way. He locks the file containing the letters in a drawer in his office at the end of the day. And he never leaves anyone alone in his office."

"There has to be a way."

"No way. You can't buy it off him. Forget—" Amaechi stopped. A glint appeared in his eyes. "Well… Well… I guess there's a way. But it will cost you a lot of wad."

"How much?"

"Five thousand."

"What! How about two?"

"It's going to be very risky. Make it worth my while. Five or nothing."

"Well, OK. I want it quick, really quick. I need to get it across to my lawyer soonest so that it can be useful. How soon can I get it?"

"Tonight. I can even get one of my hawker friends outside to deliver it to your lawyer tomorrow morning at no extra charge to you."

"Great. Make a copy too and send to me."

"How soon will I get my money?"

"Within two days."

"No! You pay before service."

"No way. I'll pay after I receive evidence that the letter has reached my barrister."

"OK. I know you're not the double-crossing type, and I'm sure you know I'm not someone to be double-crossed when it comes to payment."

"Sure. You'll get your payment. Every kobo of it."

"There's one more thing though."

"What?"

"You'll have to come along."

"Me?"

"Yes. My friend is ill. And I will need help with lookout and torch. I hope you're up to it – I can't let anyone else into our plan, as he might snitch on us. You'll have to come."

"OK. What exactly shall we be doing? How are we going to get the letter?"

"We'll be visiting Okoro's office tonight. I will pick the padlock. He won't know anyone has been in his office when he comes in the morning."

Zuba did not want to ask what would happen if they got caught. He fought off the fear creeping over him.

"But how will I be able to leave my cell?"

"Someone in your cell will cover for your absence. I'll arrange it. Wait at the Dolphin bus stop..."

"Dolphin bus stop?"

"Yes, the common toilet. Hide in the common toilet when others are going in for the final lock up. I'll come and fetch you from there. Bring one thousand five hundred naira. I'll need it to make the arrangements."

Zuba reached into his pocket and handed over the money.

"One piece of advice: don't think about what we're planning to do. Keep busy, keep your mind clear. And when the time comes, just do it. I don't want you changing your mind and bailing out on me."

* * *

"What did that psycho want? Be wary of him. Be wary of everybody here," Papa said.

Zuba bit down on the mix of excitement and dread bubbling within him and sat down beside Papa. No, he would tell Papa and Ike nothing about the plan. He would not make them accessories. It was safer this way, in case anything went wrong. "Thanks Papa," he said. "I will. He was trying to sell me a devious scheme to trap our complainants while setting me up for blackmail."

Zuba stared across Papa to Ike. "Don't you want to know what the Egbetuyis came for?"

"What else other than the same old: 'Settle us and we drop the charges'?" he said. "Zuba, you know, many a night as the mosquitoes sang and stung my eyelids from closing, instead of caressing my wife and son in my thoughts, I find myself thrashing the Egbetuyis. My blood boils in my veins, cooking me alive. I smoke through my ears, steam through my nostrils, and can scarcely breathe…"

Ike's eyes had turned red. Startled, Zuba wrenched himself from the new poetry in Ike's speech. "Ike, take it easy. Take it easy." He decided against uttering the words: *They won't get away with this.*

Papa threw an arm over Ike's shoulders. "My child, anger and hate are futile in prison. They harm only you and not the object of your fury. Had I not realized that in time, I wonder if I would still be alive here today."

Zuba was touched. "How long have you been here, Papa, and what brought you here?"

"One year, two months, five days and about three hours," Papa said. "I was only trying to help my friend. He came home to our village that Christmas in his usual flashy car, bought me expensive gifts. But a few days after Christmas, he sent me a message that the police were holding him. I rushed to the station. The police said he and some others at large had defrauded a Community Bank of millions of naira given to him as loan without any collateral, and that he had defaulted in paying back. The man had laughed and said it was only a misunderstanding that arose due to errors in the payback date. He's the head of a conglomeration of companies in the US, he said. The money was peanuts. He only needed to be free to arrange for the payback. I had believed him. I signed for his bail with the police. The police released him.

"Maybe I was a fool. But what else could I have done? His entire family were in the US, and we went way back as friends, right from childhood. I could not have doubted him. He had the money; he was the richest man in the village. He even holds a national honour: Officer of the Order of the Niger.

"He fled to the US and the police arrested me. They said I should produce him. I was charged to court, for forfeiture or something like that. I ended up here, and have not been to court again since. I thought I was doing a good deed."

Papa became silent. Zuba and Ike followed his gaze. Blue-uniformed prisoners stomped across the yard bearing a shrivelled man in tattered mufti on a stretcher. The man's left arm was raised to the skies, a salute to rigor mortis.

"If not for the kindness of the warders, I'm sure I would have been carried out on a stretcher long ago. They pity me. They call me a fool, but still pity me. And help me. They made me the prison teacher; they let me out every day to get some sun without my paying anything. Had it been otherwise, Heaven knows I would not have survived long in that concentration camp they call General Cell. Some of the warders even dole out money to me now and then. That's how I get by, buy water to take the occasional bath, buy the occasional special meal or snack, buy medicine."

"But Papa, what about your bail? What about your family?" Zuba asked.

"My child, after seeing where standing bail for someone has landed me, can you blame anybody for running away whenever anything about my bail is mentioned? My wife and I don't see eye to eye. We separated long ago. But sometimes my son travels down from Lagos, where he's attending university while staying with his mother, to visit me. He had discussed with lawyers about standing as surety for my bail. But they all say it won't work. He has nothing, and he's like a minor. One lawyer had collected twenty thousand naira from me to use in hiring one of those professional charge-and-bail sureties for my bail. But he kept telling stories afterwards whenever I sent someone to him for an update. Now, my current lawyer says bail is not the way to proceed. He would apply to the High Court and get it to quash the order of the Lower Court holding me. *Certiorari*, or something like that, he called it."

"Satior what?" Zuba said.

"*Certiorari.*" Papa dug into the pocket of his threadbare corduroy shorts. His hand emerged full of folded sheets of paper. He opened them one after the other, placing them on his lap. "Aha. Here it is."

Zuba collected the paper. It was a receipt. The heading read: *Afunanyaekwe Chambers.* He burst into laughter.

"What is it?" Papa asked.

"Afunanyaekwe Chambers: Seeing-Is-Believing Chambers. So, Papa, only believe in your release when you see it." Zuba laughed again. His laughter rose a decibel as he noticed Ike was chuckling.

"It's the man's name. His name is Barrister Afunanyaekwe," Papa said.

Breaking the Yoke

With the door fast shut and bolted from the outside, the VIP cell looked tiny, cluttered and claustrophobic. The spring bed sagged further and groaned with each twist of Vulture-king's frame. The scrape-scrape of a warder's shoes receded outside the door.

The mattresses had been unrolled onto the floor, jamming against the miscellaneous items under the bed. Zuba and four other men sat with their backs against the wall, facing Vulture-king.

"We don't have much time during afternoon lock-up," Vulture-king began. "So I will make the introductions sharp-sharp." He pointed at a wiry pint-sized man in his fifties, seated last in the line to Zuba's right, the next best position after Vulture-king's. His side was pressed against the adjacent wall, lapping up its coolness in the afternoon heat. The thick rusty bars of the cell window stood above him.

"He's 'General' Egwu," Vulture-king said. "General of a militia, and he's here in connection with the Umuleri and Aguleri communities' war."

Zuba shook hands with the General.

"And he's Chairman, an executive of a social club whose members lynched a man." Vulture-king pointed at the man to Zuba's left. Chairman flashed huge teeth at Zuba.

"Next is Baandbench, here over an OBT matter."

"OBT?" Zuba asked.

"Obtain By Tricks. That's another name for 419."

"OK," Zuba said.

"And last is 2-i-C, my 2nd in Command, here over a murder case."

2-i-C turned to shake hands with Zuba. Zuba's eyes widened. The man had a keloid. On his left ear. Fresh and glistening like a leech out of water, and fat as an index finger.

"What happened to your ear?" Zuba could not stop himself asking.

"What happened to your head?" 2-i-C asked back.

Zuba touched his keloid. "From a car crash when I was a child."

"Mine is from the police. They held a lit candle to my ear. They made me sign a confession to a murder I did not commit."

"I too am here over a murder case. It has been dragging for five years now," Vulture-king said. "My enemies want to nail me. But it was an accident. I did not know the man had a bad heart."

Zuba looked from Vulture-king's lips to his bursting biceps.

"Now tell us about yourself, if you don't mind," Vulture-king continued, "and after that, 2-i-C will tell you the few laws we have here."

Zuba blinked repeatedly. The new atmosphere, the politeness, required some getting used to.

"My name is Zuba. I'm here over a robbery frame-up that will be rectified soon."

"Amen," said Chairman. He patted Zuba on the thigh and flashed his huge teeth again.

"OK," Vulture-king said. "2-i-C, over to you."

2-i-C leant forwards. He had the dry face of a man who kept secrets. "Zuba, is it?"

Zuba nodded.

"As you can see, we in the Big Man Cells are let out every day. But it comes at a cost: we pay a booty of forty naira each day to the warder on duty. Every cell here does same. Each newcomer is expected to register his arrival by paying for a week, that is two hundred and eighty naira. And after that, the daily payments will be rotated among cell members again."

Zuba's eyes were glued to 2-i-C's keloid. He was amazed that 2-i-C's hand never reached for it even once while he spoke.

"Each newcomer is also expected to bring money for one packet of candles and one packet of mosquito coil," 2-i-C continued. "Finally, he is expected to do *cell-sho* for the provost of the cell."

"That's me," Vulture-king interjected, smiling as he placed a hand on his chest.

Cell-show, cell-show, cell-show. Zuba was sick of the extortions. "But I've already done my cell-show," he said.

"No, the one you did in the General Cell is different," Vulture-king said.

"I know. I have already done my cell-show for your Big Man Cell. A big fat cell-show."

"To whom? Who collected it?" Vulture-king sat up and scanned the faces before him.

"The Welfare officer. Hasn't he passed you your own cut?"

Laughter broke out in the cell. Chairman clapped Zuba on the back.

"Well, that means no kickback for Philippi," Vulture-king said, and joined in the laughter.

"Anyway," 2-i-C continued, "minus the booty for opening the doors, every other thing here is voluntary,

even the cell-sho. Some of us did, some of us didn't. But
if you want to do, you give him any amount that comes
from your heart."

Zuba lay down between Chairman and the General
after the introductions. He finally allowed himself to
think about Amaechi and their coming rendezvous. A
strange mix of dread, doubt and excitement swirled
within him. He pushed the thoughts out of his mind. He
remembered the Gideon's Bible he had collected from the
Welfare Office. But with Papa's words about the futility
of anger and hate in prison still in his mind, he no longer
felt like reading the Psalms. He sighed and dug out from
his pocket the pamphlet found in the food bag Nonye had
brought. *Breaking the Yoke of Adversity*, he mouthed, as
he held it before his face.

**Thus saith the Lord: "My people are destroyed for lack
of knowledge" (Hosea 4:6)**

*Many people are pounded by unending adversity, from
the left, right and centre, in their families, and they do
not know why. Premature deaths from accidents and
sicknesses, diseases that won't cure: barrenness, stroke,
paralysis, diabetes, etc.; children's lives uselessed by
drugs, teenage pregnancy and cult gangs, businesses
that never progress (the one-step-forwards-two-step-
backwards syndrome), etc. Most of such adversities
have supernatural origins. They are caused by ancestral
curses, by cultic powers and demonic dabblings (e.g.
selling soul to devil in exchange for wealth and power)
by forefathers. The Lord, Jehovah, has spoken "For I the
LORD thy God am a jealous God, visiting the iniquity
of the fathers upon the children unto the third and*

fourth generation..." *(Exodus 20:5). Break the yoke
of adversity in your family today! Turn to Jesus, turn
to righteousness and the Lord shall surely deliver you
and your family. For, if he promised to show mercy on
the whole cities of Sodom and Gomorrah if only ten
righteous souls were found in them (Genesis 18:32),
he will surely show mercy on and deliver your family
from its adversities if even only YOU reading this
pamphlet turn to righteousness; for He remains the
same yesterday, and today, and for ever (Hebrews 13:8).
For further assistance, contact Apostle Elijah Nwokolo
at Deliverance Power Ministries...*

"Are you a born-again?" Chairman asked.

Zuba looked away from the pamphlet. "No."

"That's good," Chairman said, and showed his teeth
again.

* * *

Zuba waited in the common toilet. The same toilet he had
seen prisoners washing while Philip had led him across the
yard to the Big Man Cells. The ceramic bowls brimmed
with maggots and excrement, and the floor bore clumps
and diarrhoeal streams of faeces, some pink with blood,
some green with bile, emitting a stench as sickening as
their colours were strange.

The toilet had a protruding column on either side of its
doorway. Zuba was plastered against the wall in the crook
of one of these columns. The stench made saliva pool in
his mouth, which he had to swallow each time his mouth
became full, being too scared of the sound his spitting
would make. His breathing came in short gasps, and his

heart pounded as he listened to the last footsteps of
prisoners running back to their cells, to the final clanging
of doors and jingling of keys.

Footsteps. They were not the slap-slap of rubber
slippers worn by inmates, but the heavy-booted thuds
of an approaching warder. Zuba held his breath. The
footsteps stopped a safe distance from the smells.
A baton banged on the open doorway. After some
hesitation, a head poked in and drew back instantly.
The footsteps receded amidst sounds of spitting and
coughing. Zuba breathed again.

The smells abated as darkness settled over the toilet.
So did the buzzing of flies. In the silence, Zuba became
aware that someone else was in the toilet block with
him. He could hear the heavy breathing of a man, the
kind of deep breathing that follows after respiration
has been curtailed for some time. He was sure it was
not Amaechi. Amaechi had said he would come to
get him, that he would not be in the toilet. The man
shifted, spat and emerged from his hiding. A silhouette
of a stocky frame stood in the doorway. Zuba's breath
caught in his throat as the man leant in his direction
and whispered:

"I'm off. Can't wait any longer. I've craved another real
release for so long, I'm tired of my own five fingers."

Zuba breathed again as the man crept out. Prayers
and songs of praise poured into the yard from the cells.
He kicked the air viciously to throw off the maggots
crawling up his ankle.

By the time Amaechi whispered through the doorway,
Zuba's legs were numb and the praise-singing had long
ceased. So had the occasional swing of flashlight from
patrolling warders. Amaechi took his hand. They stepped

into the night and inched their way along the shadows, heading towards the church. Zuba realized that the hours he had spent waiting in the pitch-darkness of the toilet had enhanced his night vision.

The prison yard looked serene in the darkness: a school yard after lights-out. The light of the half moon had softened the bleakness of the grey walls and bars. Coughs and snores flowed out from the cells. Crickets chirped in the distance. The twin beams from the headlamps of a remote car rose in the air, illuminating tiny particles of dust and smoke.

"We'll wait here for some time," Amaechi whispered when they got to the church. "We have to make sure no warder is patrolling." They stood in the dark shadow of the church, backs against the wall, staring across at the blackness of the office block.

Minutes later, Amaechi tapped Zuba. "Let's go." He crouched and ran across the moonlit open space. Zuba waited till Amaechi was safe in the shadow of the office block, then ran across to join him. They crept along the wall, past the superintendent's office, past the Welfare Office, until they got to the first office in the block. Amaechi turned and scanned the yard. Zuba joined him. They remained still for a while, listening for any new sounds. But all Zuba could hear was the pounding of his heart. He reminded himself that the letter was a piece in the jigsaw that would prove his and Ike's innocence and save them from being trapped in this dreary prison for years.

"Hold this, don't turn it on unless I tell you to."

Zuba took hold of a torch. He watched as Amaechi bent over his hand, looking over several metallic objects that gleamed in the moonlight.

Amaechi selected a picklock and straightened up. "This should be the easy part," he whispered as he reached for the dark shadow that was the padlock. "I studied the lock during the day. Keep a look out."

The click of the padlock as it opened was amplified in the silence, but the creak of the door as Amaechi opened it a tiny fraction was startling. They paused and listened again, scanning the yard.

Amaechi took a syringe from his pocket. He uncovered the needle, bent it and poked it between the door and its frame, at the position of the top hinge. Cooking oil, Zuba realized, as the scent reached his nostrils. Amaechi repeated the same process on the lower hinge, then returned to stand beside Zuba. "We wait for it to take effect."

Zuba sensed excitement in Amaechi's voice, and pride. When Amaechi finally pushed the door, it slid open without a sound. They stepped in and shut it behind them.

"Torch," Amaechi whispered.

The beam of the flashlight revealed torn linoleum on the floor, a cupboard stuffed with files and papers, and a desk that occupied three-quarters of the office space.

Amaechi squatted before the drawers on the desk. Each of the drawers had its own lock, and the wood was made of sturdy mahogany. He examined the lock on the top drawer. "This is where he keeps the visitors' applications file," he muttered. He handed Zuba the torch. "Hold it for me." Then he retrieved the picks from his pocket and began trying each one on the lock.

Zuba gasped when he realized that none of the picks could penetrate the tiny slit that was the lock's keyhole.

Amaechi shook his head and tried each pick again. He cursed and punched himself on the thigh. "Damn! Damn! We'll have to come back another night."

"Can't we force it open some other way?" Zuba said, squatting beside Amaechi. "We can't come this far without going back with the letter."

"No! It has to be neat. If there is any sign of a break-in the warders will fish us out. Believe me. We have to go; I'll find the right pick and we can come back tomorrow night or the next."

"No! You don't understand," Zuba whispered back fiercely. "Tomorrow may be too late. The letter has to get to the DPP in time before he takes a decision on our case file…"

"We have to go now. The warders will soon be patrolling again."

"I'm not leaving here without the letter. We must get it somehow."

Amaechi grunted. "What do you want me to do now? Use my teeth to bite open the lock?"

But Zuba had thrown himself down on his back, under the desk. Mr Egbetuyi's mockery had begun playing in his ears, driving him wild: *I see you've chosen to rot in here.* There was some space between the top drawer and the board of the table above it. He slid his hand through and into the drawer, biting down on his lip as a nail ripped at his skin. He pulled out a file. The cover had a little tear, just below the blue-lettered title: *Visitors' Applications.* Zuba held the torch with one hand and worked like a maniac, sweeping through letter after letter in the file.

A cough sounded close by. Zuba and Amaechi stiffened. The sound must have come from the courtyard.

"Hurry, hurry! They'll soon be patrolling again." Amaechi muttered.

Zuba's hand continued to fly over the pages. Then he stopped. A lightness gripped him and he felt like breaking out in crazed laughter. The letter was terse:

My wife and I have been sent by Barrister Leo Chigbo, solicitors to Zuba Maduekwe and Ike Okoli who are in your prison awaiting trial, to meet with them over the issue of settlement. Thanks for your cooperation.

Zuba recognized the scrawl of Mr Egbetuyi's signature, the same scrawl he had seen on his statement at the police station. The letter had been written using a black felt pen. He ran his hand caressingly over the expensive paper feeling its granular texture, its hardness.

A sound of shuffling, sleepy feet at the courtyard.

Zuba yanked off the letter, closed the file and slid under the table again to put it back.

A jingle of keys at the courtyard gate.

Zuba shone the torch round the office to make sure they were forgetting nothing. He dashed out to join Amaechi outside the office. Amaechi slid the door shut and jammed the padlock home. They ran along the shadows to the toilet block as the warder's footsteps descended the steps to the yard.

* * *

Zuba had spent the whole morning asleep after discarding his clothes and taking a thorough bath. "I never would have thought you were the Dolphin kind," 2-i-C had said when he saw Zuba in the morning, after the cells had been opened. Amaechi had paid him to cover Zuba's

290

absence from the cell. But Zuba had been too knackered to pay any attention.

When the cells were opened after the afternoon lock-up, he sat with Ike on one of the steps leading into the Big Man Cell block. He convinced himself again not to tell Ike or Papa anything about the night's escapade yet.

The long shadow of the block fell soothingly upon them. Behind and in front of them, other Big Man cell inmates sat in twos and threes, or clustered in groups in front of the block, before the open bathroom at the foot of the fence, where a dozen or so men bathed. Prisoners, and boys in tattered mufti, some of them looking as young as twelve, carried out buckets of water from the cells to the men, fetched towels and soap dishes. A handful of prisoners hawked buckets of water: "Do you want it? Which one? River Niger or Spring? Cheap price for the close of day."

The sounds of many voices haggling, chattering and laughing at once gave the atmosphere the feel of a bazaar.

Zuba and Ike's gazes were fixed beyond the forbidding glass-and-wire-topped fence. Heartachingly lush green trees and shrubs swayed in the breeze. Weaverbirds twittered and screeched, flashing the happy yellow and black of their plumage as they hopped from nest to nest in a palm tree several yards behind the wall. Kites soared above, scouring the length of the tarred roads below as the occasional car drove past. And looming behind the road and the few scattered, posh-looking, satellite-dish-decked houses, towering and stately, was the Nkisi Palace Hotel high-rise.

Zuba's eyes misted. Confinement hurt like a sore and formed a lump in his throat. He remembered his visit to the hotel. He and Nonye had accompanied their dad for a meal with a friend. He had been landed with an unpalatable, exotically named dish he'd picked from the menu, while Nonye made it a point of duty to smack her lips as she relished her beef stroganoff.

A bus filled with school children revved up the road under the watchful gaze of the kites.

"You know," Ike began. "What I regret most in my life is not having gone to school. Imagine me being unable to write my own statement at the police station, being unable to read what they wrote for me, hoping that what they wrote was what I told them. But I have made a vow to myself that Junior will study up to university till he becomes a professor like your father."

"Ike, it is not too late yet. You can still do something about your schooling."

"You mean like go back to primary school? At my age? The pupils will laugh at me. They will call me papa. Besides, one cannot learn to be left-handed in old age."

"No, there are adult education schools with students my dad's age. And you're only thirty, not old at all."

"No, Junior will study the thing I failed to do, for himself and for me. Same for my second child. I just have to work hard for the money. I wonder if my wife has given birth by now."

"If she has, Nonye would have rushed here to tell us. She can never hold back good news."

Zuba's gaze descended from the heights of the Nkisi Hotel to the prison bathroom. A Michelin Man, with multiple belly folds and white soapsuds all over his body, flailed his arms as he tried to soap his back. It struck Zuba that the Big Man cells had many big men: fat, flabby, pot-bellied and puff-cheeked.

Ike was still admiring the hotel at the distance. "You know, this hotel looks exactly like the one your father stayed in when we visited Abuja last year."

"Are you referring to the trip when he smuggled that pretty mulatto along?" Zuba said.

Ike stifled a smile. "No, I think he went for a meeting or something, at the National Service Headquarters."

Zuba turned to Ike. "When was that?"

"Last year, the early part of last year."

Zuba's face darkened.

"I think he mentioned something about wanting to hire *corpers* to teach in the school," Ike added, sensing he might have said something he shouldn't have. "You know, they're cheap." He attempted a chuckle.

But Ike's words only confirmed Zuba's suspicion. Recruitment of corpers, graduates doing their National Service, was done at the state National Service camps and branches, not at Abuja. There could only be one reason why his dad had travelled all the way to the National Service office at Abuja just before Zuba's National Service posting was due.

"Ike, excuse me," he said, and rose to his feet.

Ike bit down on his lips.

Zuba rushed to the Big Man Cells' toilet. It was not as well kept as the one in Philip's cell. He shut the door behind him. It had no lock, and there was a small peep-window set in it. No privacy anywhere in this accursed place. Even in the toilet.

The smell drove him out soon. He stood outside the toilet door, staring into the dungeon-darkness of the "tuberculosis" inmates' cell opposite. Then he retreated to his cell. Vulture-king was lying on his bed. His massive back was bare and filled the entire breadth of the bed. A boy was perched beside him. Fourteen or fifteen, he was painfully skinny, and his once yellow skin looked ashen beside the lustrous lightness of Vulture-king's back. He massaged the back, pressing out stray pimples and blackheads. Vulture-king's eyes remained blissfully shut.

Zuba unrolled a mattress. He slumped down in the General's post, facing the wall so closely that his breath boomeranged upon his face. Blood burned in his veins as he remembered how, on learning about his National Service posting, his father had, unusually, hugged him and said, "Oh! I'm so sorry, son. So sorry. How could they have posted you to such an uninhabitable primitive hamlet when you were hoping for a fun-filled break."

The hypocrite! The cheat! The liar!

* * *

The kick that woke Zuba caught him in the stomach. He gagged and coughed.

"Get up! C'mon get up!" a voice barked. Another kick. "I said get up."

A warder was standing over him. The same warder that had tried to get him to do cell-show for some faceless inmates. Behind him, Booty stood in the doorway, filling it with his portly frame.

The warder grabbed Zuba's shirt and yanked him to his feet.

"So, you think you can get away with burgling a warder's office, eh?"

"I… I don't…" Zuba wheezed, still clutching his belly.

"You don't know what I'm talking about, eh? What is this then, eh? What is this?" He handed Zuba a sheet of paper.

Zuba unfolded the paper and felt faint. It was the Egbetuyi letter.

The warder chuckled when he saw the expression on Zuba's face. It was the most evil sound Zuba had ever heard. He snapped the sheet back from Zuba's hand.

"Now I have you where I want you. It would have been my utmost pleasure to hand you over to the superintendent for official punishment – how do you think you'd like four weeks in the punishment cell? But my friend Booty was on duty that night, and I don't want him indicted. But I tell you, I'm going to squeeze the naira from you till you're shitting it out. Now tell me, how much did you pay that scoundrel, Amaechi? He brought the letter and said you have paid him nothing yet. But someone saw money change hands between you two."

Zuba said nothing.

"Well, Amaechi will be taught tonight never to double-cross anyone again in his life. And as for you, you'll pay through your nose to get back this letter. You might as well forget about getting out of here any time soon..."

Zuba lunged for the letter. He snatched it off the warder's hand and was about to bulldoze his way through the man at the doorway. But he stopped: the paper in his hand was light and soft, smooth and cheap – not the granular, expensive Conqueror-like paper he remembered. Amaechi was running with the hare and hunting with the hounds. The letter in his hand was a copy.

A vicious backhand from the warder lifted Zuba off his feet and slammed him against the wall.

Zuba crumpled onto the ground and passed out.

* * *

295

"Wake up, Zuba. Wake up. Is this how you sleep, slumped against the wall?"

"What? What?"

"Wake up. You have to eat something before the lock-up for the night. And bathe too."

Zuba opened his eyes but saw nothing. His head was racked by a splitting headache. He felt the side of his head and winced.

"Oh no," Papa said. He glanced across at Ike in the doorway. "Ike here said you were upset about something. But whatever it may be, I think you are taking it too far holing up here and brooding yourself into a headache."

Zuba opened his eyes again. He blinked a few times before he could focus. The sight of Papa's black face, genial and wrinkled with age, the concern in his eyes, and the reassuring grey in his hair, soothed his spirit.

"You staring at my cap of wisdom?" Papa ran a hand over his hair. "You know, my dye is one of the things I miss most badly here. And the admiration of the ladies."

Zuba managed a smile. Papa moved closer to him. Ike stared on, standing behind the kneeling figure of Papa. Nobody else was in the cell.

"Will you like to talk about it, what has upset you?"

"No. I'm all right, Papa. I'll just take some painkillers for my headache."

Ike took a sheet of paper from his pocket. "Zuba, Amaechi said I should give you this, and tell you he wants 'his thing' by tomorrow at the latest."

Zuba sat up. Sparks of pain ricocheted within his skull. He removed the stapling pin from the paper and unfolded it. Beneath a copy of the Egbetuyi letter, Barrister Chigbo had written a note: *This is great! Well done, Zuba!*

* * *

"No, Eunice. No. I won't eat."

"Daddy please." Nonye's voice was strained. She looked on from the Professor's bedside.

"Eloka, this will get us nowhere…" Aunty Chinwe began.

The Professor's gaze swung to his sister. "Is it your lies that will get us somewhere?"

Eunice sat on the other side, at the edge of the bed. Her uniform was gathered above her knees. She lifted the food tray from the bedside table and placed it on her lap. "Prof, please, I'm begging you. You can't take your medication without eating. You want to set back all the progress we've been making?"

"No," the Professor said.

"Good, my dear. OK, open your mouth." Eunice scooped up a spoonful of the food.

"No, Eunice. No." The Professor turned away from the laden spoon. He shook his head and tears spilt from his eyes. "They're lying to me. They don't want to tell me what has happened to my son. I won't eat anything until they tell me the truth." He tried to clamp his lips shut. Saliva trickled down to his pillow.

"Eloka – but Nonye has told you that Zuba has been busy travelling with Ike round the school's catchment areas: Lagos, Port Harcourt—"

"Chinwe, stop lying. He would not have stayed away for more than a week without coming to see me. Not even a phone call. Don't they have phones in Lagos, Port Harcourt?" He turned away from his sister.

"D-Daddy… tru… truly, Zuba…" Nonye stuttered.

"If nothing bad has happened, then why are you acting pious all of a sudden?"

"Eloka, why—"

"If nothing terrible has happened, then tell me: why is my daughter now wearing her face like white rice without stew?"

Nonye's voice cracked as she retorted: "But Dad, you never liked me wearing make-up in the first place…"

Aunty Chinwe drew Nonye to her bosom. "My daughter, your father did not mean it in a bad way. Your natural God-given beauty is enough…"

"Chinwe, you've started feeding my daughter with your brand of Christianity, eh?"

Aunty Chinwe chuckled. "Eeeloka. Eeeeloka. I'm not feeding her anything. She discovered our Lord herself, like Saul on the road to Damascus…"

"You people still don't want to tell me what has happened to Zuba," Professor Maduekwe cried. He lifted his right hand with his left and turned away from Aunty Chinwe and Nonye.

Aunty Chinwe rubbed the dome of his belly while her eyes smiled down at him. "Eloka, my brother, Zuba is all right. He's all right. He just can't come now."

"Why? Is he on admission in some hospital like me? Or worse? Something bad has happened to him. I feel it in my bones."

"Prof, today is Thursday. Hopefully, he'll be here to see you by Wednesday," Eunice said. "Please, give us till then, and if he doesn't come, you can embark on your hunger strike."

The Professor scrutinized her face, desperate to believe.

"You say Zuba will be here by Monday?"

"Wednesday, hopefully. Just a few days away. Shall I bring your food now?"

He nodded.

"You're a strong man, Prof. I never knew you still had such energy in you." She sat beside him and placed the food tray on her lap. "OK, open your mouth."

Professor Maduekwe opened his mouth. He chewed slowly on the mix of beans, vegetables and dried fish.

He took the spoon from the nurse and scooped another spoonful into his mouth, clinking the spoon against his teeth. He seemed to remember something as he chewed, and turned to Nonye, swallowed and began, "For all you know, Zuba might be busy having a ball with my money, checking into five-star hotels, Sheraton and Hilton, across the country..."

Dolphin Hotel

"Abracadabra! Give me a six," Zuba shouted and rolled the dice. The dice clattered on the glass-covered Ludo board: five and three. "Ooops!"

"*Champitimgwo*! I want a six," Vulture-king hollered as he tossed the dice: six and five. "Yaaaaa! Winner," he roared.

"Of course, you will win. Even an eagle would have a hard time detecting the sleight of your fat hands," Baandbench said.

"You think everyone is a scam artist, a 419, like you?" Vulture-king retorted.

Baandbench shook his head. "That's the problem with many of you people. You never go deep enough. You only skim the surface of a matter. Centuries of slavery and colonial exploitation, of theft of our priceless artefacts. And where is our reparation? I ask you, where is our reparation? Yet those of us who task our brains to balance this injustice without killing or maiming anyone, you call 419s."

"Enough of that," Chairman snapped. "Who do you think you're fooling? Are all your victims white? Was the judge white?"

"Judge?" Zuba asked.

"Let him tell you what brought him here. Why he's called Baandbench," Vulture-king said.

"Yes, I had wondered. Baandbench. Strange name."

"It is Bar-and-bench. You must give it to him though; he has balls. He had posed as the Legal Adviser of some company and tried to use one judge in his bid to defraud a white man. A judge of the Supreme Court, for Heaven's sake—"

"That's not true. He's a judge of the Appeal Court," Baandbench cut in.

"Whatever," Chairman continued. "The judge had asked him the difference between bar and bench, and he had answered: "A bar is a place where people go to take drinks, and a bench is a long wooden chair that people sit on." The superintendent couldn't laugh enough when he first arrived."

Vulture-king had laid out his dinner: one quarter of a chicken, two slabs of smoked mackerel, four eggs and tomato sauce, laid over a mountain of white rice, spreading an appetizing aroma throughout the room.

"You don't want to ask us to join you today?" Chairman asked. "So you're only generous with watery food bought from roadside hawkers."

Vulture-king did not seem to hear him. He continued chopping the fish into smaller pieces with his spoon.

"You know, your cuckolding wife continues to surprise me," Baandbench said.

Cheeks puffed out with food, Vulture-king appeared not to hear him. He crowned another heaped spoonful of rice with a piece of mackerel and shovelled it into his mouth. Another followed quickly. And another. He pushed a full egg into his mouth.

Zuba watched Vulture-king, contemplating how unlike a vulture he looked. His eyes were shiny, his head bore a thick mat of hair, and his neck was the size of a tree trunk. A searing itch drew Zuba away from his thoughts. He scratched his shoulder, pulled off his shirt and joined 2-i-C in hunting down *kwarikwata*.

301

Baandbench stood up. He rustled inside a black cellophane bag on the wall and brought out a hundred-naira note. The note must have been forgotten in some pocket and washed along with his laundry. It was shrivelled and discoloured. The rays from the overhead sixty-watt bulb pierced through the holes in it. "Anyone knows where I can get some Sellotape?"

2-i-C stopped crushing the *kwarikwata* in his shirt and spoke out for the first time. "Baandbench, throw that money away. Nobody will accept it."

Baandbench continued studying the note.

Zuba was now staring at the keloid on 2-i-C's ear. It struck him that he had not rubbed his keloid that day.

Vulture-king pushed aside his empty dish and began snacking on McVitie's shortbread. A fart trumpeted from his elephantine buttocks.

"You've started again," Chairman said.

"At least my fart announces itself," he said with his mouth full. "You, we only know you have farted when the flies start buzzing."

A putrid smell engulfed the room. Zuba held his breath. Chairman and Baandbench rushed forwards and spat through the window bars. "Urrrgh! See the kind of smell that comes from your stomach," Chairman gasped. "You need to go for a lab test."

The General remained quiet beside Zuba, chin in hand, staring up at the sprinkling of stars in the night sky. Zuba leant towards him, placing his face in the line of the breeze pouring into the room.

Sounds of singing rose from one of the General Cells:

It's not by power
It's not by might
It's by my spirit says the Lord
This iron gate must be opened
This iron gate must be opened in Jesus's name.

The yard swelled with sound as more cells began their own singing. The voices roared with pent-up yearning, deep and forceful. They reverberated in the VIP block.

The bulb blinked and went off. The darkness amplified the praise-sounds. Vulture-king hissed. He rummaged under the bed. A match sizzled and a candle came alive. He returned to his munching.

"Seems you cannot find the way to your mouth in the dark," Baandbench said, raising his voice above the din.

"If you people like, you can tease me from now till morning," Vulture-king said. "I still will not offer you any." He pushed a whole finger of shortbread into his mouth.

"Let's have our evening devotions quickly and then begin another round of games," 2-i-C said, putting on his shirt.

Vulture-king stuffed away the remaining shortbread and wiped his mouth. The General lifted his jaw from his palm and sat up.

"*I'm a fallen wall, O Lord lift me up...*" Chairman began, clapping his hands. Others joined him. Zuba clapped along. Soon, he knew the song sufficiently to sing along. Clap-clap, clap-clap. "*I'm a fallen wall...*" Clap-clap. The candle flame flickered and danced to the rhythm.

They navigated from song to song at different speeds, a jumble of flats and sharps. Seated on his spring-bed throne, bare back on the wall, oily in the candlelight, palms pounding together, Vulture-king would occasionally stop singing to stare up at the ceiling. Then he would thunder: "Yes, Lord! I hear you Lord! Speak on Lord!" Baandbench would let out a siren wail: "O Loooooooooooooooooooooooooooord! Appear! Appear!" While 2-i-C would interject with: "Jah Jehovah Armageddon! O Holy Jah!"

The clapping and singing began to die out, cell by cell, room by room, like the lights in a block of flats at bedtime. The ensuing silence was punctuated by the murmur of supplication and chants of Amen.

2-i-C rose from his post after the last Amen to his prayers. His shirt collar was bunched up on his neck and upper spine like a reptilian frill. He retrieved a plastic bottle hanging on a nail outside the window.

"2-i-C, if you sprinkle urine on my bed, this time I will exchange it with your mattress o," the General said.

2-i-C said nothing. His urine hummed against the bottle. He emptied it into a bucket outside the window and returned to his post. Others followed suit. The flame flickered wildly in the traffic, casting macabre shadows on the walls.

Zuba lay down at his post, beside Chairman.

"You don't want to play again?" Chairman asked.

Zuba shook his head.

"You seem the quiet type, as if you don't like talking. Hope no problem?" 2-i-C asked.

"Leave him. When a fowl enters a new territory, it stands first on one foot," Baandbench said.

"He didn't sound that way in the afternoon," 2-i-C insisted.

Zuba brought out the Egbetuyi's letter and the 'Breaking the Yoke of Adversity' pamphlet and began to read himself to sleep as the dice clattered on the Ludo board.

* * *

"Yeeeeeeeeeeh!!!! Warder! Waaaarder! Save me. They want to kill me here! Waar... Yeeeeeeeeeaaarrrgh..."

Zuba started awake.

The screams came from the direction of the General Cells, amplified, chilling, in the stillness of the night. He sat up and rubbed his eyes. The bulb glowed above. The General remained prostrate to his right, while Chairman, Vulture-King, Baandbench and 2-i-C had frozen around the Ludo board. The cries continued to rend the air, accompanied by the grunts and thuds of kicks and blows.

"What is happening?" Zuba asked.

"Sodomy," Baandbench said.

"*Tufiakwa*!" Vulture-king spat. "Whenever this happens, I ask myself: how can a man so hunger for a woman that he decides to settle for the shit-hole of his fellow man? What happened to his hand? Has Vaseline finished in the market?"

"It's the Devil," Baandbench said.

"Oh! How I wish I was there," Vulture-king continued. "How I wish I could give the man just one blow, just one jab." He held up his thigh of an arm.

"Order! Order!" The jangle of keys and clanking of metal against metal. "Come here," ordered a distant voice. "Quick. You're going to punishment cell."

"No, no, there has been a mistake. I was not trying to sodomize anybody. Somebody just shouted 'Sodomy! Sodomy!' and everybody started beating me..."

Zuba recognized the voice that spoke in between sobs. It was Amaechi's.

The night became quiet again.

Chairman winked and inclined his head towards Zuba.

"Is the man so poor that he couldn't go to Dolphin Hotel?" he muttered.

The Dolphin Hotel in town was notorious for prostitution, and had been ransacked by the Bakassi Boys, who said prostitutes living in the hotel harboured robbers. Chairman smiled at Zuba, who didn't smile back. He lay back on his post and struggled to get back to sleep. A lone, coughy voice started singing from the tuberculosis inmates' cells:

> I asked the blind
> The blind said our Lord is good
> I asked the lame
> The lame said our Lord is good
> Then I asked the dumb
> The dumb lifted up his hands
> The hands he lifted testify
> That, yes, our Lord is good.

* * *

"Zuba, I know it's not visiting time. But I had to see you, I had to persuade them to let me in," Tanna began as soon as Zuba stepped into the Welfare Office. Her hair still radiated a glorious sheen, framing her face.

Zuba felt a twinge as he remembered their Sunday date that would never be.

"Barrister Chigbo has forwarded the letter to the DPP?"

"He has. It got him excited. He quickly drafted an addendum to his earlier petition, attached the fresh evidence and delivered it to the DPP the same day. How did you get such a vital piece of evidence?"

Zuba smiled. "Let's just say I gave myself a hand." He moved to the table and sat opposite her. They clasped hands.

"Tanna, t-tell me. Are we free?"

Tears poured into Tanna's eyes. "Yes, Zuba," she nodded. "You two will be discharged on Monday."

They sprang from their seats and rushed into each other's arms.

The Welfare officer coughed.

They let go, smiling as they stared into each other's eyes.

"Wait, what about the Egbetuyis?"

"Oh! Yes, I was about to tell you. My principal had got the police commissioner to agree to set up an inquiry if the DPP advises that you and Ike have no case to answer. But the policemen involved in your matter arrested Mr Egbetuyi yesterday once they got wind of the DPP's position. They blackmailed him into writing a 'confessional statement' admitting he had misled them. In return for exonerating the policemen, they were to overlook his wife's involvement, allow him to take sole responsibility, as he had pleaded. He is still in police custody. I bet they will arraign him hastily to get the matter off their hands, probably by Monday. And that he would end up in prison, having made no prior arrangements for his bail."

Zuba reclined in his seat. There was something touching about Mr Egbetuyi's attempt to shield his wife. He stared out of the Welfare Office window, into the bleakness of the prison yard, into the shadowy faces that peered out through the bars of the awaiting-trial cells.

"I'll be here again tomorrow for our date," Tanna said.

Zuba shook his head.

"Why not?"

Zuba shook his head again.

"OK. I will be here with Nonye on Monday morning to drive you and Ike to court."

Zuba nodded. He remembered the *kwarikwata* that must be lurking in his clothes as Tanna made to leave. "Wait," he said. "Don't forget to soak your clothes in piping-hot water when you get home."

* * *

Zuba sat between Ike and Papa on their usual perch by the church building. His lips were wet with talk. Blood buzzed through his veins, circulating the news of their freedom to each cell of his body over and over again. Ike was whistling a highlife tune. A glow was breaking out in his eyes, a radiant moonlight in a night sky. He had drawn two babies on the sand with a stick, one male, the other female. The stick moved between the babies as he sang, as if he was practising some form of divination. He stopped and turned to Zuba. "You said Mr Egbetuyi is now in police cell?"

"Yes," Zuba said. "How many times will you ask me the same question?"

"I just like hearing it." Ike returned to his divination.

Papa was hunched up with his hands between his thighs. "I am happy for you people. Truly happy. But I cannot help feeling sad about the hopelessness of my situation. And I will miss you two so much. So terribly much." Papa's eyes watered.

Zuba placed an arm over his shoulders. "Papa, there's no way we are going to forget you here. You will be out of here in no time. I will stand bail for you. I know you won't run away," Zuba added, and pinched him on the shoulder.

"Please, my child, do all you can to get me out. I don't think I can survive another Christmas here..." Papa's voice cracked.

Zuba's eyes moistened. "Papa, I promise you, we shall feast together on goat-head pepper soup this Christmas, and drown ourselves in beer. You shall have your hair dye in abundance, and the admiration of ladies."

Papa wiped his eyes.

"It will be OK, Papa," Ike said, and squeezed the old man's knee.

"There is only one condition though," Zuba continued.

"What is it?" Papa asked.

"You must promise to let me eat all the goat tongues."

"I promise. The tongue no longer appeals to me as it used to. I now prefer the eyeballs. Perhaps they can help my waning sight."

"It's a deal then," Zuba said. "Let's shake on it."

Zuba and Papa shook hands.

"Your hand is hot," Papa said. He pulled his hand free and placed its back against Zuba's neck. "And your body too."

"Yes, I know. Let's go to the clinic. I'm beginning to feel feverish. All these mosquito bites."

"Me too," Ike said.

They rose to their feet.

There was a crowd in front of the clinic door. Zuba looked around the yard as they joined it. He saw DPP stilting his meagre frame past the front of Philip's cell. DPP scowled and looked away. "He's a Leader!" thundered out of the cell as Philip stepped out in fresh new clothes.

"There goes your Führer," Papa said. "Greet him. Raise your hand and say *Sieg heil!*"

Zuba chuckled. He waved and said, "Man Philippi." Ike waved too.

Philip's eyes flashed surprise at the exuberance of their greeting. He raised his hand in acknowledgement, with a measured smile on his face.

A prisoner strode past clutching several woodcarvings. Zuba was drawn to a black mask. There was something like a smile, the shadow of a smile, on the mask's lips. It reminded him of the Buga graffiti on the police-cell wall. It was frowning, smiling and exquisitely sad at the same time. Like the face of prison.

The prisoner stopped. "You like it? I made it. I can sell it to you if you like. I will give you good price."

"Not bad for a souvenir," Papa said.

Zuba paid for the mask without haggling. Ike collected the mask and studied it. "I used to make things like these in my youth," he said.

"Sir, sir, please find me some money," a soprano voice called out as Zuba stuffed his money back into his pocket. Zuba turned towards the sound. A boy's face was pressed against the bars of the children's cell. The spindly arm he stretched towards Zuba was covered in eczema so thick it could be scraped off with a spoon.

"If you hear the atrocities they say some of these boys have committed, your ears will tingle," Papa said.

"Don't they ever come out?" Zuba asked. He pulled out the notes from his pocket again.

"Only if they can pay for it. Or if someone else pays to get any particular one of them out for the day. I don't know how true it is, but I hear a clique here even refers to the cell as Dolphin Hotel."

Green Lawns

"Sorry, Zuba. I could not make it yesterday."

"You're here now. That's all that matters." Zuba released Nonye's hand and rested his elbow on the Welfare Office table between them. "How are you? I heard your University Matriculation Exams have been postponed till next week. Hope you still find time to prepare."

"Yes, I study at night. I'm well prepared. Can't wait to be through with the exams. And I have decided I will now go for education instead of law."

A frown appeared on Zuba's face. "Dad put you to it?"

"Not at all. I discovered a side of me that has always been for education. And through talking with Tanna, I realized I am not so much of a law person. Besides, I will want to have absolutely nothing to do with our police."

Zuba grinned and rubbed her hand. "How is Dad?"

"He has started physiotherapy, and the doctors are satisfied with his progress. He has fallen for one fine nurse in the hospital. But lately, he has been troublesome. Shedding tears and demanding to see you, threatening to go on hunger strike."

"Shedding tears to see me? Me? What do you mean?"

"Dad insisted he would not eat anything or take any medicine again until he sees you. It took a great deal of persuasion to get him to eat. It's good you're coming out tomorrow. He only gave us till Wednesday to produce you, otherwise he will embark on the hunger strike."

"Truly?"

311

"What do you mean by truly? Would I lie to you on such a matter?"

Zuba drew back, surprised by the irritation in Nonye's voice. Nonye could be saucy, yes. But never short-tempered. He reached out and took her hands. "Nonye, I'm sorry I got you into all this. The strain has been too much on you. It shows on your face, in your eyes. I'm glad I'm coming out tomorrow. I can't wait to hug you again. You're the best sister anyone could wish for."

Nonye's eyes misted. "You remember my visit with Ike's wife?"

Zuba nodded.

"We left you people and on the way back Oby started having contractions, so we drove straight to the hospital. We were there all night. The baby died, Zuba. The baby died." Her body shook with sobs. "How can I tell Ike this? Oby became so withdrawn, at first I thought I was living with a ghost." She paused and wiped her face. "But she is better now. So am I." She nodded. "From now on, surely, goodness and mercy shall follow us. Things will be better, indeed, they're already better in Jesus's name. A..."

A roar of voices shattered the peace of the yard:

Let my cry touch thy heart
O Creator of the worlds
Let my cry touch thy heart
Most merciful Father
The tears I shed every morn, noon and night
Let it touch thy heart, O Lord.

"From the church," Zuba explained, his voice weighted with emotion.

"That's good. Did you see the pamphlet in the food bag I brought you?"

Zuba nodded.

"It's from one pastor, Apostle Nwokolo. He prayed for me and Ike's wife in the hospital, ministered to us, and gave us the pamphlet. He's truly an apostle of Christ. We now have fellowship in his church. Have you read the pamphlet?" Nonye's eyes were now wide with excitement.

Zuba nodded again.

"What do you think?"

Zuba remained silent.

"What do you think of the pamphlet?" Nonye repeated.

Zuba squeezed her hands tighter over the table. "Nonye, we'll have more time to talk about this after tomorrow. Right now, all that's weighing on my mind is Ike's baby."

* * *

The church service had ended by the time Zuba stepped out of the Welfare Office. He looked up at the declining sun and counted with his fingers. About seventeen hours more. He walked on, past the crowd gathered and laughing noisily outside the church, clutching half-loaves of bread.

Vulture-king's deputy, 2-i-C, detached from the crowd. "Zuba, Zuba, come and see Baandbench o. He's not content with *419-ing* human beings, he wants to 419 the Lord too. And in His church. Remember that tattered hundred-naira note I asked him to throw away because nobody would take it? He dropped it into the offertory tray and was about counting out ninety-nine naira and fifty kobo change when the catechist rushed forwards and pushed him out of the church. Can you imagine that?"

313

But Zuba could not share in the joke. Ike and Papa would be waiting for him at the prison school. He would have to tell Ike about his baby – talk with Ike about his baby. The din behind him was fading, the grey of the walls morphing into the courthouse yellow. He strolled along on sparkling green lawns as he headed for the prison school.

Debt of Thanks

To Simon Kerr,
Sean O'Brien, Jack Mapanje,
Robin Story,
Chiemeka Ozumba, Ugochukwu Ozumba, Elisabeth Ozumba,
Anietie Isong,
Veronique Baxter,
Alessandro Gallenzi, Elisabetta Minervini,
Mike Stocks, William Chamberlain,
Newcastle University, Britain-Nigeria Educational Trust,
Overseas Research Scholarships,
and, specially, to Chigozie Ozumba.